Eat Pray Shag

www.sarahbegg.com

Eat Pray Shag

SARAH BEGG

Laura the Explorer Book 2

Published by Sarah Begg, 2020
Sydney, NSW, Australia

This book is a work of fiction. Any similarity between the characters and situations within its pages to actual persons, living or dead, or situations is unintentional and co-incidental. Any real location has been used in an entirely fictional way.

A catalogue record for this book is available from the National Library of Australia

ISBN: 978 0 9876415 1 9 (paperback)

Cover Design by Hazel Lam
Cover images courtesy iStock

www.sarahbegg.com

For all the strangers
who now know Laura

1

"**I**'m just going to put it out there. I'm really into anal sex."

The lychee martini I was sipping burned the wrong way down my throat, making me choke.

"Sorry?" I managed to splutter out as I looked up at Tristan, the guy I was on a first date with, not sure if I was feeling indignant or incredulous—or perhaps both.

"Is it something you've ever done before? Because I'd really like to have anal sex with you. Tonight." He leaned forward, an amorous gleam in his eye and an eager smile on his face.

Oh. My. God.

This really was *not* how I thought this date was going to go. I mean, honestly, from all the possibilities that run through your head when you organise a date with someone, having them proposition you for anal sex was simply not one of them. Sure, I may have imagined that he might turn out to be twenty kilos bigger than his profile picture seemed. Or that maybe he'd spend the entire evening talking about cars and suspension and paint work. I might have even deluded myself—just vaguely—into believing that he could be a prince from one of those Scandinavian countries, on holiday seeking his own Princess Mary.

A request for anal sex later tonight was *definitely* not on my list.

And he'd seemed so normal up until this point. Well, as normal as a guy sporting one of those metal earrings that stretched a big, gaping hole through his earlobe could be. I was determinedly *not* judging him by the earhole, though. Making sure I didn't even *contemplate* sticking my finger through it when he wasn't looking. Yet still, after ignoring what now appeared to be an early warning sign, my evening was deteriorating quickly.

Why was it so hard to find a normal guy for a casual fling? Surely that wasn't asking too much. Relationships were totally out of bounds for me, which I thought would have been right up the alley of most guys on Bumble. All I wanted was someone to have a flirt with, kill a couple of evenings with, and have a few rounds of brilliant sex, after which I'd never have to see them again. Surely not so hard, right?

But no. Here I was with hole-in-the-ear Tristan. And, shit, he was still looking at me and waiting for a response.

I cast my eyes around the bar, searching for a life raft. We were in a really trendy bar in Manly, just off the Corso, and for a moment I tried to mentally entreat the bartender to please, please, come over and interrupt this conversation. Unfortunately, he wasn't responding to telepathy.

I cleared my throat and met Tristan's eyes. "Is that so?" I said.

His smile deepened, like a crocodile sliding out of a swamp. "Lots of girls are really into it. It can feel great."

"Can it?" I asked innocently, and tried to look as if I were genuinely considering this. "I must say, you're very forward. Is this the line you use on all the girls you meet?"

Tristan shrugged, all confident ease. "I know what I want, and I'm not afraid to ask for it. Does that turn you on?"

Oh, for fuck's sake. This guy thought he was such a Romeo, didn't he? Was that what girls were meant to like nowadays—anal sex with a total stranger at the end of the night?

Well, let's be fair, maybe some girls *did* like that. And no judgement or anything, but as sexual adventuring goes that was one destination I hadn't visited. Nor was I certain that I ever *wanted* to visit. I mean, the *logistics* of it

2

was enough to do my head in. Wasn't there a whole lot of prep work needed? Plus, even skipping over the experience itself, what happens afterwards? Was there some rule about who gets to run to the bathroom first? Honestly, you could have nightmares about that resultant horror show.

Seriously, why was I even here? No, wait, I knew the answer to that. Kalina, my flatmate, kept giving me all these stern looks about my lack of dating life. We have this challenge, see, where I was meant to be exploring as many sexual partners as possible to compensate for having spent ten years in a relationship with the one guy—my high-school-sweetheart-turned-husband—who then announced he was gay.

I supposed, in that regard, I perhaps should consider Tristan's proposal … No! Couldn't do it. I just didn't think I was *that* much of an explorer. Not yet, anyway. (Ever? Oh God. Maybe I'd revisit the idea later.)

"Um, look, that might work with some girls, but I'm not sure I'm—"

"Oh, it does." Tristan shifted so he was a bit closer to me. "Come on, love, don't act so uptight. Isn't this why you came out tonight wearing such a sexy dress?"

I immediately felt my hackles rising. He didn't seriously just call me uptight while simultaneously slut shaming me, did he?

I felt like immediately storming out of the bar. There was no way I needed to waste any more of my time with this jerk. But then, another idea came to mind which made me pause.

Right. Game on. He asked for this.

Forcing myself to relax and appear nonchalant, I turned my most seductive smile onto Tristan. "You know what? It actually *does* turn me on."

His eyes sparked with excitement.

"I've never done that before, but I've always *wanted* to try it out," I continued. "It's a difficult topic to broach, though, isn't it? I mean, asking for something like that. Some guys might find it weird."

"I don't. I definitely don't. I find it super fucking hot."

3

"Do you? How interesting. Why don't you tell me what other things you find hot?" I smiled at him lazily, tracing my finger around my martini glass.

Tristan leaned in, the earlobe hole creeping uncomfortably close to my face.

"I like," he said too loudly in my ear, "girls who ask for what they want. Who like having their bodies worshipped and teased and rooted roughly."

Rooted *roughly*?

"Ooh," I said a bit breathily. "What else?"

"Girls who take charge when they want. Girls who enjoy playing with a thick, long cock."

I managed to prevent my snort of laughter and turned it into a strange little cough, instead, which I *think* he took to be a good sign.

"You sound like you know what you're doing. I bet you know your way around a girl's body, don't you?"

"Oh, I do." Tristan leaned back and leered at me. "I can go all night. No girl ever walks away disappointed after a night with me."

I doubt that.

Tristan's hand landed on my leg, mid-thigh, and crept upwards. I slammed my own on top of his, freezing it in place, and then placed my other hand on *his* leg and gave it a suggestive squeeze.

"My apartment is just around the corner," I said, giving him my best sultry look. "How about you settle up the bill while I go to the bathroom, then we'll get out of here?"

His nostrils flared and that crocodile smile came out again.

I tried not to jump to my feet too quickly. Taking my bag, I gave him a flirty smile before walking away towards the bathrooms. Turning back just before I was out of sight, I noted him watching me eagerly. Of course he was. He was probably imagining how hair-free my butt crack was going to be (ha!). Then I pushed my way into the dark concrete corridor and followed the signs to the bathrooms.

What an arsehole. Ironic, I suppose. An arsehole that likes arseholes.

In the ladies, while I took my time touching up my lipstick and wiping the slight mascara smudges from under my eyes, I listened to the conversation of the two girls also standing before the mirrors. I'd noticed them earlier in the bar, mainly because one of them had the most amazing long mane of blonde ringlet hair.

"He's *such* a dickhead!" Ringlets was saying. "I can't believe he'd bring her here!"

"He's a cock-face," agreed the friend, who had one of those cool Brazilian accents. "Do you want to leave? I'll leave with you if you want to go."

"I can't leave. Sasha's *my* friend. He should be the one to leave."

"Excuse me." I couldn't help myself. And I had a feeling the two women would be interested in what I was about to propose. "Sorry to overhear, but I wondered if you might be able to do me a favour?"

"Sure," said the Brazilian girl easily. "What is it?"

"Well, the thing is, I met this guy for a date tonight and he's turned out to be an absolute jerk."

They tutted sympathetically.

"And I thought, since it sounds like you can't do anything about your own moron-guy, then maybe you'd consider doing something about mine?"

The girls glanced at each other.

"What do you have in mind?" asked Ringlets.

"Nothing drastic, but as you're walking back to your table, maybe you could … spill this drink on him?" I suggested, picking up the half-full beer someone had left by the sink. "You'll know who he is. He's the one at the bar wearing a green checked shirt and he has one of those awful earlobe holes."

"It would be my pleasure," said Ringlets with a laugh, throwing her friend a gleeful look as she took the beer.

I left the bathroom with a smile, my only regret being that I wouldn't get to witness the action. Because as the door to the ladies swung closed behind me, I was presented with my escape route. If I turned left, I'd be heading into the bar and back towards anally-forward Tristan. But if I turned right, I'd wind up in a completely different restaurant. And Tristan would have no idea where I'd gone.

Of course, I tried not to look *too* smug as I strolled casually through the tables at Greektopia, wafts of garlic squid and fresh-baked pita washing over me. And then I was out in the warm evening air, a good street away from the bar on the Manly Corso, where Tristan was about to be coated in warm beer while he waited for a girl who was never coming back.

Luckily, he wasn't from around here. But I was. Manly was my town, and there were three friends waiting for me at another bar just around the corner.

2

Alright, so let me just clarify that I didn't usually ditch guys mid-date. I wasn't that mean. Not really. I'd only done it like ... twice before. And all in the last three months. But see, this was what we were dealing with in today's dating pool. You didn't need to hang around and give people the benefit of the doubt about stuff, did you? I mean, disappearing mid-date wasn't any worse than disappearing out of someone's DMs, and guys were doing that all the time, weren't they?

But anyway. I was getting quite good at dismissing guys from my mind. In fact, I'd say I was doing pretty well at the whole casual-dating thing as a whole. In the last few months, ever since I quit my job working in the incentives team at Tiger Finance, an investment bank, I'd been doing a lot of exploring. And not just exploring of men—although there had been a fair few of those—but exploring myself and my surroundings. It'd been a getting-to-know-Laura few months, and I was loving it. Plus, I had this awesome new job as an assistant location manager on a *film set* starting in three weeks, which I was super pumped about. I'd even be working with my flatmate, Ben, on the movie set, as he was the one who got me the job. Really, there wasn't much more I could ask the universe for right now. My life was pretty perfect.

Okay, so *perfect* might be a slight overstatement. There were a few ... just a couple of tiny, niggly little things that I was still trying to work out.

Like:

1. What was I going to do for money in a few months once my exciting new film-set job was over?
2. What was I going to do for money in a few *weeks* if my current rate of expenditure continued?
3. Was it normal to date so many guys and find you had zero interest in them?
4. What was the actual plan for my life?

But you know, these were pretty normal concerns I thought. No one really had the answer to these things, did they? Exactly.

Besides, I've found that the best way to deal with these little niggles was just to ignore them. See, I've been doing this thing where I just focused on the present. Just thought about this one day. How was I going to enjoy myself today? No need to worry about tomorrow. No need to plan for the future. If there was one thing my failed marriage had taught me, it was that you couldn't plan out life. You just had to go with the flow of things.

I told myself this mantra quite often. In fact, I had to tell myself this mantra when I woke up the other night in a cold sweat. I couldn't remember what I was dreaming about, but I felt like an elephant had been sitting on my chest. But then I told myself to stop worrying and things calmed themselves down again. Happiness was about the *now*, I thought. You just had to keep putting one foot in front of the other and soon you'd be climbing Everest. Right?

While Tristan sat alone, presumably in a small puddle of sticky beer, I made my way towards the bar where my friends worked.

Los Perdidos was located down a small alleyway in the back streets of Manly. Being a pop-up bar, it probably would be around for only a couple of months over summer, and it was owned by Lucas, Ben's brother.

Lucas was also … well, he was mega hot, let's just say that. He was tall and tanned with ripped surfer muscles and the bluest eyes I'd ever seen. He worked really hard on the bar and all these other businesses he seemed to have. He was driven in a way I hadn't really seen before in the one person. He could be quite intense.

I liked it when he was intense.

I mean, intense in a *friend* way. Because we were just friends.

Really.

Even if sometimes things got a bit flirty. Even if sometimes when he looked at me I felt like a crossbow bolt had just punched through my diaphragm.

But dealing with this was all part of my mantra. There was something in my gut telling me that if Lucas and I got together then it would be a massive, life-changing thing. He was like a vortex, and once you were sucked in there was no getting out again. Right now I was just orbiting gently. Not quite locked into the gravitational pull.

In any case, I wasn't heading to Los Perdidos just to see him. Ben worked there as the head chef and Kalina, my other flatmate, was one of the bartenders. It was pretty cool hanging out somewhere where the staff were all your friends. I would always get to try things off the menu for free and taste-test any new bottles of wine that were being opened. Although obviously, I made an effort to actually buy and pay for stuff whenever I was there.

Los Perdidos was fairly quiet tonight, and a number of seats at the bar were vacant. Kalina was behind the counter, drying glasses, and she grinned at me as I slid onto a stool.

"That was over fast," she stated flatly in her easy London accent as she poured a glass of wine for me.

"Not fast enough for me." My eyes slid past Kalina to where Lucas was leaning on the bar, chatting to a couple of guys. Even though we'd established that we were firmly *just friends*, I couldn't seem to prevent the lightness I felt in my chest every time I was in the same room as him.

But that didn't mean anything, did it? I also loved being in the same room as Kalina and Ben, and they were just friends, too. Besides, I'd been the one to decide Lucas and I weren't right for each other and that neither of us was ready for a relationship. He was still getting over having his heart broken by his ex-fiancée, and I wasn't sure that I'd ever be ready to dive into another relationship. Plus, the way he worked, the sheer quantity of hours he put in, meant that in reality he didn't even have time for a girlfriend.

"Let me guess." Kalina was back in front of me, her dark hair piled on top of her head in a tangled stack that wouldn't work for anyone else. "Bad BO? Or dandruff? Or ... nineties-style MC Hammer pants?"

I laughed. "Well, he did have one of those earlobe holes."

"Ooh! Did you try to throw peanuts through it?"

"I was very tempted to try to get my straw through when he wasn't looking."

"Brilliant."

"But you know, I'm a very generous person and I'm fully prepared to not judge someone by their appearance."

"Of course, Saint Laura."

"I was prepared to give him the benefit of the doubt and only judge him based on his character."

"And a very shrewd judge of character you are."

I ignored that jibe and narrowed my eyes at her as I continued.

"So, I was being very open and fair when he unexpectedly ... propositioned me."

"Like with drugs?" Kalina leaned in avidly.

I snorted. "I wish."

"Money? He wanted to pay you for sex?"

"I actually think that might have been better. But no."

"What, then? Come on, I'm dying here."

"Let's just say that Mr Darcy never asked Elizabeth Bennett to have anal sex with him."

Kalina burst out laughing. "I love that you find such weirdos, Laur."

"I do seem to attract them, don't I?" I grumbled.

At that moment Lucas wandered over towards us, and I gave Kalina a pointed look to end our conversation.

"You going to serve any proper customers tonight, Kal?" he asked jokingly.

"Laura is a proper customer!" Kalina feigned being offended on my behalf. "Aren't you, Laura?"

"I like to think so." I smiled winningly at Lucas.

"How are you, Laura?" Lucas's blue eyes creased up as he smiled back at me, and, oh …

My heart …

"Great. I'm great." Warmth flooded into my face. "How's everything going here?"

"Pretty cruisy tonight. Have you tried Ben's latest special?"

I glanced towards the kitchen, where I could see Ben working away, his shaggy hair held back with a thick black headband. It's funny that there was a time when I didn't realise he and Lucas were brothers. Now that I knew, there was a definite family resemblance, though Lucas tended to come across as serious and intense, while Ben was all light-hearted and jokey. Ben was a trained sound engineer, but he had a passion for food and had been all too eager to design the menu for his brother's bar. He would probably be rather sad when it was time for the pop-up bar to close and he would have to go back to his usual occupation.

"I haven't, no."

"Laura's been on a date," Kalina said with a wicked gleam in her eye.

If Kalina had been close enough to kick, she would have received the full force of my foot in her shin right then.

"Really?" Lucas seemed surprised. "I thought you weren't dating at the moment?"

"I'm not—not seriously," I said hurriedly, shooting Kalina a look that I hoped said *I will murder you later when we're alone.* "And it was nothing. Just a waste of time."

Lucas raised his eyebrows at me, and I swallowed the lump in my throat. Why did I suddenly feel so irrationally defensive?

Kalina's eyes were darting between us, clearly enjoying this. Then she noticed someone trying to get her attention at the other end of the bar, and with a tut of annoyance, she moved away.

"So, ah, how has the food been doing here?" I asked, simply to change the topic.

Lucas glanced towards his brother. "It's been good. Ben hasn't been making as many new items lately, but that's alright. The bar has only got a month to go, anyway."

I nodded, also looking towards Ben. Neither of us mentioned the reason why Ben might not be giving as much time and attention to the bar, though we both knew what it was. Or, rather, who *she* was.

"And you're enjoying being the owner of such a trendy establishment?" I asked.

"I am." Lucas smiled, his eyes crinkling with humour. "I like some of the regulars we get here."

"I thought I was your only regular?"

"You're one of them. By the way, how were the Chinese gardens the other day?"

I glowed with pleasure that he remembered.

See, this was part of my getting-to-know-Laura personal exploration. For the past couple of months, since I hadn't had a job to go to, I'd been taking myself out on cultural dates.

I'd done the Sydney Aquarium, Taronga Zoo, the Art Gallery of New South Wales and the Powerhouse Museum. I'd also done a load of free things, like visit the Sydney Observatory, go to the markets in The Rocks, walk across the Harbour Bridge and take a day trip out to Coogee. I did this cool art class that took place in a pub, and I also took a macramé course (annoyingly, Ben's now banned me from making any more macramé pieces for the lounge room. "Why's there so much bloody rope everywhere?" he started shouting one evening. "It's art," I tried to explain. "The art of knot tying." He didn't really get it.). It really was incredible how many different and interesting things you could do in Sydney. Funny that I'd lived here my whole life, but had never really explored the city like a tourist might do.

"The gardens were amazing! I'd forgotten how peaceful it is to just sit and relax by a koi pond."

"Is that right? Have you had much experience sitting by koi ponds?"

"Well, no. But you know—sitting by water in general is pretty nice. Or on water, for that matter."

"Sitting *on* water?"

"Yeah. Like in a boat, obviously."

"Obviously."

Lucas grinned and I rolled my eyes at him. Our conversations seemed to always deteriorate into him teasing me.

"So, what's the next cultural day out you've got planned?" he asked.

"I'm not sure yet. I need to stop doing things that cost so much, but I'm running out of ideas for free things."

"Well, if you want to come and check out some things that sit on water, I've got to go down to the marina at Bobbin Head to deliver some wine to a client there on Monday. It'll be an early start, but you can tag along if you like."

"You want me to tag along with you to Bobbin Head?"

"I'll need a hand with the wine probably." His voice was deadpan, but his eyes were teasing again.

I felt my heart stutter. We hadn't been alone together since that day almost three months ago, when I kissed him in the storeroom. And then I walked away, and neither of us had mentioned it since. Sometimes I wondered if I'd just imagined the whole thing.

But we were friends now, so why shouldn't I go along and help him out? One day at a time, after all.

"Sure," I said, trying to sound nonchalant. "I mean, if you need help with the wine, then it's definitely a good idea to have me along. I'll bring the muscle."

"Sounds good," Lucas said.

His eyes shifted over my shoulder and I saw the smile on his face freeze slightly.

I'd barely even turned around before I caught sight of the whirlwind that was racing in through the bar, long, blonde hair streaming out behind her, tanned limbs and a killer figure squeezed into such a tight dress that I found myself immediately scanning her to try to work out how she was hiding her underwear lines. If she was even wearing any, that was.

It was Amy. Ben's girlfriend.

It wasn't that we didn't like Amy. She was vibrant and outgoing and fun. But if I thought Lucas was intense, then Amy was on a whole other planet. Just being in the same room as her for more than half an hour left me feeling like I needed to have a little lie down.

Ben, of course, was absolutely smitten.

"Bae!" she cried, rushing straight into the kitchen and throwing her arms around Ben, kissing him passionately.

Honestly, you'd think they'd been separated for weeks, not the three-or-so hours it had actually been. But then, that sort of summed up their relationship. It was intense, and seemed to be on a highly escalated time scale.

"Should she be in the kitchen?" I asked Lucas as we both stared at Ben and Amy a little gobsmacked.

Lucas made a kind of non-committal grunting sound and looked away. "Not sure we'd be able to get her out of there."

"Perhaps use a hose on her?" Kalina suggested quietly, sidling up beside Lucas and joining our conversation.

We all fell silent for a moment, our mouths all agape as we witnessed the giggling, cuddling, canoodling couple in the kitchen. I mean, don't get me wrong, it was lovely that Ben was so besotted. His eyes always lit up when Amy was around, and he looked so happy right now as he squeezed her into him and nipped at her neck while she giggled.

It was just that ...

Actually no, I shouldn't even say it. Shouldn't mention it or bring it up again.

But see, there was this *tiny* little incident last week that really sent up red flags for me. Ben seemed to have just brushed it off and forgotten about it, or at least moved past it like it was nothing. I didn't really understand how he could do that. Especially because there was still the dent and the stained patch on the wall in our flat where Amy threw her entire plate of spaghetti. And the *screaming* row they'd had.

I'd been cowering in my room at the time, *Younger* on pause, listening avidly and trying to work out if I should go out and try to intercede or just stay put and mind my own business. Of course, when I'd heard the crash I'd leapt up and run out—I mean, breaking things was certainly crossing a line. But by that point, Amy was crying and Ben had his arms wrapped around her, comforting her, and he'd glanced at me looking a little shell-shocked but just kind of shrugged apologetically like there was nothing to worry about. I'd taken one look at the red spaghetti sauce and pasta still dripping down the wall, and the broken plate shards littering the carpet, and I'd grabbed the dustpan out of the cupboard. Amy was so apologetic and lovely after that, as if the plate of spaghetti had made it to the wall simply by accident, that I couldn't work out what to say about it.

Of course, I hadn't told Kalina about the incident. She thought the stain on the wall was from a rainbow lorikeet flying in through the open balcony door and flattening itself on the wall (not my most brilliant story, but I panicked under pressure). But see, Kalina already had this weird kind of suspicion going on about Amy. She hadn't been able to articulate what, exactly, was off about her, she just kept shaking her head and saying weirdly cryptic things like, "The game is on." I personally thought it was entirely down to the fact that Kalina was going through a bit of a detective obsession at the moment. I kept walking in and finding her sitting on the couch watching all these old *Sherlock Holmes* episodes, and just last week she took it upon herself to "solve" the case of the never-empty bins at the units. She set up Ben's go-pro camera in the stairwell window, camouflaged by a plant, pointing down at the trash cans, determined that she was going to catch whoever it was that kept filling them up straight after bin day.

"You don't mind if I take off, do you, Lucas?" Ben called from the kitchen, his eyes all crinkled with laughter as Amy noisily kissed his cheek. "I've already cleaned down, and we haven't had a food order for the last half-hour."

I looked to Lucas to see his reaction. The muscle in his jaw was clenching, but then he took a deep breath and smiled. It looked a bit forced.

"That's fine. If you're sure you're all done for the night?"

"Yeah, totally," Ben said, giggling, Amy pressed right up against his side. "See you tomorrow."

"Bye, everyone!" Amy waved and beamed at us all cheerfully as she and Ben walked out the door.

"Bye." I raised a hand as they left.

"Did you notice she had *another* Dior handbag? Different to the one she had three days ago," Kalina said, her eyes still pinned to the spot where Amy had last been seen.

"So?"

"*So*," Kalina turned to look at me triumphantly, "how does a uni student afford *that*? There's something up with her, I'm telling you, Laura. It's the little things that are infinitely the most important. My awareness is attuned."

I rolled my eyes, sure that was one of those Sherlock quotes.

"'Scuse me, mate, can I order some of the meatballs?" a customer asked.

Lucas looked pained.

3

Sitting in the car with Lucas as we drove down the winding road to Bobbin Head, I was trying really hard to act normal.

But he was *right there.*

His arm was mere inches from my arm. I had to keep my hands tucked in lest they decide to stray of their own accord. And my eyes kept sneaking looks at his hands on the steering wheel, at his legs spread apart on the seat, the way they'd shift each time he changed gears.

Stop it, Laura!

God, what was wrong with me? We were *friends.* Every rational part of my brain knew that was the most sensible relationship for us. I didn't want to ruin that with thoughts of him naked.

And well, let's just say, there were many, many of those thoughts.

"So, now that we're alone and you can be completely candid with your answers, I'm dying to know. What do you think of Amy?" I asked, more to distract myself.

"I'm not sure it's really a good idea to have an opinion on my brother's girlfriend."

"Oh, come on. None of that copping out. I'm not going to say anything to Ben."

Lucas grinned. "Well, how do you feel about her? You've obviously been thinking about this."

"Nope, I asked you first. Ben's your brother, so you must have a viewpoint on the matter."

Lucas's mouth tensed as he looked out at the road, and I wasn't sure if he was trying not to smile or grimacing.

"I think Ben is young and hasn't had any real relationships before," he said eventually. "And I'd probably assume the same thing about Amy."

"What makes you think she hasn't?"

"Just a hunch. I'm sure she's dated guys … but I'm not sure she would have had anything very real."

"And?" I prompted.

"And I think they will have to work things out on their own."

"Aha. So, you don't see this lasting in the long term, then? It won't be a proper first relationship for either of them?"

Lucas raised his eyebrows at me. "I'd say this relationship will be like a wild fire. Hot and intense, but it'll burn itself out pretty quick."

I laughed. "You sound like you know a lot about relationships."

Lucas shrugged. "I've had a few."

There was an awkward pause in the conversation, and my mind immediately jumped to the last relationship Lucas had had, with a girl named Holly Kovarnik. I'd stalked her online, of course. Lucas had *proposed* to her, and they'd been engaged for a few weeks, but then she'd cut and run. I found pictures of her on her Facebook page. I was probably hoping she would look like a nightmare or have three heads or something, but to my dismay she was pretty and petite and looked not only normal, but like one of those down-to-earth, nice people who would make an excellent friend. There were photos of her dressed up like Snow White at a toddler's birthday party. There were pictures of her smiling amidst a group of people having a picnic. There was one of her dressed up nicely at a wedding, and frankly, she looked quite stunning. The photos were sporadic—she clearly didn't live her life on social media. But the worst picture was the one I came across from two years ago, of Lucas and her together. She was laughing delightedly and he had his arms around her, pulling her in tightly, with his nose and lips pressed into her cheek. I felt weird when I looked at that picture, like I was witnessing something I shouldn't see. And now, of course, I couldn't forget it.

Honestly, sometimes I felt like the internet made my life *worse*, not better.

"Anyway," I cleared my throat. "Relationships are overrated."

Lucas shot me a raised-eyebrow look. "You still think that? You know, I wondered, months ago, where you'd gotten your stance on dating from. Now I realise it's probably come from Kalina."

"It hasn't! I mean, so what if it has? She's right, isn't she?"

"You're the one drinking the Kool-Aid."

"Kalina isn't Kool-Aid!"

Lucas grinned but didn't respond.

"Oh, come on, you think she's wrong?" I pushed, looking at him incredulously.

His lips twitched.

"There's nothing wrong with just wanting to sleep with people for fun and not wanting to get involved in a relationship," I said, folding my arms and staring resolutely out the window.

"I'm not judging if that's what you want to do," Lucas said. "But Kalina's got her own issues to deal with. Just don't take her opinions as gospel, is all I'm saying."

I made an annoyed tutting sound, and refused to look at him. But I heard him laughing softly beside me.

Before I had time to think of anything else to say, we rounded the final bend and the trees that had been blocking the view suddenly ended as we drove down the last steep stretch of road into Bobbin Head. The water stretched out before us, sparkling crystal in the morning light, with forested hills rising up all around. Clustered in one area was the marina and the jetties with boats all closely docked. And spread around the wharves, dotted here and there, fishermen sat peacefully with their fishing lines and buckets of supplies.

"Have you been here before?" Lucas asked as he cruised towards the empty car spaces.

"Yeah, my parents love coming down here, so I've been quite a bit. There's the cool mangrove walk over that way." I gestured over the bridge towards the other side of the river, where wide green parks nestled between the rock face and the water. "You?"

"Only to the marina. I didn't know there were mangroves over there."

"It's pretty cool. There are heaps of crabs you can see in the mud."

"Sounds ... great."

"No really, it is!" I laughed. "Okay, it might not sound great, but it's beautiful. We'll go check it out after."

"Will we now?"

"Yes. Call it part of your own cultural education."

"Mangroves and mud crabs. Definitely something I need to experience."

I rolled my eyes at him, even though he was parking the car and wasn't looking at me.

As I opened my car door and climbed out of the seat, the almost deafening sound of cicadas greeted me. The air was still and humid, and despite it being early, I knew that very soon it would crank up into a scorcher of a day.

I walked around to the boot and popped it open, all prepared to start carrying wine, but was stopped when I saw the contents.

"Is this seriously all for the one client?" I asked incredulously. "There have to be hundreds of bottles here!"

"Yeah." Lucas came around to join me at the boot. "He's a good client."

"Are we actually carrying all this?"

"I thought you were the muscle here?" Lucas teased me, giving my bicep a poke.

"Hey!" I swatted his hand away. "You didn't say there would literally be *hundreds* of bottles of wine!"

Lucas laughed. "Come on." He shut the boot. "We'll get trolleys."

"Oh, thank God."

So, it turned out that when you had a friend with a boat, then marinas were pretty cool places. Instead of being restricted to the public areas, we got buzzed into the private jetties. And let me just say—wow. Future goal for my life: being able to afford an awesome boat.

The marina staff were all super friendly once we were on the inside, too. We were able to get these two giant carts that we raced back to the car and loaded with all the boxes of wine, then pushed at a much more reasonable pace back to the marina. As we passed boats of ever-increasing size, I wondered which of the boats we were heading to and just how wealthy Lucas's client was. I supposed, based on the amount of wine they'd ordered, it shouldn't have been hard to guess.

"There he is!" a deep, raspy voice called when we'd almost reached the end of the jetty. I looked around for the speaker and realised it was the man standing on the enormous, three-storeyed yacht parked right at the end. "Perfect timing, Lukey!"

He was probably in his late sixties and his uber-tanned skin was covered in a fine layer of white hair. He was the kind of man who could have looked fit, except for the enormous beer gut sticking out over his board shorts—the only thing he was wearing aside from fluoro-yellow sunglasses, which were perched on top of his bald head.

"Frank, my man!" Lucas called back warmly. He dropped the handle of his cart and jumped up easily onto the deck of the yacht, gripping Frank in a handshake and simultaneously pulling him in for one of those man-hugs.

I waited awkwardly on the jetty.

"Come on up, Laura," Lucas said easily, smiling at me and stepping aside so I could also climb aboard.

"So, who's this, then?" Frank was appraising me with friendly interest, shooting one of those knowing looks to Lucas. "New girlfriend, eh?"

"Laura," Lucas said, holding my hand to steady me as I climbed onto the boat. "She's a friend."

I didn't know why, but I felt quite a stab of disappointment by his words.

"Laura, this is Frank, nomad of the seas," he continued, and Frank roared with laughter.

"I like that! Are you both going to stay for a drink?"

"Ah, wish we could, but I've got a busy day ahead," Lucas replied. "Maybe next time?"

"I'll hold you to that, my boy! You're always welcome here."

"Thanks, Frank."

"Sorry to hear about Maurine, by the way," Frank went on, rubbing his hand over his bristly chin. "The old girl went well past her use-by date, didn't she?"

"Yeah." Lucas laughed softly, almost apologetically. "And she was still running rings around people a good thirty years younger than her."

"Great genes, right here," Frank said, clapping a hand on Lucas's shoulder and giving me a wink.

I looked at Lucas quizzically, not knowing whom they were talking about. He smiled apologetically at me, looking a bit uncomfortable, but then he turned his attention back to the jetty.

"Well, this wine isn't going to get itself on board!"

And that was the end of that conversation. We all pitched in and helped to get the boxes of wine up onto the boat, and Frank even gave me a tour of the yacht (it was *beyond* amazing). Then we were saying goodbye, and

Lucas and I were leaving the private marina area.

I was shocked when I checked my watch to see that more than an hour had gone by. But then I spotted the cafe and the huge ice-cream poster stuck up outside it.

"Come on! It's traditional to get ice-cream when you come to Bobbin Head," I said, pushing Lucas ahead of me up to the counter. "And I know you said you've got to get back, but we need to check out at least part of the mangrove walk before we go."

"Alright, I don't need telling twice." Lucas smiled as he looked at the ice-cream poster. "I don't actually need to hurry back, though. I just said that, because otherwise it's almost impossible to escape once you've had a drink with Frank."

"Oh, you cheeky liar!" I shoved him playfully.

"What can I get you?" A middle-aged woman had appeared behind the counter and was smiling at us.

"Vanilla Cornetto," I said.

"Golden Gaytime," said Lucas.

"What?! You're not seriously getting a Golden Gaytime, are you?" I laughed as the woman turned to fetch our respective ice-creams.

"Why not?" Lucas asked.

"No one eats Gaytimes anymore!"

"They're my favourite."

I shook my head as the woman handed me my Cornetto. "Alright. Weirdo."

We paid for the ice-creams then went back out to the marina front.

"Lead the way to these mangroves, then," Lucas said, dropping his ice-cream wrapper in the bin.

I did just that, and we marched away from the marina, the sun burning down on our heads. The cicadas were still going, sounding louder next to the rock wall, which bounced the sound back out at us. We crossed the carpark again and I led Lucas over the large bridge and across the road, through the open park and around the children's playground. As we reached the end of the park, where the pathway disappeared around the rock wall, we found the sign heralding the start of the mangroves.

"Well, you weren't making it up!" Lucas said jokingly as we walked around the water's edge. Ahead, a steel-structured pedestrian bridge crossed the water again, leading to a boardwalk raised up over the water and disappearing into the mangroves.

"Did you think I was?" I grinned at him as we crossed the bridge.

"Could have fooled me. I had no idea this was here."

"Being able to surprise you must be a special talent of mine."

Lucas laughed. "One of them, I'm sure."

I looked away so he couldn't see my smile.

We paused at the first small open lookout on the boardwalk, both gazing down at the mud below.

"Crabs, see?" I said smugly, watching them scuttle in and out of their holes.

"I see."

For a moment we were silent, watching. Then I cleared my throat. "So, how do you know Frank really?" I asked.

"He's an old family friend, and was one of my first clients, actually."

"He seemed to know you well. And ... Maurine?"

"Ah. My great-aunt. She passed away a couple of months ago."

"Oh no, I'm so sorry! I had no idea. Were you close to her?"

"Not really. She lived down near Adelaide, and I hadn't seen her in about five years. Ben was the closest to her out of all my brothers. He lived with her on and off during high school."

"He did? Why?"

Lucas shrugged. "Household of five boys. Ben's right in the middle. I didn't really think about it at the time, but I think he needed some space.

Besides, Maurine's estate is pretty awesome. It's this huge ten-acre property and I used to love when we took family holidays there. It's got a giant, sprawling villa for a house, and there were always cleaners and gardeners and chefs all working. My parents are actually down there now, helping sort out her estate and all that."

"Right! Gosh, was there a funeral? I mean, I didn't think ..."

"There was, but Ben and I didn't go. My younger brothers went down for it with my parents, but we were busy with work, so ..." Lucas trailed off, shrugging.

"That's a shame. I mean, that you—and Ben—missed it. Especially if he was so close to her."

"I kept telling Ben he should go. But he knew Maurine wouldn't have cared. She hated funerals. She'd rather just get pissed with everyone and call it a day. Ben and I did have a couple of bottles of wine in her honour."

We moved away from the lookout, walking together further along the boardwalk so that we were right in the mangroves, their reedy stalks rising up high above our heads. I loved the way the boardwalk snaked around through them, so you quickly found yourself in a whole little isolated world, with cicadas chirping and crabs scurrying across the mud, and this kind of muted dampness to the air.

"Right, hypothetical question," Lucas suddenly said. "If you were a multi-billionaire, what is the most creative thing you can think of to do with your money?"

I gave him a disbelieving look. "How have I magically become a multi-billionaire?"

"It's a game. Say you're rich, and you've already done all the standard stuff, like buying a house, going on holidays and donating to charities. What would you do that was original?"

"Is anything original?"

"Think about the most eccentric billionaires. You've got Michael

Jackson, who created his own fantasy land. There's Elon Musk, who is literally building space rockets."

"Oh, I did read that Lindsay Lohan has apparently bought her own island near Dubai and is turning it into 'Lindsay Land'!"

"Exactly. You're an eccentric billionaire. So, what would you do with your money?"

"Hmm. I would ... build an underwater palace and breed mermaids."

"Are you just saying that because you're looking at water right now?"

"Er ... no. Though there wouldn't be any crabs allowed in my underwater palace."

"How would people get there?"

"Teleporting."

"Of course."

"So now, if you were a multi-billionaire, what would you do with your money?"

"I'd buy a really old, really good winery and work on the cellar door."

"Hey! That's not something you need billions of dollars for!"

Lucas grinned. "The billions of dollars would ensure that I don't actually have to worry about the business side of the winery. If people came and bought wine, then great. But if they didn't," he shrugged, "well, it wouldn't matter."

I frowned at him. "Is that your real goal, then? To work in a winery?"

"My goal is to make as much money as I can now so that I don't need to worry about working at all in the future."

"Right." Oh God. And I said I wanted to breed mermaids. "I wouldn't mind working in a winery. But I'd probably need to know a bit more about wine first. They're so nice to visit, though, always so laidback and everyone's friendly and in a good mood."

"You'd actually want to work in a winery?"

"Maybe one day."

He smiled at me then, and I realised what I seemed to be implying.

Abruptly, my heart started thudding really hard, and I found my eyes flitting away, trying to focus on something else. "Hey look! Did you see that massive crab down there?"

I peered down at the mud and tried to spot another of the huge crabs I'd just seen scuttling away. Lucas came up beside me and also looked down.

"Careful you don't fall in," he said.

I turned to ask what he meant, but he was looking at me with a cheeky smile, and then I felt the jolt of his hand on my back, giving me the smallest prod forwards before grabbing my shoulders to prevent me from actually falling off the boardwalk.

"Hey!" I protested, but I also started laughing. "You make sure *you* don't fall in!"

I went to push him, but he jumped away, and then we were running and zigzagging across the boardwalk, giggling like children as we tried to both get the other person and protect ourselves at the same time.

We called a truce when we reached the end of the boardwalk, the wooden planks ending with wide stone steps leading up into the bushland beyond.

"Shall we head back?" Lucas asked.

"Not yet. There's one more thing here you should see."

I led him up the steps and past the trees, squeezing through the narrow rock canyon and up to the bush trail beyond. There were ancient carvings in this area, created by the Aboriginal people of this land thousands of years ago, but that wasn't what I wanted to show him. I steered Lucas a little way along the track, and then we stepped off it and crossed to the beautiful lookout that cast a view across the sparkling water of Bobbin Head in the distance.

"Nice, isn't it?" I asked, turning to observe Lucas.

His eyes were looking out over the water, an expression of delight on his face. He glanced at me and we shared a smile, then I turned to look at the view as well. A moment later, I felt him shift beside me. He was gazing down at me, a pensive look on his face.

"Hey, Laura." Lucas stopped, seeming unsure, and I raised my eyebrows. Aside from the sounds of cicadas and birds, we were completely alone up here, and it was as if we could have been the only two people left in the world.

"What we were talking about before," Lucas said quietly, a fierce kind of intensity in his gaze. He hesitated again and I frowned.

"About being a billionaire?"

His expression cleared into humour for a moment. "Not that. What we were talking about in the car—about relationships. Look, it doesn't have to be me. But don't close yourself off from the world and start seeing men as nothing. I know Kalina makes a convincing argument, but I also know she just hasn't met the right guy yet. I'd hate for you to end up so jaded and closed off that you can't remember what it's like to be with someone. I know you were hurt really badly by your ex, I know that. But let someone else in again before you forget how to."

I'd frozen during his speech. He was still looking at me intensely, and I suddenly felt hot and unable to breathe. I looked away, trying to centre my gaze on the horizon, but my vision was swimming. I blinked rapidly, desperate to dispel the tears so they couldn't fall.

Lucas must have realised I needed a moment, because he turned back to the view, giving me time to compose myself.

But what could I say to that? What was he expecting me to say? My heart was racing, and I thought I might start hyperventilating. And every second that passed, I realised the moment was disappearing along with it. But what moment? What was this? I couldn't process this. Not right now. I wasn't ready.

My eyes still felt hot, but I cleared my throat determinedly. "There's not much else to see up here," I said, knowing that I was completely ignoring what he'd just said as if it meant nothing. And then I finished it right off. "We should head back." And I turned and started climbing back down.

INSTAGRAM FEED

Erika Healin:

If you can dream it, you can do it.

Gina Reed:

The only one who can stop you, is you.

Charlotte Levids:

Not all who wander, are lost.

        NEW COMMENT

        Laura Baker:

        Do you know this quote is from The Lord of the Rings?

4

We should head back?

For fuck's sake, was that all I could come up with?

Brilliant, emotionally retarded me. Well done.

I tossed and turned all night, unable to stop replaying my conversation with Lucas. Had he just put himself out there and I'd completely ignored it? What was *wrong* with me? Unsurprisingly, I was tired and groggy when I finally made it out of bed late the next day, and I had to suppress a groan when I realised Ben and Amy were in the kitchen, cooking. Or rather, Amy was in the kitchen wearing these miniature little Peter Alexander PJ shorts with a matching lace cami (and zero bra—her nipples were sticking out like little bullets), making a total mess with flour everywhere and about three frying pans all going at once, while Ben just kind of hung back gazing at her in adoration.

Kalina's door was wide open, but there was no sign of her. I wondered, briefly, if she'd stayed at Maverick's place last night. I thought she'd gone off him a bit, but since Amy had been hanging around at our place so much, Kalina had been making herself more and more scarce. I couldn't blame her. If I had a lover whose house I could go and hide at, I probably would too.

"Morning," I forced myself to say cheerily as I entered the kitchen. This was still my home, I reminded myself as I walked around the other side of the island bench and went to the fridge.

"Morning, Laura!" Amy said with far, far too much enthusiasm. "I'm making pancakes for Benny. Would you like some?"

I peered around the fridge door and dubiously eyed the strangely coloured globby batter which was not only swimming in a mixing bowl, but also decorating the floor, the cooktop and the kettle.

"No thanks, I'll stick with yoghurt this morning."

"Suit yourself." Amy shrugged. "These are red velvet pancakes, and they're going to be amazing."

Ah, so that explained the brownish hue.

"Benny, can you get the butter out for me?" Amy asked sweetly. I pulled it out of the fridge along with my yoghurt and blueberries, and handed it to Ben. He took it with a goofy smile on his face and I had to work hard not to roll my eyes. He was just so smitten with her, it was a little bit sickening. In a sweet way.

Rather than attempt to get a bowl from within Amy's disaster zone, I poured my berries straight into the yoghurt tub and sat at the bench. Amy dropped a giant knob of butter into the too-hot saucepan, and within moments the kitchen was filling up with smoke. Ben casually leaned past her and switched on the extraction fan.

It must be killing him, I thought, not being the one doing the cooking. Ben *loved* to cook, and he was really good at it, so watching Amy doing such a hashed job in his kitchen surely must bug him to no end. Weirdly, he didn't seem to mind. He just leaned back on the counter, his arms folded, and stared at her again with the sort of look on his face that a faithful dog has when gazing at its owner. I guess that's Ben, though. He was super easy-going. Amy could probably do anything and he'd let her get away with it.

"So!" I said brightly. "What are you guys up to today?"

Ben, finally, appeared to snap out of his love-struck fugue and looked around at me. Amy answered first, however.

"We're going to have such a fun day. After breakfast we're going to go shopping, then we're having lunch up at Jonah's and we're going to do the lighthouse walk at Palmy, aren't we, bae?"

Ben looked a little caught out. "Were we? I didn't realise we had plans. I told Hobs I'd go surfing with him later."

"Ben!" Amy dropped the spatula she was holding with a clatter, and gave him a look full of hurt, shock and just a flash of anger.

I was pretty sure I felt the temperature in the room drop. Plus, it couldn't be a good sign that he'd gone from "Benny" and "bae" to now just "Ben".

"I've already booked the restaurant! I can't cancel it now, it's too late notice! There's no way we'll be back in time for you to go surfing."

"But ... Hobs is pretty keen ..." Ben trailed off, and I saw that Amy had such a look of devastation on her face that her eyes had filled with tears.

"You'd rather go surfing than take me out for a beautiful lunch that I've organised especially for the two of us?" she said, her voice wobbling. "Don't you want to spend time with me? I want to spend all my time with you, but you'd rather go surfing with your friend than spend the afternoon together?" She blinked and a tear rolled down her cheek.

I realised I'd frozen, my yoghurt spoon hovering midair, watching this interaction like it was playing out on a movie screen in front of me. Honestly, Amy had *really* missed her calling as an actress.

"Oh, babe, I'm sorry." Ben was moving to her, wrapping his arms around her. "I didn't mean—of course I want to spend time with you. There's no one else I'd rather be with."

"So, you'll come to lunch, then? You won't try to hurry off to go surfing?" Amy lifted her face from his chest and peered up at him, her eyes wide and glassy.

"Of course, babe." Ben kissed her on the forehead. "Whatever you want to do, we'll do that."

"Good!" Amy beamed, and she turned back to her pancakes with renewed energy. If I hadn't just witnessed the tears of a moment ago, I could swear blind that she'd been in a sunny mood all morning.

"Here you go! I've made you eight pancakes!"

"Eight?" Ben looked at the stack in surprise. "Aren't you having any?"

"Me? No, these are all just for you, bae!"

"Right. Eight might be a bit much ..."

"I made them *just* for you, though!"

Shit, here came the tears again.

"Eight is great!" Ben said quickly, taking the stack. "You're the best, babe."

"I know," Amy replied sweetly. While Ben began attacking his pancakes, Amy glanced to me and gave me a smile that should have been radiant, but it made my insides curl.

It was a smile that you'd usually reserve for a friend when sharing an inside joke. On Amy, the smile seemed to say, *Look how well I control him.*

∽⚭

Later, once Ben and Amy had left the apartment, I gave my mum a call.

"Hello, darling!" came Mum's cheery voice down the phone. "How's the holiday going?"

Bless Mum, she kept referring to my current unemployed status as my "holiday". I took another sip of tea, and wiggled my toes in the sunshine on my balcony before responding.

"It's great! I'm really enjoying myself."

"What are you getting up to in your leisure time?"

"Oh, plenty of things! Going to the beach, and the museums and the art galleries. I've read a few books. I even went to Bobbin Head yesterday."

"Lovely. Baxter, down. Baxter, no! Bang! Baxter, bang! BANG!"

"How's the dog training going?" I tried not to laugh.

About a month ago a good friend of Mum's had to fly to Europe suddenly, and Mum offered to host Margaret's two toy poodles who were show dogs. Apparently, the dogs were capable of doing a large number of tricks, such as playing dead when a human pretended to shoot them. Unfortunately, and despite Mum's best efforts, the only trick she seemed to have witnessed so far was the wee-on-the-carpet kind.

"We're getting there!" Mum replied, sounding a bit strained. "Baxter definitely *leaned* to the side just then. And Muffin has started staring at me whenever I'm in the kitchen. Like, really staring. I think she's interested in cooking."

"Isn't there that dog show next week that Margaret wants you to enter the dogs into?"

"Oh yes, that's happening! We're working on it." Mum definitely sounded strained now. "The dogs are certainly excited. Aren't you? *Aren't* you?"

Dad told me last week that there was no return date set for Margaret, so he didn't know how long the dogs would be living with them. He was a bit worried Mum had decided they were her new replacement children, since I'd moved out of home again and Elle was still off in South America.

"So anyway, have you spoken to Elle lately?" I asked. "I tried skyping her last week, but she couldn't get online."

"Yes, I just spoke to her yesterday. She's in Mexico now, which I was very upset to hear. But apparently, it's their last port of call, and I suppose if nothing bad happened to them in Columbia or Bolivia, then they should be alright in Mexico."

"Has she set a return date, finally? I thought she wasn't coming back for another four months."

"Marika wanted to cut it short, it seems, so Elle is also coming back. She's arriving in two weeks, can you believe it! And she's already got a job lined up."

"She has? Doing what?"

Considering Elle went straight from her communications degree at university to travelling through South America, with no employment history other than coffee shops and retail, I couldn't imagine how she could line something up from the other side of the world.

"She's starting work at an advertising firm in the city."

"Really?" My stomach did an awkward kind of drop and swoop. "That's … well, wow. Good for her."

"Yes, it's quite a good job, actually. She's done very well in securing it. But then, she's always managed to fall on her feet."

Something clenched in my throat.

"Muffin, no, that's not for you! Drop it. Drop it! Muffin! Give. *Give* it. Give it here. Muffin, do you want a treat, instead? I've got a treatie here for you, Muffin. Muff-in. Treatie! Treatie for Muffin!"

"Mum? Mum!" I tried to get her attention again.

"Hmm? What? Muffin, let go."

"I'm going to go. Sounds like you've got a lot on."

"Okay. Muffin, come here. Come HERE."

"Bye, Mum."

"Bye, darling. Baxter, what's that in your mouth? No, don't chew faster!"

I hung up the phone with a sigh, and stared out to the small patch of ocean I could see from my balcony.

Elle was coming home in two weeks! I couldn't wait to see her. To hear all about her trip. All the amazing stories she'd have, the adventures she had been on.

And fancy that, already having an amazing job lined up here waiting for her? I shouldn't be surprised. Elle had always put zero planning into anything, yet just as Mum said, things always seemed to fall into place for her. She was lucky like that.

Not that I was jealous. Of course not! I too had an amazing job lined up. I was making a career change. Plus, I was enjoying my own sort of holiday right now, which was helping me get my life back together.

Really, I shouldn't have a care in the world.

Only ... well, was this movie job *really* going to turn into a career? I'd been trying not to think too far ahead, trying to just focus on the here and now. But say the job was amazing, and I absolutely loved it and was great at it. Well, then what? It was only a two-month contract. And realistically, not many movies were made in Sydney. Ben said that getting jobs on movie sets was rare, even for him. So what was an assistant location manager going to do after the job wrapped up? Should I be worried? Should I be planning ahead more?

Maybe it would just be best to not think about it.

5

There was a knock on the front door, and I looked up from my book with a frown.

It was still mid-morning and I was alone in the apartment. Ben and Amy presumably were on their way to Jonah's, and Kalina was still out.

I was half thinking it must be a delivery guy—Kalina was always ordering stuff online, and half the neighbours left the front security door propped open in the day time—but when I pulled the door open I was surprised to find a strange guy on my doorstep. He had short, spiked brown hair and a wash of stubble on his face, bright brown eyes and a slightly crooked nose. He was tall and skinny, though I could see just enough muscle beneath his shirt to know it was that kind of artistic skinny that was quite attractive. He looked as surprised to see me as I was to see him, and I realised he had one of those enormous backpacking travel packs on the ground behind him, as if he was a friend coming to stay.

"Er ... yes?" I said hesitantly.

"Does Kalina live here?" he asked, an indeterminate British accent to his voice.

"Yes, she does, but she's not here at the moment. Was she expecting you?"

His eyes had lit up when I said she lived here, but now he looked a bit cagey.

"Ah no, not exactly. I was going to surprise her. Do you know when she'll be back?"

I shrugged, eyeing him curiously. Who *was* he? I knew Kalina had a brother back in the UK, but I thought she'd mentioned he played rugby. This skinny guy would get flattened if he ever set foot on a rugby field.

"I can give her a message if you want?" I offered.

He scratched his chin, looking a bit lost. Based on the backpack alone, I'd say he'd probably come straight from the airport.

"Can I wait for her here?"

No way was I letting a strange guy into the flat to hang out with me, even if I *was* dying of curiosity.

"I'd have to give her a call first and check that's okay. Sorry, what was your name?"

He looked cagey again. "Ah, no, that might ruin the surprise. Tell you what, I'll just come back later. What time will she be home?"

"I don't know," I lied. "Might not be till tomorrow. And, sorry, but how do you know her?"

He gave me a smile that seemed engaging, but he didn't answer my question. "I'll come back later, then. No need to tell her I was here."

"Who *are* you?"

"I'm a friend. An old friend."

"And your name is?"

"Don't worry about it." He waved a hand as he hoisted up his backpack. "Just forget you saw me."

I watched, confused, as he lumbered off back down the stairs, pulling a phone out of his pocket and unlocking it as he went. As soon as I heard him leave the building I grabbed my keys and ran down to the front door, kicking the wedge the neighbours used out of the way so the security door swung shut. Honestly. The security door was there for a reason. I thought about pinning a rude note to the door but knew everyone would just ignore it. Then I ran back to the flat and called Kalina.

It rang out and went to her answering service.

"Kal, it's me. Call me back when you can. Some rando guy just turned up at the flat looking for you."

Los Perdidos was almost full on Friday night, no doubt due to the beer and tapas special that was on. I hadn't seen Lucas since our outing to Bobbin Head, and even though he was here now, working behind the bar, I was avoiding him.

Well, avoiding him as much as I could. I did wave in a friendly way when I arrived. But luckily—I mean *coincidentally*—he was really busy, so I hadn't had an opportunity to speak to him. Besides, I was at the bar with a friend.

Rose and I used to work together at Tiger Finance, and I hadn't seen her at all since I left two months ago. There'd been a bit of … unpleasantness between us around the time, but we'd buried the hatchet, as they say, and were back to being friends again. Sitting with her then, I realised just how much I missed my morning coffee breaks with Rose, probably the only thing I really missed about my old job.

"No way! Cara actually resigned?" I said in response to news that my former boss had also left the company.

"Yeah! Apparently, she went on a week's holiday to this health retreat thing in Bali, and then when she came back she announced that she was leaving to go and work with them. Literally, just decided she was going to move to Bali!"

"That's so bizarre. I can't imagine Cara in Bali. I can't imagine Cara *relaxing* anywhere. Ever."

"I can picture her there. She'd be scaring everyone into holding their downward dogs for way too long and they'd all end up with burst blood vessels in their eyes."

"Nup. Still can't imagine it."

"Philippe does yoga, did you know? He's amazing at it. We go to Bikram together on Saturday mornings now."

"Does he?" I raised my eyebrows suggestively. "And how are things going with *Philippe*?" I couldn't resist putting on a French accent as I said his name.

Rose had been in a pretty stable, long-term relationship for the past few years with a guy called Christian, but had recently decided things weren't working out (*after* she'd cheated on him with a guy at work—but you know, no judgement). Yet, I'd long known that Rose was one of those people who could never be single for long, and the fact that she looked like a Swedish goddess cemented this—she was all long, blonde hair, amazing legs, perfect skin, etcetera. Anyway, it was no surprise to learn that she was already in a serious relationship with a sexy Frenchman, and had practically moved into his artsy loft apartment in Pyrmont.

"Things are *wonderful*," Rose gushed now. "He's just so relaxed and laidback compared to Christian. We get up early on weekends and have coffee at this gorgeous little cafe on the street corner near his place. Then we wander around the markets or take a picnic down to the water. And in the evenings we drink wine and eat cheese, and his place has the most amazing view out over the city."

"You don't miss going out at night?"

"Definitely not! Besides, I feel like I *am* out. Honestly, you have to come around and see the view from his place. It's better than half those bars in the city that claim to have a view. Plus, there's another reason we stay in so much." Rose dropped her voice and leaned in closer to me with a sly smile. "You wouldn't *believe* how good he is in bed. Our sessions last *hours*. It's incredible!"

I couldn't help bursting into giggles.

"Seriously, Laura!" Rose was looking so earnest and excited, and she gripped my arm even though I could see she was trying not to laugh too. "Christian was such a dud in bed by comparison. I mean, he was so unfit and he drank so much and played Xbox all the time, so it was no wonder! But now that I'm with Philippe, I mean, really, you don't know what you're missing out on until you try something new."

My giggles dried up and I huffed a sigh. "Well, to be honest, I'm going through a bit of a dry spell at the moment. I just haven't … I mean, one-night stands aren't actually as easy to engineer as you might think. Plus, I'm not sure I really want any more of them. But I still don't want a boyfriend, either. So I'm kind of in limbo right now."

"What about …?" Rose's eyes slid across the bar suggestively and I felt my stomach squeeze as I realised she was looking at Lucas.

"That's him, isn't it?" Rose asked. "The volleyball guy you had a thing for? He's hot, Laura."

"I know he's hot! Stop staring at him," I hissed, hoping Lucas wouldn't look over and see us both ogling him. Luckily, he was occupied talking to a guy at the bar. "And no, nothing has happened between us. And it won't, at least not now. We're just friends."

Rose raised her eyebrows and her gaze skated back to him again. "I don't know," she said in a kind of knowing way. "You'd better be careful. A guy like him won't stay single for long. You should snap him up while you can."

My eyes darted back to Lucas in sudden, inexplicable fear, but he was still talking to the same guy. As if feeling my eyes on him, he glanced up and our eyes met for a moment.

I turned quickly back to Rose. "Anyway," I said. "We're talking about you and Philippe, not me."

Rose quirked an eyebrow at me. "My advice? Hook up with a guy who does yoga. They're amazing in bed. So … experimental."

"Well, I'll try." I rolled my eyes at her. "But you know, Lucas doesn't even do yoga, so that counts him out."

"He's fit, though. Fitness is just as good."

"I'll bear that in mind."

Just then, Kalina appeared next to us and slid into the vacant seat at our table.

"I'd ask if you guys want more drinks, but I can't be bothered getting up again," she announced.

"Rose, have you met Kalina before?" I grinned at them both.

"Not properly. Nice to meet you, finally." Rose smiled at Kalina, her accent slightly more posh than it had been before.

"Rose." Kalina gave a nod of the head, her voice curious but cool as she swept Rose with a shrewd look. Kalina knew all about the "scene" at work Rose had caused for me just before I left. See, back when I was just starting to date again, Rose was in a rut with her then-boyfriend Christian, and I think hearing about my dating adventures made her miss being single. So, unbeknownst to me, she began sleeping with this guy, Pete, from our work. But then *I* slept with Pete, thinking she'd been encouraging me to do so. And then she had a meltdown and yelled at me across the department floor, basically implying that I slept with anything that moved and humiliating me in front of everyone.

It's all water under the bridge now, and I'm doing my best to forget the incident. But, with a cringe, I suddenly realised that Kalina wasn't going to forget it so easily.

I secretly loved her for that.

"There hasn't been any sign of the A-monster tonight," Kalina said, turning her attention to survey the bar. There were groups of people at every single table, and others loitering around the bar, holding their drinks and watching for a table opening.

"Who's the A-monster?" Rose asked.

"Amy," Kalina supplied. "Ben's girlfriend."

"Right. And Ben's your other flatmate? Does he work here, too?"

"That's him in the kitchen," I pointed out.

"Ah." Rose's eyes gleamed in understanding as she spotted him. "And he and Lucas are brothers?"

"You'd *think* his brother would have a word to him," Kalina said, ignoring Rose's question. "I mean, Amy is clearly bad news. Plus, she's an idiot! Do you know what I heard her telling Ben the other day?"

"What?" I glanced at Rose with a grin.

"She was telling him that if he ever encounters a shark in the ocean, then the best thing to do is to *spin around in a circle*."

"Seriously?" I laughed.

"Yeah! She was really serious about it! She reckons that if you start swimming round and round on the spot then the whirlwind or currents that you make will somehow confuse the shark and it will swim away and leave you alone. She reckoned she'd seen it on TV!"

"I think if I ever came across a shark, my first reaction would be to swim to shore as fast as possible," Rose said with a frown.

"Or try to punch it in the eye. Apparently that works," I suggested.

"Surely, if you're near its eye you're also a bit too near its teeth, though?"

I shrugged. "I think if I can see its eyes or teeth, then my reaction would be, right, I'm dead."

"Is that her?" Rose sat up, her eyes tracking over my head, and Kalina and I whipped our heads around. Sure enough, Amy had appeared in the kitchen, and was doing her best to pull Ben's attention away.

"Surely not," Kalina huffed, glaring towards them. "We're way too busy tonight for him to leave."

"I'm sure he knows that," I said, attempting to be generous. As we watched, it seemed that he was trying to gently extricate himself from Amy's grasp, while smoke started pouring up from the stove behind him.

I was half expecting to see the waterworks come out, and for Amy to stamp her foot in a huff. But to her credit, she just kissed him on the back of the neck again and then slipped out the back door.

"Well," I said, turning to Kalina and Rose. "That wasn't so bad. Maybe she's calmed down a bit."

Kalina just grunted, her eyes still fixed intently on Ben. Then she stood, grabbing up the dish cloth she'd previously brought to the table with her. "Right. Back to it."

"Can we get another drink, please?" I smiled sweetly at her. She rolled her eyes in response as she left.

6

"You don't know what you're doing with your life."

"Yes, I do. I'm drinking cocktails in a bar. That's what I'm doing."

"That's not very good. Drinking cocktails is just a fluffy waste of time."

"Well, I'm not *just* drinking cocktails. I'm drinking them with people. With friends."

"Your friends all know what they're doing with their lives. Are you just their tag-along, cocktail-drinking friend?"

"No, I'm the friend who's going to be really successful. And they will be *my* tag-along, cocktail-drinking friends."

"Wisdom is found at the source."

"What?"

Cara blinked at me again, her six arms arranged around her body like concentric haloes, a blue bindi on her forehead.

"I said this is none of your damn business. You don't like her. You've never liked her."

"Who don't I like?"

Cara gave me a weird look, opened her mouth to keep speaking, but then she vanished. And suddenly, I was blinking around in the dark, seeing bright morning light peeking around the blinds in my bedroom.

And there were raised, shouting voices coming from down the hallway.

I quickly got out of bed, trying to shake the bizarre dream version of

Cara. While yawning and trying to blink myself awake, I realised it was Kalina and Ben yelling at each other that had woken me.

"You just can't stand to see anyone else happy, can you?" Ben shouted so loudly that I could hear him through my closed door. "Just because you're miserable doesn't mean everyone has to be!"

I opened my door quietly and hesitated, unsure if I should butt into their fight or wait it out and hope they resolved it on their own.

"Shut up! I am not *miserable*. And this has nothing to do with me—absolutely nothing. I'm talking about your crazy girlfriend, no one else."

I decided to wait it out. And you know, just listen, so maybe I could help analyse it later.

"Don't talk shit about her! You don't even know her! You haven't made any effort to be nice to her."

"How could I? She doesn't want to spend time with anyone else but you, Ben. And she doesn't want *you* to spend time with anyone else, have you noticed?"

"Oh and that's a problem, is it? That's such a bad thing that we want to spend so much time together? You're really scraping the bottom now, Kalina."

"You think it's all fine now, but I've seen shit like this happen before."

"You're not the fucking expert!"

"I know more than you do!"

"Just fuck off out of my life, okay? Amy's right about you—you're toxic."

"I'm *what*?! So, she's already been talking shit about me, has she?!"

I could hear movement now, the sounds of things being picked up, keys scratching on the table.

"That's rich. You're the one who won't stop talking shit about her! I'm fucking over this, Kalina. I don't need people like you in my life."

I heard the front door open and a moment later it slammed shut with a resounding echo through the apartment.

Then there was a thumping sound followed by an exclamation of pain and a curse from Kalina.

I took a deep breath and hurried into the kitchen.

"Hey," I said, completely inadequately.

Kalina glanced at me and I saw tears in her eyes. She quickly turned away, wiping furiously at her face. "This is *such* bullshit," she muttered.

"I heard—well, a lot of it," I said, feeling completely useless and wondering if I should have tried to intercede.

"He's making such a mistake. I wish I could make him realise that. She's going to completely railroad him and he'll be lucky to come out the other side in one piece."

"Kal," I said gently. "What makes you so sure? I mean, do you think maybe you're overreacting? After all, we don't really know Amy at all."

"I don't need to know her. I know people *like* her."

"But that's a pretty big leap, isn't it? I mean, you're making quite an assumption that you know what she'll do to him."

Kalina made a grumbling sound and shook her head.

"Plus, I hate to say it, but don't you think you're risking your friendship with Ben by trying to turn him against his girlfriend?"

"It's *because* I'm Ben's friend that I'm doing this. No one else will tell him."

"But by trying to tell him it's as if you're undermining his own judgement. You're implying that he can't make his own decisions."

"He's blinded by her."

"Yeah, but that happens to everyone. And I think being a friend means that you just have to watch from the sidelines, be supportive, and just be there to pick up the pieces when it does all fall apart."

Kalina started pacing up and down in the kitchen. "It's not ... I mean, there's more to it than that. Do you know that his great-aunt just died?"

"Yeah, Lucas told me. I thought he said it was a couple of months ago?

But he and Ben didn't go to the funeral."

"They couldn't because of the bar. Or, at least, that was the excuse. But Ben once told me all about his great-aunt. He used to live with her, on and off. It was almost like she was a second mother to him. And yet he didn't go to her funeral."

"Lucas said she wouldn't have cared. That Ben knew that, or something."

"Maybe. But I feel like Ben should have done more to process her death. And then—don't you see? Right around the same time that she died, when Ben was all vulnerable and sad, Amy arrived. It's like he's just transferred all his emotions into this new thing with her, and he's convinced himself he's in love. It's classic transference, or whatever they call it."

"That might not be a bad thing. Amy might be just what he needs to help him get through this sad period."

Kalina made another grunting sound. "If she was someone else then maybe, but there's just something about her ..." She trailed off.

"Hey, that reminds me. Did you get my message the other day? About a guy turning up looking for you?"

I was sure Kalina stilled slightly. "Oh, yeah, I got that. He didn't say who he was?"

"No, he was pretty sketchy about it. I kept asking what his name was and he wouldn't tell me. Looked like he'd come straight from the airport, though—and I'm sure he was British."

Kalina definitely blanched this time.

"Who was it? Do you know?" I pressed.

"He's no one I care to see. If he comes round again, tell him I don't live here anymore."

"Right ... so ...?"

Kalina shook her head. "He's just a fuckwit."

I watched her carefully as I turned the possibilities over in my mind. Kalina was pretty cagey when it came to talking about her life before she moved to Sydney. I knew she'd been in a serious relationship, had lived with a guy in London before she'd found out he was cheating on her with her best friend. She'd never said so, but I was pretty sure that was what had caused her to flee to the other side of the world. Could her mysterious caller be him, come to try to win her back? Or was he someone else entirely? To be fair, Kalina could tell me that she used to work in a drug trafficking ring in London and I would find it totally plausible.

"He did say he was going to come back and try to surprise you," I said in an attempt to needle her into telling me more.

She froze momentarily, her eyes wider than normal, then shook her head sharply as if trying to dislodge a thought from her mind. "Let's get back to the Ben-and-Amy problem," she said curtly. "What are we going to do about them?"

I sighed. "Honestly, Kal, I know you have Ben's best interests at heart, but I think you really need to step back and just let him go through it. Just be there for him, and only give your opinion when he asks. *If* he asks."

Kalina started chewing on her thumbnail, but I could see her turning my words over in her mind. Or was she thinking about the British guy who'd come looking for her? Either way, she eventually stopped gnawing at her nail and looked up at me with a huff.

"I suppose I've been acting like a total bitch about Amy, haven't I?"

I laughed gently. "A bitch with the *best* intentions."

"Fuck. Poor Ben. It's just that—"

"I know."

"And he needs to know—"

"I *know*."

Kalina gave me a rueful look, which then turned into a half-laugh. "Fine," she said. "I'll stop talking shit about Amy. But, I'm telling you, I have a really bad feeling that things are going to turn into a huge clusterfuck for him."

"They won't. You'll see. He'll make up his own mind about her, and we won't need to worry about him."

"I hope you're right."

"I will be."

7

I wasn't right.

The next day, Kalina and I got up in the morning to discover Ben's bedroom door wide open.

And all his clothes cleared out.

"What do you mean, he's not coming back?" Kalina demanded.

We were standing in Los Perdidos, hours before opening time, watching as Lucas cleaned the bar. Kalina and I had spent all yesterday telling ourselves that Ben was being overly dramatic, and that he needed some space, and that he'd be back soon. But now we weren't so sure, and Lucas seemed to agree.

"He's taking an extended break," Lucas repeated, looking strained. "Matty's agreed to run the kitchen until he gets back."

"But *where* has he gone?" I asked. "Surely, he gave some indication of when he's coming back?"

Lucas rolled his shoulder, bringing his hand up to knead the muscle behind his neck. My eyes devoured the movement, before I had to remind myself to firmly stop it.

"I don't know," he said, sounding a bit uncomfortable. "I probably should have asked more questions at the time, but I didn't realise he was going to turn off his phone and go full communication break as well. All I was thinking about was the bar and getting through till the end of the month when the lease ends."

"But realistically, how many places can he disappear to?" I offered. "Your parents' place maybe?"

Lucas shook his head. "He's not there. I spoke to Charlie last night—he hasn't spoken to or seen Ben in over a week. He also said he'd call me if he saw or heard from Ben."

I frowned, thinking. Charlie was the youngest of the Hartcoats' five boys—Lucas being the eldest, and Ben right in the middle. With their parents still down in Adelaide sorting through Aunt Maurine's estate, the two youngest boys who still lived at home would have the place to themselves. They'd also have no reason to lie to Lucas about Ben being there.

"What about Adelaide, then?" I asked. "Could he have gone down there to be with your parents?"

Lucas shook his head. "Spoke to Mum this morning. I didn't want to worry her—she's got enough to deal with as it is. But neither she nor Dad have spoken to Ben in a few days. And I'm sure he would have called ahead, if that's where he was planning on going."

"I can't imagine Amy would agree to go hang out with a bunch of old people clearing out their old relative's estate," Kalina said. "No offence," she added as an afterthought.

Lucas smiled ruefully. "Nah, you're right. I don't think they'd have gone there."

We fell silent, all thinking. I was chewing on my lip, my brows furrowed when I realised Lucas was looking at me. Not just looking—staring, in that intense way he had. For a moment, I made myself stare right back.

What was he thinking?

What was I thinking?

What did this stare mean?

If I was a bit more intuitive, maybe I could work it out. His look could be saying: *Laura, you are the only one of us who can solve this puzzle and work out where Ben is.* Or it could be saying: *Laura, I'm mentally ripping your top open and running your tongue across your nipple right now.*

I blushed and looked away. Shit. Not the time for those kinds of thoughts.

I felt, rather than saw, Lucas's eyes crinkle with amusement.

Kalina, meanwhile, had been trying to call Ben again. She scoffed and hung up the phone. "Still straight to voicemail. What a joke."

"Could he be on a plane?" I asked. "I mean, you have to turn off your phone when you fly ..."

We all looked at each other in alarm.

"Oh fuck," Kalina said. "What if she's taken him off to Mexico? She could be involved with a drug cartel! Maybe she's convinced Ben to become a mule."

Lucas snorted. "Ben would make a terrible mule. Have you ever tried playing poker with him? Besides, let's give him some credit. He's not *that* stupid."

"He's stupid enough to be with Amy," Kalina muttered.

"Kal!" I couldn't help saying sternly. "I thought we agreed you weren't going to talk badly about her! Isn't that why Ben's left in the first place?"

"But this is different!" Kalina insisted. "Don't you see—she's a leech! The girl's got no job and no money. Remember when I suggested she buy some milk for our place? She told me she couldn't *afford* to buy milk! So, wherever they are now, guess who's funding it all?"

I glanced to Lucas, and based on the look of shock on his face I could tell he hadn't considered this before.

"He's always been too generous with people," Lucas said, sounding strained.

"Exactly." Kalina looked triumphant, but in a sad way, like when you don't really want to be right. "This is what I've been trying to say. She's *using* him. She's the kind of person who uses people. She has champagne taste and a beer budget—or no budget at all. And Ben is too nice to be able to see that."

"Well, even if she is a bit of a leech, maybe that's just a mistake Ben has to make," I offered, attempting to be the voice of reason. "He's not that silly that he'd spend so much money on her, is he?"

Based on the looks Kalina and Lucas were exchanging, they thought he was.

"It's only been a day," Lucas said eventually. "Let's give it another couple before we really worry."

If only Lucas's confidence had been correct. But two days turned into three, which then turned into four, and there was still no word from Ben.

He'd left his parents a short message on his mum's voicemail, wishing them a happy wedding anniversary, but hadn't mentioned anything about where he was staying. His parents, at least, seemed completely unaware that anything was wrong.

And we didn't want to alarm them. After all, we didn't know anything *was* wrong exactly. It was quite possible that Ben simply needed a break from us, and trying to force communication on him might not be the best.

But as the days ticked past, Kalina became more and more agitated, more and more restless and convinced that something wasn't right. And perhaps because I had nothing better to do, I found myself growing equally concerned with Ben's wellbeing.

"But where the fuck *is* he?" Kalina asked again, rhetorically. "I still think we should go to the police."

We were sitting in the flat alone that morning, torrential rain preventing us from venturing outside. I was lying across the couch, examining the cracks in our ceiling, while Kalina was sprawled on a beanbag on the floor.

Outside, the rain was so heavy that the day felt unnaturally dark, and I couldn't help thinking it was a bad omen.

"What would we say to the police? That we drove our flatmate away, and now he's refusing to talk to us, and oh yes, would you mind checking his phone records and bank account details and letting us know where he is, please?"

"He could be in serious trouble. He's absconded with a crazy woman!"

"He's gone away with his girlfriend. Besides, he remembered his parents' anniversary, so he can't be in any real trouble."

"Something's not right, Laura, I'm telling you. Maybe we should hire a private investigator to track him down?"

I frowned, thinking. I was trying to be rational about this, but the truth was I *did* have a bad feeling about the whole situation. I could see why Ben might want to block Kalina—at least (hopefully) temporarily—but why was he ignoring *my* phone calls and messages? I hadn't said anything negative about Amy, at least that Ben knew of. Plus, Ben was also ignoring Lucas, his own brother, and he'd just ditched the job Lucas had entrusted him with. So long as I'd known Ben, he was professional and rational and loyal to his friends and family. What on earth could motivate him to do that to Lucas?

"If he was still using Facebook and Instagram, I might not be so worried," Kalina said. "But he's gone completely silent on social media. And his phone is *still* switched off every time I try calling it."

"Could he have blocked your phone number?" I asked. "*Would* he have done that?"

"I never would have thought he'd be that dramatic. But with Amy now ... I don't know, it's like he's been brainwashed."

"It is really strange. I mean, the fight you guys had wasn't even that bad, and now he's disappeared without any word? That seems so ... unlike Ben."

"Exactly. It's not at all like him. I kept trying to tell everyone, Amy is a terrible influence on him."

"Hey, what about Amy!" I sat up suddenly, looking towards Kalina.

"Have you checked *her* social media stuff?"

"Of course I have. I've even sent her a few messages on there, but she's ignoring me. She just keeps posting stupid motivational quotes on Instagram."

I caught my phone off the coffee table and looked up Amy's Instagram account. Sure enough, in the last week she'd posted three photos—all just stock backgrounds with obscure quotes written in swirly writing.

I clicked over to my feed, and as it refreshed I was startled to see that the first image to come up was from Amy—posted six seconds ago.

"Hey, Kal! She's just posted something!" I exclaimed, feeling the adrenaline surging through my veins. "An actual photo this time—look!"

Even though Kalina could check her own phone, she crowded around mine and we both squinted at the picture.

"That's Ben's arm!" Kalina pointed excitedly. It was an image taken at a cafe, the main focus of the photo being the trendy lattes and fancy brunch laid out on the table. But there was also a distinctly male arm in the picture, one wearing a black plaited string looped around his wrist, which we both recognised.

"Wherever they are, it looks sunny there." I frowned. "Unless this photo was taken on another day ... but it's been raining for the last few days here."

Kalina started chewing her thumbnail and stared out at the rain with a frown. "Shit. Where could they be?"

My eyes honed in on the corner of the picture, where the menu was just visible.

"Ennota Cafe," I read excitedly.

"What? Where's that? I don't think it's around here ..."

But I was already on Google, looking it up. In a flash, I was remembering a conversation I'd had with Ben, months ago, about places in Australia we'd both been to or wanted to go to. I couldn't believe I hadn't remembered it before. And as soon as I saw the search results I knew I was right.

"Bingo," I said, handing my phone to Kalina. "I know where they are."

She took it eagerly and stared down at it. Almost immediately, she broke out in deep, relieved laughter.

"Byron Bay—of course! He's always wanted to go there!"

"What should we do about it?"

Kalina looked outside at the torrential rain again. Then turned to look at me with a growing smile on her face.

"Pack a bag, Laura. We're going to rescue Ben."

PUSH NOTIFICATION
Lunar Period Tracker App
Tender breasts? Based on your predicted period cycle, you have a high chance of nipple sensitivity today.

NEW MESSAGE
From: Rose Spencer at 10.17 am
OMG Laura—Philippe is serious man drug right here. I still can't believe you're not here to talk to in the mornings!! I'm talking serious 🔫🔫

NEW MESSAGE
From: Mum at 12.22 pm
Hi darling, do you know anything about Clicker training? All the good dog trainers live in your area and they all seem to be doing the clicking thing. Can you walk past the dog park near you and ask about it?

8

Byron Bay. A town famed for being the most chilled-out place in Australia. It's all surfers and hippie culture, and alternate, well, *everything*. It's where cool kids go to hang out and take drugs and connect with nature. It's where celebrities buy their holiday houses.

Of course, I'd never been there. Never had the right friends who wanted to go. But the moment Kalina suggested we should follow Ben, the excitement in me started building. And okay, yes, I knew the whole point in going there was to find Ben and that was a very serious task. But, Byron Bay! I couldn't wait!

Not even the nine-hour car journey dampened my mood, though by the time the GPS said we were fifteen minutes out from our destination, Kalina and I were both feeling pretty sore and stiff. We'd also literally sung ourselves hoarse, and were now trying to recover our vocal cords by drinking Powerade. "Chandelier" was probably the song that did it. People doubtlessly could have heard us a kilometre away. Anyway, my butt had gone completely dead, despite the multiple breaks we'd taken, my back and shoulders hurt, and I was fantasising about getting out of the car and going running.

Running. Unbelievable.

We turned off the highway as the sun was beginning to set, giving a cheer as we went. The diminished light lent a warm glow to the burnt-brown paddocks and palm trees we drove past, and the cows placidly ignored us. Kalina was driving and I zoomed in on the GPS location to see where we were staying in relation to town.

"Are you sure it's a hotel?" I asked, frowning at the street location which was just outside the main town area.

"Nope," Kalina replied. "I get carsick if I look at a phone too long in the car."

"Brilliant," I said with a laugh. Kalina had organised the accommodation during the first leg of the journey, while I was driving. "So, what did you book?"

"It was on Airbnb. Looked like a cool house."

"You booked a whole *house*?"

"It was super cheap. But ... maybe?"

I frowned but decided not to worry about it. We'd be there in seven minutes, apparently, so we'd work it out then.

We passed a sign by the road that read, "Welcome to Byron Bay. Cheer up. Slow Down. Chill Out", and Kalina and I both squealed, then we started passing properties with signs for hotels, holiday rentals, caravan parks and backpacker hostels. Soon, we turned into a residential street and then pulled up outside an enormous, sprawling beach house, its front garden looking like it was in desperate need of some maintenance. The weatherboard exterior had peeling turquoise paint just visible behind the jungle of palm trees and shrubs out the front.

"Is this it?" I leaned forward excitedly. "Oh my God, what an amazing deal! Is this seriously where we're staying?"

"Yeah. Wow. This does seem ... a bit too good to be true."

I turned to look at Kalina quizzically. She pulled out her phone and looked a bit frantic as she searched for something.

"Kal?" I said slowly. "Is this the right place?"

Kalina was frowning down at her phone. "This is definitely it," she said after a moment. "The pictures look right. I just ... hang on ... ah."

"What do you mean, 'ah'?"

Kalina looked up at me and made a face. "Surprise! We've rented a room in a share house."

"Oh God. Is that even safe? Maybe we should just go and stay at a backpackers' hostel or something."

"The hostels here were all booked out—I checked them first. Honestly, Laur, *everything* was booked out. This was one of the only things available. Well, the only thing we could afford that was available."

"Shit." We gazed up at the house. Eventually I said, "Well, I guess let's go take a look, then."

Kalina turned off the engine and unbuckled her seatbelt. "Right. How bad could it be?"

"Seedy old men?" I offered as I unclipped my own belt. "Or family with ten screaming children?"

"Old lady who wants to cook for us and tell us stories about her grandsons?"

We looked at each other in alarm.

But despite my lack of enthusiasm for our accommodation, it was a relief to get out of the car and stretch my aching back. We grabbed our bags out of the boot and approached the front door.

After knocking loudly a few times, we eventually heard footsteps approaching from within. And then the door swung open and we were looking at a girl who was probably about the same age as us, holding a large, fat, ginger cat in her arms.

"Hi, Kalina, is it?" She gave us a huge, friendly smile that offset the cat's glare. In fact the cat, I thought, looked like there was something a bit wrong with its face—kind of like grumpy cat, but a bit more smooshed and downturned. It was giving me the most definite scowl.

"Yeah, that's me. Hi, Meadow, right?" Kalina replied. "This is my friend, Laura."

"Come on inside. I'll show you around." Meadow stepped away from the door, the cat rotating its head over her shoulder so it could continue glaring at us with its fat, pouty cheeks as we followed Meadow down a hallway. Meadow's caramel-blonde hair fell in a long braid that scraped the top of her waist, and aside from her bare feet and toe rings she looked more Bondi than Byron. Her tanned skin and toned physique were clearly visible beneath her Lululemon three-quarter leggings, slouched waterfall top and sports crop top that was a mosaic of straps across her back. She looked like she'd stepped right off the page of a yoga catalogue.

"This is your room down the end of the hallway here," Meadow said, showing us the small bedroom with one queen bed and a single bed crammed in. Kalina dumped her bag on the queen bed and I dropped mine on the floor before we followed Meadow out again.

"Bathroom's there," she continued, nodding through a doorway. "Out here's the kitchen and lounge. Upstairs is the other bedrooms, but you shouldn't need to go up there. Oh, and through there is the yoga room—feel free to use it, but remember if you break anything I'll charge you for it."

"Thanks," I murmured, looking around at the living area we were now standing in. There were large glass doors facing out onto a small and completely overgrown backyard, and pretty much every item of furniture within the room looked like it was probably picked up during kerbside clean-up. Then I noticed that a guy was sitting on one of the couches, a laptop perched on his leg, a beer in his hand, and huge headphones on his head. Just as I noticed him he glanced up, did a small double-take, then stood up and pulled off his headphones.

My first thought was: that is a *lot* of hair.

His beard was on another level. And his hair was long and shaggy, that kind of wild surfer-hippie look that girls would kill for. If it weren't for the fact that I could see the top half of his face and most of his torso beneath his Bintang singlet, I would have put his age somewhere in the vicinity of sixty-five. But he wasn't old. He looked, if anything, no older than thirty.

"Hey," he drawled. "How're ya going?"

He had the most bogan Aussie accent I'd ever heard.

"Hi," I replied.

"Do you live here?" Kalina asked, sounding immensely unimpressed.

"Yep." He grinned at her.

"This is Echo," Meadow interjected in her serene way. "He's renting one of the rooms upstairs."

"Brilliant," Kalina replied. I hoped I was the only one who detected her sarcasm.

Echo sat back down on the couch. I was pretty sure the way he was grinning at Kalina meant he knew exactly what she thought of him and that he thoroughly enjoyed it.

Then a cat—a *different* cat, this one was black and white—sprang up from beneath the coffee table onto Echo's lap, circled a couple of times, then promptly started kneading its claws on his thigh. He winced, but patted the cat, anyway, his eyes still watching us with keen interest.

"There are a few cats that live here," Meadow said mildly. "Hope that's not a problem?"

"No, not at all." I glanced to Kalina, who was frowning and looking a little disgusted at the cat on Echo. Or maybe she was simply disgusted by Echo? Either way, she didn't seem impressed. But she didn't say anything.

"Cool. So, how long were you guys staying again?" Meadow stroked the back of the ginger cat, who was clinging to her arms and glaring at me again. I could see the tiniest little pink tongue sticking out of its mouth, as if it didn't all fit inside.

"We're not sure yet. We're trying to—"

"We don't have any set plans," Kalina interrupted me. "I've booked four days, but we can let you know tomorrow if we need to stay longer—is that alright?"

"That's fine. I'll let you know if someone else wants to book and give you the first option of staying then."

"Great, thanks. Laur, let's go and … unpack."

I raised my eyebrow at her, but after a friendly nod to Meadow then Echo—who was still watching us curiously—I followed Kalina down to our room.

"What?" I asked as soon as I'd closed the bedroom door behind us.

"Let's not tell them why we're really here. I just think … detectives never reveal more than they need to. Plus, their names are *Echo* and *Meadow*. What's with that?"

I laughed. "Well, this is Byron Bay. Maybe we found a genuine hippy house. They do have a yoga room. But we're hardly detectives."

"Yes, we are! That's why we're here!"

"Alright, well … I suppose it doesn't matter. They wouldn't know who Ben or Amy are, anyway."

"Exactly. So, we'll just say we're here for a holiday."

I rolled my eyes at her. "Sure. Whatever you want, Sherlock."

"Cool. I'm also bagsing the big bed."

As if I hadn't realised that already.

We got changed and decided to head straight into town to "survey the landscape" as Kalina said. The house, at least, was extremely close to the town centre. We crossed over an old disused railway line and straightaway we were walking past takeaway-food joints and seeing restaurants with people spilling out onto upstairs balconies or sitting at tables stretched across the pavement.

Everywhere we looked the place was buzzing with people. There were families out walking together, teenagers shouting and laughing, couples wandering along with their arms around each other. There were shops selling dreamcatchers, and places offering tarot readings. Street artists sketching caricatures and musicians playing guitars. Gorgeously healthy-looking smoothie shops next to hole-in-the-wall kebab joints. My eye caught on a sign outside the tiniest coffee shop, which was no wider than a doorway, offering medicinal mushroom coffee.

What the ...?

The streets were practically gridlocked with cars trying to navigate their way around all the wide tree-filled roundabouts, but unlike other cities, there were no car horns or aggressive driving. Pedestrians wandered across the road directly in front of the cars, and the drivers just waited good-naturedly for them. It was as if everyone had taken the welcome sign coming into town very seriously.

Kalina and I went to cross a road and we were almost flattened by a girl riding a bicycle, who came zooming around the corner way too fast, completely oblivious of the cars and people around her. Given the fact that she was wearing no helmet or shoes, and looked a bit spaced out, I wasn't surprised.

"Alright." I released Kalina's arm from where I'd pulled her out of the way, and we crossed the road cautiously while our heart rates recovered. "Where shall we go from here?"

Kalina was blinking around at the streets and I thought she looked about the same way I felt—completely overwhelmed. How on earth were we going to find Ben?

"I think ... let's just get some dinner first. I'm starving."

We did just that, choosing a gorgeous little pizza restaurant that had a table available outside. We ordered a bottle of red wine and two pizzas, and soon we were having a lovely time.

"I wonder if we'll see any celebrities while we're up here?" I said, while using my knife to try to fish a fruit fly out of my wineglass.

"Why do you ask that?"

"Because so many live here! I mean, aside from Chris Hemsworth, there's also Gemma Ward and Olivia Newton-John and—"

"Wait—what?!" Kalina had frozen with her fork halfway up towards her mouth. "Does Chris Hemsworth live here?"

"How do you not know that?" I grinned at her totally amazed expression.

"Oh my God! Oh my God, that's *awesome*! Imagine if we see him!"

"What would you do if you saw him? I'm pretty sure there's some unspoken rule up here about not disturbing the celebrities. That's why they like living here so much."

"You can't see the sexiest man on the planet and not try to talk to him!"

"Kal! He's married! And he's got kids!"

"Oh, that's hardly ... I mean, I wouldn't *flirt* with him or anything."

"Uh-uh. So, what would you talk to him about?"

"Erm ... I'd ask him where you can get the best coffee from?"

"Well, that sounds like a brilliant conversation that will last all of ten seconds."

Kalina shrugged. "Actually, I'd probably just try to take a sneaky selfie with him."

"How do you get a *sneaky* selfie? I'm pretty sure he'll notice."

"It's all about perspective. See, if I'm in the foreground and he's way behind me, I can just sort of position myself in the shot. Like this." She picked up her phone and held it out to the side, leaning in and angling it just so.

"Right, so, like, if I just move a bit like this ..."

I raised my eyebrows in amusement.

"Done." She handed me the phone and I looked at the picture she'd just taken.

"Kal!" I tried not to laugh. "That woman in your background is glaring at you in this photo!"

"I know," she dropped her voice, "just don't make eye contact with her."

I glanced over and saw the woman glaring at us still.

"Laura!" Kalina hissed.

I looked back at her, laughing. "Well, this is a great strategy, Kal. I'm sure it will work perfectly with Chris Hemsworth."

She shrugged. "I got the photo, didn't I?"

We stayed at the restaurant for another hour, and then I found myself yawning and glancing at my watch. "God, it's later than I thought!" I exclaimed. "I know we haven't even talked about finding Ben, but is it too early to just call it a night?"

"Definitely not. I'm exhausted. It's inefficient to operate on sleep deprivation, anyway. We can sort out our plan for finding Ben tomorrow."

"I'm so glad you said that! I'm starting to feel like a zombie."

Kalina smiled. "Come along, Doctor Watson. Off to bed with you."

9

Where am I?

It was dark—night obviously—when I woke. I was disoriented for a moment, wondering why I could hear someone else breathing heavily, then remembered where I was and whom I was sharing a room with. I scrabbled around on the floor for my phone, my throat feeling completely parched, and managed to find it and determine it was 12.30 am.

I really need some water.

Feeling more awake, I swung my legs out of the small single bed I was sleeping in and quietly left the room, shutting the door softly behind me.

There were lights still on down the end of the hall, and as I came into the lounge I could see a lamp switched on. There was another light coming from the kitchen, and as I crossed over I realised the fridge door was open, most of the light streaming out from within.

I could also see a guy's naked back poking out from the fridge door, shadowed from the light within, and he had long dreadlocks tied behind his head with a leather cord.

I cleared my throat and he stiffened, then slowly leaned out to look at me.

Beautiful, was my first thought. He was wearing loose linen pants in a sort of earthy colour, and his bare torso was chiselled, lean and ripped, the light from the fridge casting shadows across the ridges of his abs. His face was clean-shaven and he had the most amazing cheekbones I'd ever seen, all high arches and angular. A sprawling tattoo covered one of his pecs with swirling lines and arrows and dots—it looked tribal. When his eyes focused on me—the intruder in his kitchen—he smiled easily and reached up with one arm to lean casually on the fridge door.

"Hello there." His voice was deep and rich and sexy, and his eyes glinted in the artificial light.

"Hi," I squeaked in response. Oh God. Was I dreaming?

He regarded me quietly for a moment and I tried to think of something witty to say. And failed miserably.

"Can I get you something from the fridge?" he asked.

"No, thanks, I was just going to get some water," I replied, gesturing towards the sink. Suddenly, I was super aware of how brief my PJ shorts were, and I prayed I didn't have erect nipples under my cami.

Unless … would he like that?

He kept looking at me, a playful smile on his face. "Go on, then." He nodded his head, not moving from the fridge.

I had to squeeze past him to get to the sink, and I could feel his eyes on me, hot like the midday sun. I didn't know where the glasses were kept, so I started opening cupboards at random, completely aware of him still watching me and feeling hugely embarrassed.

"I assume you know where the glasses are kept?" I asked, casting him a questioning look.

"You assume correctly."

He was smiling again. Playful. And oh God … way too sexy. Who was he? Was he Meadow's boyfriend? Shit, I couldn't start flirting with Meadow's boyfriend!

"Can you please tell me where they are?"

"That one there." He raised his arm and pointed at the cupboard above the sink.

I had to force myself *not* to look at him. To not let my eyes focus on that curve of tricep, or the lat muscles under his arm that sloped downwards. He was still standing with the fridge door wide open, as if he was using it to cool himself down, and the light washed around his figure, highlighting his narrow waist and hips, and drawing attention to the linen pants strung a bit too low across his abdomen.

I was glad there wasn't much light in the kitchen, so he hopefully didn't notice my eyes devouring his body.

Shit! I quickly turned back to the cupboards and located the glasses. I grabbed one out and hastily filled it up, then drank the water all down thirstily as if I could drown the butterflies in my stomach.

With a gasp, I refilled my glass, then mentally prepared myself to act like a regular human being before turning to look at him again.

"So, are you planning on standing in the fridge all night?" I asked with a smile.

He shrugged. "It's cool in here."

God, he had a nice voice.

"But does the food inside like being warmed up so much?"

He leaned against the edge of the fridge, still with the door propped open, and placed his hands in his pants pockets. With a yawn, he rolled his shoulders forwards, his fists going even deeper in the pockets, and causing the pants to slip even *lower*.

I felt my eyes going wide. I didn't know if it was just the low lighting in here, but he looked like a living Adonis. So many rippled lines of muscle. There wasn't a shred of fat on him. Plus, the pants were so low now that I was sure I could see the shadow of hair beneath his waistband. And ... was he even wearing underwear? A second later he finished his yawn and rolled his shoulders back again, and then he looked at me with a friendly smile.

Was he even aware of the effect he was having on me? In this sort of situation, I think it's normal to assume he'd be doing it deliberately. You know—deliberately, accidentally, showing off his drool-worthy body. But this guy just seemed, well, tired.

"The food'll be fine. Besides, it's my house so I can do what I want."

"Oh, right. So, you must be Meadow's boyfriend, then?"

"No, we're just housemates. I assume you've rented the spare bedroom?"

Hallelujah!

"You assume correctly."

We smiled at each other for a moment. Teasing. Playful.

"My name's Truth."

Of course it was. "Laura."

"Nice to meet you, Laura." Oh, I *loved* the way he said my name. "I guess I'll see you around, then?"

"I hope so," I replied, taking my water glass with me as I went to leave. I had to pass so close to him in the narrow kitchen that I felt the cold air from the fridge on my skin and the hairs on my arm prickled and stood up. I also could *smell* him, a kind of hot, earthy but sexy scent that made my heart race a little. I glanced back, quickly, before I got to the hall and he was still standing with the fridge door open, leaning out slightly and watching me with a smile.

"Goodnight," he said softly, his voice sending shivers down my back.

"Night." I bit my lip and turned away, suddenly wishing quite desperately that I wasn't sharing a bedroom with my flatmate.

10

"Wake up, Laur."

I came to blearily, feeling thick and heavy and with a furry mouth. Kalina was standing over me, dressed in denim cut-offs and a cami, her wet hair slicked back off her face. She was holding a steaming mug out towards me.

"How long have you been up for?" I asked her groggily while I managed to sit up in bed and take the cup of tea off her gratefully.

"Hours," she replied, sitting on her own bed and picking up a second mug of tea from the little table between us. "It's almost eleven."

"Really? Shit, I've been asleep for ages!"

"I know." Kalina picked up her laptop and opened it up brusquely, all business-like. "But I haven't. I've spent all morning brainstorming ideas on how we can try to find Ben."

"You have?" I was instantly feeling much more awake. "Why didn't you wake me earlier?"

Kalina shrugged. "To be honest, I wasn't expecting you to sleep this long! But it didn't matter. That Echo guy has been helping me brainstorm."

"I thought you didn't want to tell anyone what we were doing up here?"

"I didn't mean to. But then, I figured we could use someone with some local knowledge. I need all available information so that my mind can start putting clues together."

"Right. So did he have any ideas on how we can find Ben?"

"He actually did have some good suggestions, which was quite surprising. Especially because he looks like a homeless hippie and sounds like he grew up on a farm."

"I'm sure Sherlock Holmes wouldn't let his prejudice interfere with deeming someone useful," I teased her.

"Exactly. Which is why I've been speaking to him for so long."

I raised my eyebrows. "Sure you don't like his beard?"

"No! He looks like a Wookiee! But anyway, the point is we've now got some ideas on how to find Ben."

"Right! Okay, tell me what you've got."

"First of all, it turns out that Byron Bay is a whole lot larger than I thought it was going to be before we came here."

"Promising start."

"There are literally *hundreds* of accommodation options here, and they're spread out not just in and around town, but all over the hinterland, too. I spent ages looking up hotels online and marking down the ones that would be in Ben's price bracket, and then I spent about an hour phoning them all up. I kept asking to just be put through to Ben Hartcoat or Amy Richards, but none of the places have anyone staying there under those names."

"Could they be using fake ones?"

Kalina shrugged, looking helpless. "They could be. In which case, we'd have no chance of finding them at a hotel. But even so, it's just the *hotels* I've been trying, you know, places that have phones in the guests' rooms where they can patch you through. The majority of accommodation places around here are all holiday rentals, and those places won't disclose guest names even if you ask. Echo reckons it would breach their privacy policies or something. So, if they're staying at an Airbnb or private holiday place, we'll have no way of knowing where they are."

"Kal, why didn't you wake me up! I can't believe you've spent hours trying to track them down while I've been asleep!"

She snorted and waved her hand at me dismissively. "There hasn't been much point, anyway, has there? Besides, Echo proved quite useful."

"Alright, but now I'm properly helping! We might not be able to work out where they're staying, but surely they'll be moving around each day and doing stuff? So, we just need to work out where they're likely to go and what they're likely to do."

I clambered out of bed and grabbed my own laptop from my bag, then returned to sit on top of the quilt, facing Kalina.

"Let's start by profiling each of them," I said.

"Amy. Psychotic," Kalina replied, sounding deadly serious.

"Ben." I ignored her. "Loves the beach and loves to surf."

"Loves food. He has a thing for tapas."

"He's also into Italian stuff, isn't he? Maybe we should put he's into all Mediterranean food."

"I think he's into trying anything new. We should probably just put 'loves all food.'"

"Well, that's helpful," I grumbled, but I wrote it down, regardless. "What food does Amy like?"

Kalina scrunched up her nose. "Anything Instagrammable?"

I nodded thoughtfully. "That could be a thing. We can probably look up what are the trendiest restaurants on Instagram that do pretty servings and list them as places she'd likely go to."

"I bet she's one of those girls who stands up on their chair at the cafe to get the best aerial shot, and makes everyone wait ages before they can eat so all their food goes cold."

"People don't really stand on their chairs, do they? In public?"

"Yeah! I've seen someone."

"Honestly, *what* is our society coming to? Alright, so we have a good starting place for restaurants that we can scope out at lunch or dinner time.

What about outside of that? Is there anywhere, apart from the beach, we think they'd go?"

Kalina pursed her lips and tapped her chin a few times. "I think Amy does yoga, doesn't she? Like hot yoga or rope yoga or something like that?"

"*Rope* yoga? What is that?"

"Oh you know, there are all these weird trendy yoga things now."

I laughed. "Ben wouldn't be likely to tag along, though, would he?"

Kalina sighed. "Truthfully? I think Amy can convince him to do anything."

"Right. So, we just need to work out where the yoga places are around here, then."

Kalina checked her watch. "It's still brunch time. Let's go into town and see if we can find some trendy cafes first. I reckon that's where Amy would be right now."

So, in hindsight, attempting to find someone in a large, buzzing town with only minimal knowledge of where they were was really, really hard.

I was exhausted. And drained. And demoralised.

And it hadn't even been a whole day.

We'd spent over two hours that morning walking through the streets of Byron Bay, using Google to guide us to every single cafe. We'd started on a positive note, of course, and for the first half-hour we were in good spirits. We bought coffee and pastries at one of the first cafes (we needed fuel for our hunt, of course), but pretty soon I just felt like a walking puddle of sweat as the sun increased its heat expenditure, and the shadows diminished under the midday glare.

We checked out leafy-green cafes with tables spilling onto the pavement, and trendy bar-style establishments serving organic vegan granola and tofu scramble. We ticked off all the most Instagram-worthy places we could find—from the beautiful Egyptian-themed cafe serving crispy falafels and Cairo eggs, to the tiny but famed juice bar selling an impressive array of chia puddings and smoothie bowls.

And even though we saw girls dressed in boho skirts and bikinis, and guys who were barefoot and sandy, we didn't see Ben or Amy.

Finally, after we realised it was well past lunchtime, we decided to try the beach.

And OH. MY. GOD. The beach at Byron Bay was *enormous*. The bloody thing stretched on for kilometres. Plus, walking through sand was very difficult. Your feet sink in. Your calf muscles ache after a while. I'd never really noticed how hard it was to walk through sand before, because it was such a romantic thing to do, wasn't it? Just taking a nice stroll along the beach. Playing chase and runaway games with the waves.

Usually, when I went to the beach, I'd arrive, walk in a straight line towards the water, then plonk my towel down and sprawl out for the day. But walking up and down a long beach, trying to get a good look at the faces of the people underneath beach hats, or sunbaking on their stomachs with their faces planted in their towels, was really bloody difficult.

And we did *two entire* laps of the beach.

But anyway. The whole day had been a total bust. And Ben's phone number was still just going straight to voicemail. Either his phone was switched off, or he'd blocked us, but either way he wasn't responding to calls or texts. And the messages we'd been sending him on WhatsApp were showing that he hadn't even read them.

"If one of them would just post something useful online," Kalina huffed for the umpteenth time, as we traipsed back to the hippie house late in the afternoon. I was struggling to think of anything positive to say about the day at all.

"I wonder if they realise we're here, looking for them?" I pondered aloud.

We'd made the decision not to tell Ben we were in Byron Bay—at least not until we could actually get him on the phone or speak to him in person. We didn't need to add any more fuel to the idea that we were meddling in his life too much (at some point, he would understand we were doing it for his own good).

"I don't see why or how they'd know that. As far as they're concerned, we don't even know *where* they are."

As I followed Kalina into the share house, I was surprised to find Meadow sitting at the breakfast bar, tapping away on a laptop that had yellow flower decals stuck to the outside. Just as we entered, her phone rang, and she tapped the small handsfree device sitting in her ear to answer.

"Hannah! Thanks for getting back to me ..."

"I'm taking a shower," Kalina said to me as she checked her watch. "Let's give it an hour then head out to check the bars and restaurants, yeah?"

"Yeah," I agreed, trying not to sound too put out by the idea. Traipsing around town for hours again and peering in at all the restaurants while everyone was eating their lovely dinners did *not* sound appealing, but I couldn't argue. Currently, we didn't have a better plan to find Ben and Amy.

Kalina disappeared off down the hallway, and I crossed to the kitchen to get a glass of water, giving Meadow a friendly smile as I did so.

She acknowledged me with a nod while she kept speaking on her call. I sipped my water and admired her laptop at the same time; it was a gorgeous pearl-white colour, though the sunflower decals spoiled it a bit. Then again, maybe Meadow just had an inexplicable urge to showcase her hippie lifestyle across all of her possessions.

"Absolutely, I'll tell her. So, did the funds clear? ... Excellent. That'll make a dint in it. And we're on track for the next quarter, then? ... Yes, almost, I know. I'm still working on it ... Okay, thanks, talk soon."

She hung up and I tried not to look like I'd been listening.

"How's your day been?" Meadow asked me, closing her laptop and taking out the earpiece.

"It's been good! We just ... went to a cafe for lunch and then hit the beach," I replied. "How about you? Do you work from home?"

"Sometimes I do," Meadow said, perking up with interest. "I'm all over the place usually with meetings, so sometimes it's easier just to come back and finish up the day here. I work for Yogatainable," she added smugly, in the way I imagined someone would say if they were announcing they worked at Google.

"Oh, right. What is that?"

"You don't know Yogatainable? Oh, you'll *have* to go while you're staying here in Byron. It's the hottest new wellness retreat in the whole southern hemisphere."

"Really?" I asked, feeling genuinely interested. "And it's here in Byron Bay?"

"Of course! Byron is Australia's capital for alternative medicines and health practices. Yogatainable only opened a month ago, but already it's had Katie, Taylor *and* Selena all come and do health retreats."

"Er, right."

"You should definitely come check it out. There are day packages you can do, or you can just stop in for a class. Here, I've got some free guest passes." Before I knew it, Meadow had slipped a couple of business cards from her phone case and was holding them out for me.

"Thank you! This looks great," I said automatically as I took them.

Meadow's phone rang again, and this time she picked up her laptop and answered the call as she moved upstairs, her long legs once again wrapped in printed Lululemon leggings.

I looked closely at the cards she'd given me. They appeared to be made of finely sliced bamboo with a beautifully designed lotus logo on one side, above the words "free class pass". Pulling out my phone, I quickly googled

Yogatainable. Sure enough, the website was all tranquil greens and wooden decor, with inspiring photographs of an amazing eco-building with yoga studios, palm trees and toned people all holding a warrior pose.

A video popped up on the home page of beautiful people all stretching gracefully in a lush forest sunrise. A montage of shots of girls sipping smoothies, walking through deserted forests and stretching exotically lithe bodies followed, and I was surprised to see that I recognised half these girls. They were all models and celebrities, the kind of girls that would break the internet when they posted a group Christmas photo. There was even a couple of guys in there, ones that I thought I'd definitely seen on TV somewhere.

The video ended and I felt a bit stunned with how glamorous it all was. And then I realised that Yogatainable was exactly the kind of inspirational, Instagrammable place Amy would love.

11

"I don't know about this, Laura. I bet this is going to be one of those weird hippie communes where everyone sleeps in twenty-person dormitories and plays tambourines together."

"I'm sure it won't be!" I replied with more confidence than I was feeling.

To be fair, Kalina's assessment regarding where we were going wasn't looking like too much of a stretch of the imagination. I mean, Yogatainable's website had looked all sleek and impressive, but we'd been following the directions on Google Maps for twenty minutes already and we were now driving through burnt-brown farms with cows that mooed at us in the morning sunlight.

"Meadow works there, and she's not a weird hippie, is she?"

"She's got a disturbing thing for cats, though. What young, single girl owns eight cats, I ask you?"

"Are there eight of them?"

"Might as well be."

"Well, we're almost there, according to Google. So, let's just wait and see."

"And cross our fingers that we have more luck today than we did yesterday."

Last night we'd gone out into town again and spent about three hours bar hopping in the hopes of finding Ben and Amy. We visited open-air pubs and small wine bars and I wished we had the luxury to just slow down and enjoy being there. But Kalina was insistent that we kept moving and looking, so I continued to remind myself that we were in Byron Bay for one purpose and one purpose only. But still, I'd made a few mental notes on some places I'd really like to go back to and just relax at. Once we found Ben, obviously.

Kalina was in the driver's seat and she turned off down a side road as directed. The open paddocks suddenly gave way to huge, ancient-looking trees, and we abruptly found ourselves in a mini-forest.

"Look, there's a sign!" I pointed to the side of the road where a big wooden billboard featured a familiar swirling lotus logo above the words: "Yogatainable—turn right 500m".

And then we were turning into a driveway that had the most impressively massive Morton Bay fig trees growing on either side of it, each one probably about three hundred years old, and up through a long driveway shaded by a medley of tree boughs. The sunlight dappled the driveway and I had the distinct feeling of driving into some secretive fairy land, hidden away among the arid plains of the Byron hinterland.

The driveway opened up at the end and before us was an immense, architecturally modern building, made of deep-brown wood, with frangipani trees and honeysuckle shrubs all gloriously wild out the front. We followed the discreet sign to the carpark, and Kalina pulled into an empty spot.

"Well," I said, gazing up at the building before us. "I don't think we need to fear it being a hippie commune."

"Could definitely be a cult, though," Kalina replied.

Another car pulled into a spot near us and a girl climbed out holding a yoga mat. She had long, wavy hair with feathers threaded through it, darkly tanned skin wrapped in tie-dyed yoga shorts and a matching crop top, and her bare feet and hands were awash with rings, anklets and bracelets.

After a furtive glance at each other, Kalina and I got out of the car and followed the girl up to the main entrance of the building. The reception space was all open air, with a huge cathedral-style ceiling and wicker fans pushing a gentle breeze downwards. The calming lull of tinkling water came from a stone fountain that was ringed by armchairs, and the soft gonging of acoustic music echoed faintly through the hall.

The feather-girl had already disappeared while Kalina and I were staring around, so I made my way up to the reception desk, which came with smoky incense weaving through the air.

"Good morning." The girl behind the counter had striking blue eyes, long, dark, wavy hair, and about fifteen different facial piercings. She smiled serenely at me, her voice so low and calm that I almost couldn't hear her.

"Hello. We were given some guest passes by Meadow?" I said, holding out the cards.

"That's wonderful. Is this your first visit here?" She took the passes from me, her movements all slow and calm-like, as if she were moving through water.

I nodded and glanced towards Kalina. Rather than join us at reception, she was looking suspiciously at two girls sitting on some plush couches nearby sipping tea.

"Welcome to Yogatainable. I'll just get you to fill in some details here." The girl placed two clipboards on the counter with forms attached to each. Kalina finally came up next to me and started flipping through the papers on her clipboard with a frown.

Ignoring her, I quickly filled in my form.

"Do you know which class you were thinking of doing?" the girl asked me when I handed the form back to her.

"Is there more than one on?"

"Oh yes. Vinyasa is beginning in fifteen minutes, or we have aerial starting in five. If you wait forty minutes then Yin is beginning—that's a ninety-minute class."

"Oh, right. Which is the one for beginners?"

The girl smiled at me, but didn't laugh. "Why don't you do the Vinyasa class? It's easy enough to follow along."

"Great. I guess we'll do that one."

"Excuse me," Kalina suddenly asked. "We're meant to be meeting our friend here, but now I can't remember which class she was doing. Do you have any way to see if she's booked in for any classes?"

"We don't take bookings, I'm afraid. It's a first-come basis for all our classes."

"Oh. Do people check in when they arrive? Are you able to see if she's here?"

"What is her name?" The girl turned to her computer screen and started clicking a few times.

I glanced at Kalina hopefully and saw the excitement shining in her eyes.

"Amy Richards," Kalina said, leaning across the counter and trying to peer at the computer screen.

The girl was frowning, and she sucked her two lip rings into her mouth in concentration. "Sorry, the computer won't let me look it up," she said eventually. "It's a new system and we're still working through some teething problems here."

Kalina deflated and I couldn't help a little groan of disappointment from escaping my lips.

"You're welcome to walk around and look for her, though. It's a big complex—here, I'll give you a map."

She shuffled around some papers behind the desk and then she placed a piece of paper in front of me that had a detailed map drawn of the place.

"We're here at reception," the girl used a pen to circle the building. "You'll need to head up here through the treetop walk to get to your yoga studio here. And if you go over this way past the mindfulness walk, you'll find the peace complex which includes the meditation room, peace cavern and salutation space. And up here is the organic, vegan nourishment hub located next to the spa. Your friend might be enjoying the solitude at any of these places. Was she here for a day retreat, do you know?"

"Er, I'm not sure. We'll just take a look around, thanks." I took the map and stared at it in alarm. The complex was *huge*. Aside from the places the girl had circled for us, there were accommodation villas, and a whole lot of other buildings that I didn't have time to identify.

"There's accommodation here!" Kalina pulled the map closer and eyed it with a frown. Then she fixed her attention on the receptionist again. "Actually, our friend might be staying here—can you look it up?"

"Oh." The girl frowned down at the map again. "Sorry, I've given you one of the new maps. Those villas aren't open yet—only the resort lodgings are open, and they're invitation only at present. Is your friend a vlogger or a celebrity?"

"No," I said, feeling a bit dumbfounded. "She's not."

"Can you check though? Amy Richards, again. Or it could be under Ben Hartcoat," Kalina asked, smiling winningly at the girl.

With the same calmly serene smile, the girl typed one name, then the other, into her computer system. "Sorry," she said after a moment. "No one by either of those names here."

"Worth a try." I smiled gratefully at the girl.

Oh my God, I *loved* this place.

We had to walk up through an amazing wooden boardwalk that was suspended in the trees and then literally came to a large treehouse room built between two enormous boughs. It had glass windows all around, and was, apparently, the yoga studio. Kalina handed me her water bottle, insisting she had to go back and find the bathroom, and so I was alone as I stepped through the doorway into the most magical yoga studio I'd ever seen.

Okay, full disclosure here. I had done yoga a couple of times (including a—very brief—Bikram phase), but it was always so wildly different wherever you went that I'd never really got into it. When I was back at home with my parents after my marriage fell apart, my mum dragged me along to do a yoga class with her. She hadn't done yoga either in about fifteen years, but she was very excited to learn that Gaye, her old yoga teacher, still taught. Well, it turned out that Gaye was about ninety-five years old and so impressively flexible that I was a bit blown away. But she made us do all these weird positions called things like "happy baby" and "embryo pose", and there was another old lady in the class who kept farting every time she stuck her bum in the air, and then snored really loudly during the meditation. I told my mum flat out that I was never going back.

I was pretty sure she was relieved.

But anyway. I was almost completely certain this was not a yoga studio like Gaye's one. For a start, it wasn't Gaye's downstairs rumpus room, so that was a good sign.

The treehouse studio at Yogatainable was so calm and serene. There was soft music playing, the sort of deep gonging sounds that I imagined came from Buddhist monks when they all sat around quietly playing the bowls together. There were a number of people lying on mats already, most on their backs with their legs bent in frog position, their eyes all closed as if this was the most natural way to lie.

I went over to the pile of mats and grabbed two of them, quickly positioning them so Kalina and I would be near the back of the room. At the front, a solitary mat sat with a few candles burning around it—evidently the teacher's mat, although there was no sign of the teacher yet. I sat quietly on my mat and looked around at the beautiful view of the forest around me.

And honestly, I kind of felt like pinching myself just to check this was real.

It was so tranquil. And Zen. The gonging notes were interspersed with harp trills and I felt like I could feel the vibrations reverberating through my bones. More people were quietly coming into the room and placing their mats down. I made eye contact with a couple of them, which seemed a bit awkward, so I lay myself down in the same frog-on-the-back pose and closed my eyes.

Almost instantly, I felt warmth and calmness flowing through me. It was like that feeling you get when you sink into a beautiful, warm bath. It was a sense of peacefulness and solitude. Of expanding and embracing and comforting. It was ... oh my God, it was *yoga*. I was a natural at this!

This was where I belonged. Suddenly, I could imagine myself wearing one of those orange Buddhist robes, sitting on top of a giant plinth of rock in the middle of wheat fields, calmly meditating while the sun passed overhead.

Why had I never taken yoga more seriously before? It was all about getting that connection between your body and nature, all about *knowing* yourself. Yes, this place was where I belonged—here, on the yoga mat.

"Good morning, everyone." A male voice, deep but softly spoken, roused me from the trance I'd fallen under. Or had I been asleep?

I blinked my eyes open, feeling a bit wonky, and wondered why the sunlight now seemed exceedingly bright.

I realised everyone else in the room was now sitting cross-legged on their mats, facing the front of the room, so I quickly pushed myself up into a sitting position and looked around.

Kalina had slipped in beside me while I was trancing, and the room was full. There were a number of guys present, all young and fit, and most of them weren't wearing shirts.

Hmm. This class was shaping up already. Plus, not a single person in here looked over thirty-five.

"Today we'll start on our feet," the male voice said, from somewhere over my right shoulder. He spoke slowly, his voice calm but deep and rich, and I thought it sounded familiar.

I quickly clambered to my feet, and looked around to try to locate the teacher.

My eyes found him, roaming between the mats near the back. His bare feet made no sound as he walked gracefully across the wooden floor, and I froze.

Chiselled cheekbones. Dreadlocks pulled up in a loose bun on top of his head. A tribal tattoo swirling across his bare pec.

Oh my God, it was *him*, the guy from the fridge. Truth. He was shirtless again, wearing nothing other than loose linen pants, and his tanned skin rolled smoothly across his leanly muscled torso. As he walked towards the front of the room I caught sight of his back and was momentarily stunned. Tattooed from the base of his spine up across his ribs and shoulderblades was the most intricate and beautiful depiction of a tree. Immediately, I began imagining tracing its lines across his skin, and found myself desperate to get a closer look.

It was beautiful. *He* was beautiful. My eyes devoured him as he stepped gracefully up to the teacher's mat and then turned calmly to survey the class, that same open, genuine smile on his lips that I'd encountered last night.

"Plant your feet firmly into the earth, feeling all of your toes, your heels and the outside of your feet making contact with the mat. Bring your hands up to prayer, close your eyes, and draw your attention to your breath."

I knew I was supposed to close my eyes, but I couldn't. I didn't want to stop looking at him. He had his own eyes closed, and everyone else in the room was following suit. But I couldn't look away.

Oh, stop it, Laura! Take this seriously.

I tried to match my breath to the beats he was counting, but I couldn't slow it down enough. I felt like my heart was pounding, demanding more and more oxygen, and in response I was breathing almost twice as fast as everyone else. I watched as Truth inhaled deeply, his ribs expanding outwards, and then his stomach muscles contracting as he slowly exhaled.

God. He had really, *really* nice abs. And I wanted very much to run my hands over them.

Truth opened his eyes and I quickly shut mine.

Shit. I shouldn't be getting the hots for the yoga teacher!

Then again … if more yoga classes had teachers like this, then maybe I *would* become a regular.

"Sun salutation." His tranquil voice coiled around the room. "Raise your arms slowly up above your head." His voice was a deep caress as I floated my arms up in front of me like everyone else. "Reach them up towards the sky. Feel your back lengthening while your shoulders are down and relaxed. Feel the connection to the earth through your feet and each of your toes. And as you exhale, bring your arms slowly back down to your sides."

That voice. It was so smooth, so sexy. I was trying to breathe deeply and copy what the girl in front of me was doing, but I was struggling to peel my awareness away from the teacher. He began walking slowly through the mats again, watching the students, his hands clasped behind his back. He moved as silently as a cat, and if it weren't for his voice I'd have no idea how to locate him in the room. At one point he walked directly behind me, and I found myself stretching that little bit further, trying to show off just how good I was at the moon pose. Even though the girl in front of me was practically sideways and I was still mostly vertical.

Did he recognise me? Would he? It was pretty dark in that kitchen two nights ago, plus I'd been wearing pyjamas. Here, he had at least twenty students to watch, and I was just one in a sea of many. Plus, as far as I could tell, he hadn't looked me in the face yet.

"Scoop and roll, hands down on the floor in front of you. And hold as you inhale deeply, feeling that stretch through the backs of your legs. And now step one foot back, followed by the other, into downward dog."

He was right near me! Shit, well I didn't suppose he was going to recognise me with my hips in the air. I was trying to do the stretch properly, surreptitiously checking the girl next to me to compare our postures (Kalina, on my right, seemed able to execute a flawless downward dog. How on earth was she so flexible?!), when suddenly I felt hands on my hips. *His* hands.

"Just move a bit further back here," he whispered quietly to me, his hands gently tugging my hips so they moved further over my legs. "And press your back down, shoulders flattening, here." His hand was firm but soft between my shoulderblades, easing my spine gently into a straighter position.

Oh my *God*. I was upside down, he was touching me, and all I could think, ridiculously, was—what if I accidentally farted like that old lady in Gaye's class?

But no, I didn't even *need* to fart, so that was a stupid thing to think. But my heart did abruptly start beating a whole lot faster and my stomach muscles all contracted spontaneously, so I'd say it was definitely very lucky that I didn't eat anything like cauliflower or lentils yesterday.

I was practically panting like a dog (while in downward dog, yes I noticed the irony), when he leaned down and whispered, "Much better." Then his hands disappeared off me, and I saw his feet turn and move away from me.

Okay. Okay, I could breathe properly again. And oh God, I had such a rich, warm feeling flowing through me from his praise. How ridiculous that nailing a downward dog could make me feel like I'd really achieved something.

"At your own pace, *chaturanga dandasana*. Then up into cobra, or up dog if that's available to you."

Bewildered, I looked around under my armpit to see what everyone else was doing. They were all now lying flat on their stomachs, and some were pushing themselves up on their elbows or hands to make a backbend. I quickly followed along.

"As you flow with your out breath, back into down dog," Truth said, and everyone pushed themselves back up again. "Hold while you inhale. And when you're ready, jump to bring your feet between your hands."

From under my arm, I saw everyone do these very graceful handstand-style jumps where they kind of hovered midair for a moment then landed gracefully with their feet perfectly between their hands. I tried it out, and felt like a very heavy bunny rabbit hopping on the spot. My feet landed nowhere near my hands, and I quickly scrambled to get them up in place.

Shit. I hoped Truth wasn't watching me just then.

"Slowly, come up on your inhale and bring hands to prayer. Take a deep breath, and on the exhale melt down again. When you're ready, either jump or step back into down dog."

Oh God, we were doing it all over again. I didn't remember yoga being quite this acrobatic. Or having this many transitions. Back in Gaye's lounge room, we all just rolled around on the floor with our legs bent up in the air and our fingers hooked around our big toes.

Beside me, I noticed Kalina, the traitor, looking like a total pro. She was *definitely* a closet yogi.

We did the whole sequence a few more times, and once I'd memorised it I was able to move between the poses a little easier, trying to match each transition to my breathing. I also found myself eyeing up everyone else in the class and making mental notes of all the things I wanted to go shopping for later. (Plaited wristbands, hair feathers, stylish anklet and toe rings. Also, those yoga tops that looked a bit unflattering and shapeless when you put them on in the fitting room, actually looked quite lovely in a yoga class. I was going to have to revisit them.)

"*Virabhadrasana*," Truth directed from somewhere nearby, while we were all in down dog again. "Step your right foot forward into a lunge. Then on your inhale, lift yourself up and exhale into warrior two."

I peered out from under my arm again, wondering if I was going to end up with a neck injury soon. I followed what everyone else was doing and quickly got myself into the correct position, arms out horizontally and body twisted to the side.

I could hear Truth nearby, slowly walking through the mats. This was the first time he'd come near me when my face was visible, and I stared resolutely forward, trying to look all serene and yogi-like while wondering if he'd recognise me.

Slowly, I could sense him stepping towards me. I breathed out, trying to sink further into the lunge. And then my leg started trembling with the effort.

Oh, bloody hell.

I hoped he didn't notice. Everyone else in the room seemed to be holding the pose with ease. And of course, just as I was hoping he *wouldn't* notice me, he stopped right beside me.

"Long arms, out here," he whispered, his hands pressing up on the underside of my wrists as he guided my arms out and up further. I couldn't help the little gasp that escaped me and had to bite my lip to prevent making any further sound. Then his hands were on my hips again, and I swear my heart literally paused.

"Lunge further, this way. Can you feel that stretch in your back leg?"

I nodded, breathless. In my peripheral vision, I could see his face, so close to mine. Was he looking at me a bit too intensely?

"Good," he said softly, right by my ear, and then his hands disappeared off me and he moved away. My eyes devoured his back as he left my side, following the symmetrical whorls of tree boughs tattooed over his shoulderblades, and the graceful arch of leaves that extended up his spine.

I watched him stop and correct another girl a few mats away, his hands lifting her arms like he'd done to mine, and I felt an almighty stab of jealousy.

Oh, grow up, Laura. He's the teacher and he probably doesn't even remember you. It's his job to correct everyone's postures.

I noticed Kalina darting me a curious look and I determinedly looked forwards, concentrating on my pose.

But I wanted him to touch me again. I wanted to feel his warm, firm hands on my skin. I wanted to hear him tell me what to do.

"*Trikonasana*, triangle pose," Truth said, and I tried to copy the girl next to me, straightening my lunging leg and moving my arms so they were now vertical.

I must have looked particularly awkward, because Truth moved back in my direction. This time he stopped directly in front of me, and even though my head was tipped on an angle so I was looking at him on a diagonal, we finally made eye contact.

He smiled, that gorgeous, genuine, open smile he had, and I marvelled again at his amazing cheekbones, framing eyes of such a light brown they were practically amber. I smiled back; it was impossible not to.

"Tilt your head up," he said softly to me. "Look up towards the sky."

I twisted my face in the direction of the ceiling, but my eyes only lasted a second up there, before they flitted back down towards him. He held my gaze for a moment, and I was sure his smile increased. Then he *winked* at me, just a quick, fleeting acknowledgement, and I realised he knew exactly who I was.

12

I don't know how I managed to get through the rest of the class, but somehow I did and hopefully no one could tell how totally in love with the teacher I'd already fallen.

I mean, overstatement, obviously. But he just seemed so *nice*. And flexible. And spiritual. And mega hot.

Plus, he lived at the house where I was staying.

The class culminated with some stretches and deep breathing while lying on the ground, and even though I wished Truth would come back over and correct me again, he didn't. We all sat up and there was a resounding "om" to finish the class, followed by everyone saying *namaste* and bowing their heads, and then people started rolling up their mats and leaving.

My eyes followed Truth to where he'd returned to the front of the room, and I had the overwhelming urge to go and speak to him. But it looked like I wasn't the only one with that idea. A girl had already grabbed his attention and was talking animatedly at him, while three—no *four*—other girls were hanging around waiting for their turn.

"Laur?" Kalina was eyeing me expectantly.

"Sorry, coming." I quickly packed away my mat, and shot a last wistful look in Truth's direction as we headed out the door. He was demonstrating a complex pose, his body lithely contorted and balancing on a single arm, and he didn't see me leaving. Of course he didn't. Why would he be watching for me?

But I couldn't help the stab of disappointment in my chest as we left the room.

"This place is pretty epic," Kalina said as we walked across the treetops pathway.

"Isn't it?" I agreed, my eyes now caught on the greenery of the trees around me, the sounds of birdsong filling the air. I was distracted by how energetic and positive I felt, and there was this wonderful feeling of lightness and strength flowing through me. I felt like all my muscles had been lengthened and toned, plus I could swear my posture had corrected itself, as if before I was walking around as a bit of a hunchback, and now I was all straight and willowy.

I decided, then and there, that I was going to start doing yoga regularly. Daily, in fact. I'd be one of those girls who got up early and wore a uniform of yoga pants and stylish tops. I'd be a barefoot goddess with tanned skin and long limbs and I'd change my name to something like Serenity and I'd stop shaving my armpits.

Well, maybe I wouldn't go *quite* that far. With a sudden flash of memory I remembered my high-school cooking teacher who had these long, bushy armpits, and how all the students would try not to look repulsed as we watched her chopping up herbs or reaching for the saucepans.

But I couldn't deny the euphoria coursing through my veins, and I was sure my vision and hearing were crisper.

"Let's get a coffee," Kalina said, pulling my awareness back to the present. "There's a cafe here, isn't there?"

"There's the organic vegan nourishment hub." I pulled the map out of my bag and studied it. "Hopefully, it sells something with caffeine. This way."

The nourishment hub looked more like a co-working hub at Google than a coffee shop. The room was decked out in every style of seating imaginable—there were lounges in one corner, egg chairs and pods, deck chairs and even swings hanging from the ceiling. Throw blankets and cushions were scattered everywhere, there were books and magazines with names like *Yoga Culture* and *Organic Living* placed invitingly on coffee tables, along with gorgeous little jars of fresh flowers and sprigs of herbs. The cafe was about a third full, people in ones or twos sitting comfortably and eating smoothie bowls or sipping kombucha.

We ordered organic coffees and perched ourselves on some Moroccan ottomans while we waited.

"So, what's the plan now?" Kalina asked. "We go and check out all those meditation caves and stuff that are on the map to see if Amy's there?"

"I guess so. We could try showing the staff her photo and asking if anyone recognises her?"

"*Would* anyone recognise her? I mean, I've seen those documentaries where they test that stuff in shopping centres and ask someone if they recognise a kid who was literally just paraded in front of them a moment before and they never do."

I pulled the map out of my bag and studied it again. "This place is crazy. Look, there's a whole meditation *complex* over here. Would Amy be into meditating?"

Kalina frowned, then sighed. "Honestly? I doubt we're going to find her here. I mean, there are heaps of yoga places in Byron Bay, and I can't imagine she'd be able to *get* here. They would most likely have flown to Byron, right? Which means they wouldn't have a car."

"Yeah, I suppose so. Though they could have rented one."

"For this long? Again, Ben would be paying for it all. I can't imagine he's that silly."

"We might as well check out the whole place since we're here, on the off chance we see them." I didn't bother mentioning that there was a certain yoga teacher I wouldn't mind bumping into.

Once our coffees were ready, we took them and followed the tree walk away from the cafe and down into a forest trail that had signs positioned along it saying things like, *The journey starts now* and *Agenda for today: breathe in, breathe out, repeat.*

"So, that teacher guy was getting a bit handsy with you, wasn't he?" Kalina said as we wandered along through the forest.

"Yeah. I didn't mind at all." I couldn't help the goofy smile that took over my lips.

"Ugh, I suppose if dreadlocks are your thing. He was pretty hot, minus the hair."

"You know who he is? He lives at Meadow's house, where we're staying."

"Really? Echo did say there was another guy who lived there, but I hadn't seen him. How do you know?"

"I ran into him the first night. I forgot to tell you. I got up to get a drink, and he was there in the kitchen. His name's Truth."

"Get out! Not another hippie name!"

"I know! Although, it kind of suits him."

Kalina rolled her eyes. "Well, no wonder there's a yoga room in the house—they're all off their rockers. They probably all chose their spiritual names together or something."

"*You* can't have a go at yoga. You looked like you were born doing it!"

Kalina snorted. "Hardly. I did gymnastics when I was younger, that's all. And I've always just been really flexible without trying."

"Oh, boohoo, what a problem to have!"

"It does make for a good sex life, I can tell you that."

"Overshare! But speaking of, what's going on with your boys at the moment? Did Ethan ever come back? And are you still into Maverick?"

Kalina made a sort of disgruntled huffing sound. "I haven't seen Ethan in months. And I think Maverick and I are just getting a bit over each other. It's like, when I see him we'll have a great time in bed together. But after that, and *before* that, we just have nothing to say to each other. And, to be honest, there's only so long that booty calls with the one person can stay interesting."

"Right. So, what about that British guy who turned up at the door? Are you going to tell me who he is?"

Kalina was silent for a while and I was about to keep pressing her when she finally answered, "He's someone I don't ever want to see again."

"Even though he flew halfway around the world to see you?"

"Yep." Kalina folded her arms.

"And is there any chance that our spontaneous trip to Byron Bay to go look for Ben has anything to do with avoiding seeing this nameless man?"

Kalina didn't respond, but I noticed she was scowling.

I was distracted from questioning her further because we suddenly reached the end of the tree path and came out to a startling sight.

My first thought was that it was a construction site. My second thought was that it was quite simply just a disaster zone.

There were half-finished treehouses everywhere. Some were missing roofs, others were just the shells. Across the whole ground, there were trees cut down and sawdust coating the ground and cranes sitting dormant.

"Whoa," Kalina said.

"Are we meant to be here?" I asked, glancing around. The whole place was deserted, and I felt the hairs prickling on the back of my neck, as if we were being watched by some malevolent force. The spirits of the half-finished treehouses.

"I'd say not," Kalina answered after a moment. "Is this on the map?"

I pulled it out and we both peered at it. "This is that area the girl said wasn't open yet," I said, pointing out where I thought we were.

"Well, I don't know much about building things, but I'd say this place is far from finished."

"Yeah, it looks almost abandoned. Are the construction workers just having a day off or something? It's not even the weekend."

"Let's take a closer look." Kalina grinned at me, and then started approaching one of the treehouses that looked almost finished.

"Yeah, 'cause walking through a construction site in our thongs is a great idea."

Kalina was already off though, peering in at the treehouses and stepping carefully over debris.

"Kal!" I hissed, hurrying up to her as she stepped closer to one that at least had all of its walls. "I really think we should head back. I don't—"

There was a sudden noise from within the enclosed treehouse, and Kalina and I both froze. A second later there was another sound, this time resolving itself into a voice.

Shit! We weren't alone here after all. I was all set to bolt back out towards the pathway again, but Kalina gestured at me urgently and ran forwards to crouch underneath the treehouse, in the shadows.

For a second I stared at her, aghast, but then I saw the door starting to open and I too dashed under the treehouse before anyone could see me.

Why we were hiding I had no idea. I felt like I was back in high school, skipping class and trying not to get caught.

"Stop, alright, just stop," a woman's voice barked. "I want to hear solutions, Carol, not problems. All you're bringing me right now are problems."

Footsteps crunched down the stairs right above us, and Kalina and I pressed ourselves back into the shadows. A woman stepped down onto the ground, a phone held up to her ear. She was wearing a business suit, and looked to be in a very bad mood.

"That's not an option, I've told you that," she said curtly into the phone. She'd paused at the bottom of the staircase, one fisted hand resting on the rough, untreated wood of the railing. "The date is set and there is no way we are compromising on that. I've made commitments. If you can't make it happen then you can fuck off right now and I'll find someone who can. I am one *thousand* percent sure that this is achievable. If it's not finished on time then it's due to your incompetence."

I hardly dared to breathe as we cowered there in the shadows. If the woman turned around she'd spot us, and though I wasn't entirely sure we were doing anything wrong or illegal by being here, I was pretty sure we'd lost our opportunity to play the lost-visitor card.

"Fuck the supplier, I don't give a shit about the terms!" The woman finally pressed away from the stairs and started striding back towards the pathway out of the treehouse zone. "Tell Ronnie that whatever it takes he's got to ..."

I didn't hear what Ronnie had to do, because the woman left the clearing and Kalina sagged beside me with a soft groan.

"Jesus fucking Christ!" she said. "Why do I feel like we almost just got caught doing something really dodgy?"

"Yeah." I tried to laugh but it sounded fairly skittish. "Come on, let's get out of here. This place is creepy."

13

Alright, so our main purpose in coming to Byron Bay—locating Ben—was turning out to be far more difficult than expected.

We'd left Yogatainable without any further incidents, though also without miraculously running into Amy. Nor did we run into a certain hot yoga teacher, but that's *totally* not relevant or important. I mean, not really.

But we needed to get back on task. We'd been in Byron now for almost forty-eight hours and we still had zero leads on Ben's whereabouts. What was that thing people said about missing persons? Something like the first few hours were crucial and then every hour after that it became less and less likely you'd find them? Well, exactly. I probably shouldn't think about that.

"Right, so where do you think we should go now?" I asked Kalina as I navigated the car back down through the forest-lined road. "Should we try town again?"

"I don't think I can handle traipsing around all those streets right now." Kalina rubbed her temples. "Let's go to the beach. I'm hot and sweaty and I need a rest. Besides, Ben and Amy will probably *be* at the beach."

Less than an hour later I was stepping out onto beautiful white sand, feeling the sun on my skin, hearing the water rushing and swelling, that smell of sun-baked seaweed in the air. God, I loved the beach. It didn't matter which one I went to, it always felt like a heavy weight was lifting off my shoulders every time.

I should just live here, *at* the beach. Not bother doing anything else. Not caring about anything else. I should become one of those hippies who lived in a van by the beachfront and did dawn yoga on the sand.

Hmm. Not a bad idea.

Of course, I still had my mind firmly on the Ben problem. I *did*. But that didn't mean I couldn't also enjoy being at the beach, did it?

"Looks like all the surfers are over that way," Kalina said, shading her eyes against the sun's glare as she peered out across the water.

I followed her gaze to the sea and picked out where she meant; there was one main area where surfers were congregated, bobbing up and down on their boards as they waited for the next wave or paddling back out if they'd just caught one.

We made our way down the beach in that direction, diligently scanning every sunbaker we passed in case we stepped right over Ben or Amy. But aside from some people who were really going to regret not wearing sunscreen, we didn't see anyone to spark our interest on the sand.

Once we were in front of the breaking waves and the surfers, we both spent the next five minutes scanning them all.

"This is hopeless," Kalina finally said. "I can't see Ben anywhere amongst them."

"Nor is Amy anywhere on the sand around here," I added. "Maybe we should just stake out a spot? If Ben is planning on coming surfing, surely he'll come past. We can take it in turns to keep an eye on all the people coming in and out of the water?"

Kalina chewed on her lip, her brows creased.

"Plus, I'm sure it wouldn't kill us to do a *tiny* bit of relaxing. You know, we are in Byron Bay, after all," I wheedled.

Kalina rolled her eyes. "Okay, fine."

"Hooray!" Without any further prompting, I spread out my towel on the ground, stripped off my beach dress and lay down with an audible, "Ah."

"Are you watching first, or am I?" Kalina asked.

"Hmm?" I replied sleepily.

She tutted. "Fine, then."

I could understand why some people became sun worshippers. There was just something so wonderful about feeling the warmth soaking into your skin. The heat of it, lighting you. I wriggled down further in the sand, adjusting the bumps under me. And wondered if perhaps the sun was just a *little* too scorchy.

Opening my eyes, I noticed Kalina was gone.

I pushed myself up on my elbows and frowned down at the water. After a moment I spotted her, bobbing around in the water, her face turned up to the sky. So much for keeping an eye out.

And, wow, the sun really was extremely hot right then, wasn't it? My towel felt damp beneath me, and I hadn't even been in the water yet.

Climbing to my feet, I walked the few steps down to the surf and swam out to where Kalina was.

"Hey," I called.

She blinked around, looking all zen and relaxed. "Nice sleep?" she asked me with a grin.

"Yeah, it was. Sorry," I added, feeling a bit guilty.

"It's alright," she said with a sigh. "To be honest, though, I'm starting to run out of ideas."

"About finding Ben?"

"Yeah. What do we do? This whole staking-out places feels hopeless. And his phone is still going straight to voicemail. I'm starting to think this was all a stupid idea and that we should never have come. Maybe we should just go back to Sydney."

Instead of replying, I stared out at the water around me. If I was honest with myself, I didn't want to go back home, not yet. And I wasn't sure if that had anything to do with Ben.

"We've come all this way," I eventually said. "I don't think we've given it enough time yet. But maybe we need to ... I dunno, just let the universe help us a bit."

"Huh?"

"I mean, we've been so determined to look for Ben that we've been charging around to all these places and restaurants and things trying to find him. But what if we just slowed down a bit? Maybe if we stop trying to force ourselves to find him then we might happen upon him, anyway?"

"What are you suggesting?"

"Maybe we should just relax a bit? We're here at the beach, in Byron Bay, but we're not really *enjoying* ourselves, are we? I mean, I know we're trying to find Ben, but maybe if we just stopped forcibly searching for him and instead enjoyed where we are, we might end up finding him? After all, Ben and Amy are probably enjoying themselves up here. So if we do too, then maybe we'll end up in the same place."

Kalina scowled but looked like she was considering my words. "I suppose so," she eventually said. "Although, I really don't think that's what proper detectives would do. But if we still haven't found them in another couple of days, then we go back to actively searching."

"Agreed!"

For a little while, we bobbed up and down in the water, enjoying the waves, and I couldn't help but smile. We could relax for a while! Finally! Of course, finding Ben was still paramount. Absolutely.

"Oh, here we go," Kalina suddenly muttered, planting her feet on the sand so she was half out of the water and looking over my shoulder with a distinctively unimpressed look.

"Wha—" I started to say, but instantly stopped as I turned and spotted what Kalina was looking at.

It was Echo emerging from the waves, a surfboard under his arm. He was wearing those half-wetsuit leggings that clung to the legs like seal skin, dipping down low on his hips so that more than just stomach hair was on show. Surprisingly, he was rather hot, in a meaty, solid sort of way, although the beard was streaming water and still made him look far older than I presumed he was.

"Don't you have a job to be at?" Kalina asked incredulously, planting a hand on her hip.

Echo grinned at her wolfishly through his streaming beard, his eyes sparkling with delight to have found Kalina in the water. "I'm on holidays, love. How about yourself?"

"You know what we're doing in Byron Bay," Kalina answered, her voice dripping with annoyance.

"Of course." Echo put his surfboard down on the water and sat on it like it was a bench. "How's the hunt going?" He looked questioningly at the water around him. "Your flatmate hiding under the waves?"

"Oh shut up!" Kalina folded her arms. "We're taking a break. We've been looking for him *all* morning, for your information."

Echo shot me a grin. "She's slacking off, isn't she?" he said with a nod towards Kalina.

I tried not to laugh, but couldn't help the giggle that escaped, especially when Kalina looked apoplectic.

"I'm not slacking off! Ben could definitely be here, at any moment, so if you don't mind you can leave now and we'll keep looking for him."

"Uh-uh." Echo kept grinning at her, making no move to leave. Then he switched his attention to me again. "Laura, right? You look like you're the real brains here. I've got a tip for you."

"Don't listen to him!" Kalina interjected, looking furious.

I couldn't help returning Echo's grin, though, finding it highly amusing just how much he was getting under Kalina's skin.

"And that would be?" I asked him.

"There's some cool bands playing at the Beach Hotel tonight. There'll be a big crowd. If your friends are around, chances are that's where they'll be."

"Great! Hear that, Kal? We'll have to go to the pub tonight!"

She made a non-committal kind of scoffing sound.

"Thanks for the tip." I turned back to Echo with a smile.

He nodded, hopped off his surfboard and hoisted it up under his arm. "You might even be lucky and run into me there," he called back to us as he walked away, a cheeky grin flashing in our direction, before he strode out of the waves.

"I like him," I said, grinning at Kalina.

"Ugh." She rolled her eyes.

"He seems to like teasing you," I needled.

"Yeah, he's an annoying knob-head."

"Uh-uh."

We were silent for a moment, and I kept grinning at her thoroughly annoyed expression.

"Stop it, Laura." Kalina scowled at me.

The Beach Hotel was packed out when we arrived late that afternoon.

Located right across the road from the main beach of Byron Bay, the huge outdoor spaces overlooking the street were filled with groups of people drinking beers and chatting, and families eating pizzas and ignoring their kids, who were giddily running amok. We'd been in there the previous evening when we were hunting for Ben, but had done nothing other than walk through the place then leave. Now, I couldn't wait to get a beer and find somewhere to sit, so we could relax and finally just enjoy the atmosphere!

"Keep your eyes peeled for Ben," Kalina said to me as we made our way past a group of youths wearing carnival-style clothing and having a heated debate about politics. Where on earth you could even *buy* corduroy suspenders and a matching fedora, I had no idea.

"We're enjoying ourselves tonight, remember?" I said pointedly. "But yes, don't worry. My Ben-dar is on."

"Ben-dar?"

"Yeah. Like a gaydar, but a Ben-dar."

Kalina shot me an incredulous look.

"Okay, I'm aware my gaydar has a terrible track record. That was probably a bad example."

"I'll cross my fingers that your Ben-dar is better. Let's just both keep our eyes open."

I didn't need reminding. Currently, my eyes were devouring every sight around me. I *loved* walking into a buzzy pub, especially one that had such a unique range of patrons. It was like a fashion show in there, albeit a hippie version.

We made it to the bar, and after waiting an interminable amount of time to be served drinks, we took our beers and found a solitary table that was free.

"This place is great!" I couldn't help enthusing as I placed my drink down. "When do you think the bands will start?"

"Seven, it said on the sign at the bar," Kalina answered. She took a sip of beer and then stiffened, narrowing her eyes over the top of her glass at something in the distance.

"What?" I followed her gaze, trying to work out what she was looking at.

"Echo," Kalina answered before I could spot him. "Seriously, he's got the *worst* beard. I keep thinking I'm imagining it, and then I see him again and I realise that—hang on, I'm not imagining it. It's really bloody awful."

I spotted Echo on the other side of the pub, turned half away from us and talking to another guy who also had a terrible beard (though Echo's was the most epic).

"I think you love it really," I teased Kalina.

"As if! Imagine sleeping with him. You'd get pash rash *everywhere*."

I raised my eyebrows at her. "So, you've imagined sleeping with him, have you?"

"Oh, shut up."

I laughed and looked back over to where Echo was. He seemed to be with a group of people, some standing and some sitting on the couches nearby. The guy Echo was talking to shifted slightly and I saw that sitting on the couch among the group was a guy with dreadlocks and amazing cheekbones.

I gasped and grabbed Kalina's arm. "He's there!"

"Who?"

"Truth—the yoga teacher! He's there with Echo!"

I could sense Kalina raising her eyebrows at me, and when I glanced back at her she was smiling slyly.

"Someone's very excited about this."

I didn't respond, but just slapped her arm excitedly a few times. "Come on, let's go join them!"

"Really?" Her smile dropped instantly.

"Yes, please! Come on, it'll be fun! You don't have to talk to Echo, there are loads of other people with them."

Kalina groaned, but I knew she was caving. "Fine. But only for your benefit."

We walked towards the group and I suddenly realised that my mind had gone completely blank. What do you talk to strangers about? What's a witty opening line? *Oh God, have I forgotten how to make conversation?*

As we joined the group a girl and a couple of the guys eyed us curiously (or coldly? I couldn't tell), making me feel extremely awkward.

"Look what the cat dragged in," Echo drawled, a cheeky smile directed at us. (Well, mainly at Kalina).

"*Such* a surprise finding you here," Kalina answered, sweeping the whole group with a friendly acknowledgement.

Echo started introducing us to the group, and I immediately forgot each person's name as soon as he'd said it. Until he got to Truth.

"You know Truth, or do you? He lives at the house," Echo was saying.

At the mention of his name, Truth had turned away from the guy he was chatting to and finally looked at the two people who had just joined his group. He glanced first at Kalina then registered me, and he smiled warmly in recognition.

"We haven't properly met," Kalina said. "But we did manage to stumble into his yoga class this morning."

"You went to Yogatainable?" Echo asked, sounding surprised.

"I thought you looked familiar," Truth said to Kalina. "I'm Truth."

"Kalina," she replied.

"And Laura," Truth turned his attention back to me. "Nice to see you again."

"Likewise." I smiled back at him.

The guy who'd been sitting beside Truth on the bench stood up and headed towards the bar, and Truth beckoned me over to sit with him with a nod.

Trying not to look too delighted with this development, I sat beside him, aware of the space between us as if it were filled with magnetic charges.

"So, you teach yoga?" *Oh, well done, Laura. Standing ovation for your opener.*

"I do," he replied, regarding me with warm, golden-brown eyes. "I didn't realise you were a student. Have you been practising long?"

"Oh, I'm not really a student, just a casual drop-in yoga imposter. As I'm sure you realised," I added with an embarrassed laugh.

He shrugged. "Everyone's got to start somewhere. And you weren't bad. I've seen students a lot worse than you."

"Thanks for saying so. But, well, I'm pretty sure I'm terrible."

"A lot of people don't give yoga a proper chance. There's a yoga room at the house if you want to practise there. I think Meadow lets guests use it when they stay."

"Yes, she did say that. Well … maybe. I'll see."

"I always try to get up and do a dawn practice," Truth added. "It can be the best thing for the soul."

Dawn! Well, I supposed if you were an instructor then that made sense. Actually, if Truth was going to be there at dawn, then the prospect of getting up that early wasn't so bad.

"Have you taught yoga for long?" I asked, trying not to imagine him shirtless and stretching again.

He nodded. "Years. I've been very lucky to be able to study different styles with a range of masters both here and abroad. I've studied yoga for over eight years now, though even I know that I'm still learning."

"Wow. What overseas places have you studied in?"

"Oh, not too many. I spent a lot of time in Southern Asia—Sri Lanka, India, Burma—all just backpacking around and living in yoga communes."

"Wow," I repeated. "And did you always know you wanted to be a yoga teacher?"

Truth raised an eyebrow at me, his eyes glinting with humour.

"Sorry!" I cringed. "I'm not trying to make this like twenty questions. I'm just so … curious. I don't know any other yoga teachers."

"That's okay." He nodded his head. "I'll start firing questions at you in a minute. But to answer your question, no, I didn't always know I wanted to do this. It was only when I went travelling through Asia with a friend after high school that I discovered yoga. Before that, I'd never even done a class."

"Right. So fascinating. But, okay, your turn. Fire those questions at me."

He turned so that he was sitting at an angle, his body facing towards mine. I sat up a bit straighter and waited while he narrowed his eyes and rubbed his chin in a deliberately pensive manner.

Gosh, his cheekbones really were amazing. And his eyes, that sort of burnt-honey colour, framed by dark brows and dark dreadlocks falling across his shoulders. Despite him wearing a ripped and faded t-shirt, I was aware of the inkscape across his back, like a hidden secret just begging to be revealed.

"First question, then," he said. "What's the reason you're up here in Byron Bay?"

I hesitated for only a moment, wondering if I should tell him the truth. Then decided that there really wasn't any reason to lie.

"We're looking for our friend," I said. "He's in a bit of a bad place, emotionally, and he's met this girl. And, well, they've sort of run away up here together. We want to find him before he does anything he'll regret later."

Truth listened to me with what seemed to be genuine interest, and he nodded his head when I was done. "Not what I was expecting, but a very noble answer. This will make my second question sound very lame."

I smiled. "Well, you get three questions, so two to go."

"Three, do I?"

"Fair's fair."

"Alright. Since you know that I'm a passionate yoga teacher, tell me, Laura, what are you passionate about in your life?"

My smile faded as my brain tried to formulate an answer.

What was I passionate about? Shit, this should have been a really simple question. I was passionate about things, wasn't I?

Truth was looking at me, his eyes friendly and encouraging, as if he had all the time in the world to wait patiently for my answer. But I couldn't think of anything. I sipped my beer, playing for time, but it was as if my mind had gone completely blank. *Passion*. What was I passionate about?

"I don't ... I mean ... I'm still ..." I mumbled, casting around for an answer that sounded half decent. Then I just sighed and met his gaze again. "Honestly? I don't know. I think I'm trying to work that out now."

To my relief, Truth nodded, as if I'd just given the right answer to an exam. "Being honest with yourself is one of the hardest things to do."

I coughed a half-laugh. "Yeah, well. I'm hoping that some direction might appear in my life at some point soon."

Did I really just say that?

But Truth was nodding again, his dreadlocks slipping over his shoulder. "You'll get there. Yoga was that for me, really. I found it at a time when I needed help, and it's guided me ever since. What's going on in your life that seems so difficult or confusing right now?"

I looked at him in surprise. He was giving me his full attention, his expression open and reassuring and warm. For a second, I was barely even conscious of the fact that he was absolutely gorgeous. I just felt like I could share anything with him and he would listen patiently and without judgement.

"I'm trying to work out who I am," I said quietly, my voice hesitant. "I mean, I know that sounds stupid, but I thought I knew who I was and then my whole world kind of fell apart. The guy I'd been together with pretty much my whole life, left me. Well, he didn't really leave me, he realised he was gay and so we split up. And since then, I've been trying to put my life back together. Actually no, I've been trying to get a *new* life. To find out who I am by myself."

"That sounds very brave."

I huffed out a laugh again. "No one calls me brave. They call *him* brave—

my ex. You know, for coming out after all this time and realising who he is. He gets all this support and encouragement from people, and of course I can't resent him at all, can I? It's not his fault. He's had to live his whole life struggling with his identity. I have to be empathetic and understanding, just like everyone else."

I had no idea why I was telling Truth all this. I barely knew him. Plus, I was pretty sure I wanted to sleep with him, and this conversation certainly wasn't a flirty one. But he was still looking at me with so much care and understanding. It was as if we were the only two people at the pub, everyone else around us just moving in and out of some other dimension. I felt like he could guide me, like my own personal Gandalf. But a sexy one.

"My mothers told me once that no one would ever choose to be gay in this world."

"Mothers?"

"Yes. I was raised by two women. One of the original same-sex couples from back when that wasn't very common." Truth shrugged nonchalantly, as if this was something he'd always found completely normal. "It was tough for them. Really tough. I've had conversations with them both, separately, where they've told me that even though they're happy with who they are, they still wouldn't have actively chosen that life. At the very least, they could never have children that were biologically related to them both. And the very act of having children was challenging, because suddenly third parties needed to be included."

"Gosh, that's ... amazing. I mean, it's amazing that you were raised by two, I'm going to guess, very strong women."

Truth smiled. "They are both very strong. Very resilient. They learned long ago to not worry about what others thought of them, and they've given me so much respect and appreciation of women."

"Do you have brothers or sisters?"

"No." Truth's smile faded. "After Nita—my biological mum—had me,

Sophie was going to have the next child. But she couldn't get pregnant. They spent years trying, and when it didn't happen they decided that our family was complete just as it was."

My heart broke a little for Truth's mums. How hard it must have been, especially when every attempt to get pregnant would likely have been challenging instead of joyful.

"I guess my ex will have to come to terms with those difficulties if he ever wants to be a father," I said quietly, thinking of Jack. "But I'm not sure he wants children, anyway. At least he didn't. Or at least not with me."

"Do you want children?" Truth asked.

"Not now! I did … or at least I thought I did. But definitely not anytime soon. It's now moved to one of those vague 'in the future' events, I think."

"Well, presuming you end up with a male partner—if indeed you do want another partner—then you're lucky that things should be straightforward in that regard."

I laughed. "Yeah, at least there's that. And how about you—do you have a female, or male, partner?"

Truth smiled. "I don't have either. Though I have been with both, I do more strongly lean towards the female energy. Many of the theories I've studied revolve around the balance of masculine and feminine energies, and the healing nature they can bring."

I frowned. "I didn't realise yoga was about that."

"These are ideas that come from the philosophical matrix out of which yoga grew."

He must have noted my confused expression, because he clarified, "Tantra."

I choked on my drink and looked at him sharply to see if he was joking. He had a serene calmness to him, and this might sound weird, but it was as if he just sort of radiated happiness. If that was a thing.

"Tantra?" I repeated. "As in …"

"Tantric sex, yes," he said with a laugh. "I'm a Tantric-sex instructor, as well as a yoga instructor."

I didn't know what to say, so I just stared at him. My mouth was probably hanging open a bit.

My expression seemed to amuse him even more. "Tantra is about much more than just sexual practice. It's about seeing the divine in the worldly. Non-duality. Though, of course, Tantric lovemaking really is quite an experience. I've worked with many couples to help them find a deeper connection and joy with each other."

"Right. Couples. Um, that sounds very … interesting."

Truth nodded. "And I do the odd individual lesson."

I choked on my drink again (why was I still sipping it?) and spluttered and coughed a fair bit before I could respond. "What on earth do you teach someone in an individual lesson? I mean, or do you …?"

He didn't seem at all bothered by my ongoing questions. In fact, he looked like he was enjoying responding to them. "Lessons are usually clothes on."

"Of course. I mean, I wouldn't have presumed …" I trailed off, feeling my face heating up.

A Tantric-sex *instructor*? I wasn't sure now if I *really* wanted to sleep with him, or if I wanted to run a mile away.

Truth laughed softly. "I'm not actively teaching Tantra at the moment, except by request from former clients. So, you don't need to worry about strange goings-on at the house."

"Oh, I'm not worried about that! I'm just … curious, I suppose."

Truth gave me a quizzical look, but before he could say anything further Kalina appeared out of nowhere and plonked herself down on the bench next to me. I jolted, suddenly remembering that Truth and I weren't the only two people here, and as if on cue someone else sat down on the other side of Truth and drew him straight into a conversation.

"Okay, seriously, Laur," Kalina said, leaning in and gripping my arm hard at the same time. "That guy over there. Is it Chris Hemsworth?"

NEW MESSAGE
From: Yogatainable Lifestyle Retreat at 10.42 am
Namaste and Welcome to Yogatainable. For us to curate your journey to health and wellbeing, please take a moment to fill in our <u>online questionnaire</u>. We look forward to seeing you on the mats 🙏

NEW MESSAGE
From: Rose Spencer at 11.15 am
LAURA!!! I have no one else to tell this stuff to, so you're it! Philippe has introduced me to the land of TOYS and OMG you should see his collection! Things are starting to get very ... experimental. 😂 *We need to have drinks again soon!!!*

INSTAGRAM NOTIFICATION
Your contact "Mum" is on Instagram as @MuffinandBaxtervacation

INSTAGRAM NOTIFICATION
@MuffinandBaxtervacation started following you

INSTAGRAM NOTIFICATION
@MuffinandBaxtervacation wants to send you a message:
Hi darling this is your Mum 🙂

14

Things I had decided since arriving in Byron Bay:

1. Yoga had many more hidden benefits than I initially thought.
2. Byron Bay could quite possibly be my spirit town.
3. Ben had either lost his mobile phone or was going through some sort of early-life crisis.
4. Kalina had the hots for a bogan Aussie guy with a terrible beard whose name was Echo.
5. I definitely had the hots for a yoga-teaching Tantric-sex instructor whose name was Truth.
6. I was prepared to do things I hadn't done in a while (i.e. get up frighteningly early) in order to improve my overall wellbeing (see point one) and advance the likelihood of meeting my hot housemate (see point five).

I was woken the next morning by my pillow vibrating. I groggily fumbled around for it in the dark and switched off the alarm before it could wake Kalina. Not that it mattered. Kalina's sleeping-bear impression was still going strong.

I climbed quietly out of bed and changed into my yoga clothes. It was still dark outside, but dawn would be happening any moment now. I just hoped that when Truth mentioned he did dawn yoga, he really did mean at the crack of dawn. Our conversation at the pub had been cut short last night, right as it was becoming super interesting, and I hadn't had a chance to speak to him again before he left. And even though Kalina and I had stayed at the pub for an extra couple of hours, hoping Ben and Amy might appear (they didn't), I hadn't been able to stop thinking about Truth and wondering what exactly being a Tantric-sex instructor involved.

The home yoga studio was silent and empty when I entered, and I wondered if I should turn on the lights. But the sky outside was rapidly lightening, the stars now completely invisible, and I knew within minutes that light would be flooding the room through the huge glass doors.

I spread one of the mats out on the floor and then stood and closed my eyes, trying to remember what Truth had started with in the class the day before.

Breathing. That was it. I focused on my breath and made it slow down. *In. Out. In. Out. In.*
Woo, feeling a bit light-headed.

Alright, maybe I should try something else. I took a breath in and raised my arms above my head. And then I rolled my body down slowly so that my fingertips brushed the ground and my hips were in the air.

Hmm. I couldn't help thinking that this would be a rather unflattering time for Truth to arrive. I had my bum in the air again, poking out right at the door.

Planting my hands firmly, I stepped my feet back and came down into a high-plank. Was that right? We definitely did some planking in the class yesterday. So, if I just held it there for a while … Yes, planking was great. *Definitely* yoga-ish.

Although, my arms were shaking already. Had I lasted a minute yet? Surely I was close.

Deciding I'd done enough planking, I dropped to the ground and did a bit of a back stretch. Which was called snake pose, wasn't it? Or lizard?

Something like that. Anyway, after that I rolled over and tried a side twist. I couldn't remember what that position was called, but it was definitely stretching something.

"Good morning," came a deep, husky voice from behind me. "Mind if I join you?"

Smiling in delight, I untwisted to look at the door and saw Truth standing there, wearing nothing other than loose track-shorts that were cut and fraying at mid-thigh, and riding waaay low on his hips.

Holy shit. He was *beautiful*.

His stomach and chest were a mosaic of lean muscles and deeply tanned skin, that tribal tattoo rippling and curling its way across his pecs and just tickling his collarbone. His dreadlocks were tied back behind him again, and he wore a collection of leather and string ropes on his wrists.

I realised my mouth was hanging open and I quickly closed it.

"Of course." I gestured invitingly at the room. "This is your house, after all."

With a smile, Truth walked in and laid a mat out next to me.

The next few minutes were spent in total silence. I tried to do my own version of poses (though to be honest, I'd totally run out of ideas and was just cycling back through the same ones I knew) and pretended I wasn't watching Truth.

He started out just lying on the floor, on his back, with his eyes closed. I tried not to imagine running my hands up and over his chest, but failed dismally.

Then he began a series of flowing movements, which had him transitioning through all these different poses with hardly a pause between each one.

And then he planted his elbows on the ground in a kind of triangle position and pushed his body straight up in the air, so that he was balancing like a candlestick in an arm-stand.

I didn't even bother pretending that I wasn't looking then. His whole body was taut with the effort, looking like a sculpture of Ideal Man (if Ideal Man was also Upside-down Man).

He stayed there for a while, then bent at the waist and slowly lowered his legs, his toes the gentlest silent caress on the floor as they touched down. And then he was planting his hands on the ground and swinging his legs beneath himself, crossing one over the other and balancing with them out to the side, a good foot off the ground.

I felt a bit feeble doing my lizard pose after that.

"It can take a lot of patience to really understand and feel the benefits of yoga," Truth said suddenly, while slowly unwinding his legs.

"Oh?" I paused, watching him as he moved until he was sitting on his ankles. He looked up at me with a warm smile, his skin flushed and his amber eyes sparkling in the morning light.

"I remember when I first started," he continued. "I thought yoga was simply all about the poses—the *asanas*—and that there wasn't much more to it than just stretching. But there are so many deeper benefits that most people have no idea about."

"Right." Well, count me in with that group of people. "Such as?"

"Mindfulness. Stillness. Inner strength and wisdom. In the royal yogic tradition, there are eight limbs of yoga, each one vital to master in order to achieve overall balance. The asanas are only one of these limbs."

"Oh. So, I'm even more of an amateur than I realised."

Truth laughed. "Everyone's journey and experience with yoga is personal. And I don't believe there is such a thing as an amateur. Right from your first practice you will start to feel the benefits of yoga. Tell me, how did you feel this morning, doing yoga in here?"

I was basically just waiting for you to arrive because I want to sleep with you.

Shit. I couldn't say that.

"I felt … calm. And peaceful. Energised."

Did those things contradict each other?

Truth nodded. "I think it's the best way to start the day."

"Yes, I'll have to, I mean, I *should* make it a regular thing. It can really help me get some … *direction* … for my day."

What was I saying?

Truth tilted his head to the side, considering me. "You know, I've been thinking about our conversation from last night."

Oh no. What had I said?

"About how you're trying to work out who you are?" he continued, and I felt my cheeks immediately heat. Shit, I had said that, hadn't I? How embarrassing.

"I know who I am, it's just—"

"You're recovering from a broken heart?" Truth supplied.

That silenced me. I quickly found the garden *very* interesting to look at. But Truth waited me out, silent too. I could feel his eyes on me, waiting. *Shit.*

I cleared my throat. "It's been ages. I'm pretty recovered. As in, I'm not in love with my ex anymore, if that's what you think."

"But love can leave the deepest scars."

I threw him an incredulous look. "Well, of course it can! And yes, I probably am a bit scarred. But so are most people."

Truth just nodded. "I know. I work with people all the time who struggle with love. Sorry if you think I'm out of line asking you this. I'm just trying to understand you more."

I raised my eyebrows at him, feeling wary. "Right. Well, is that necessary?"

Truth smiled gently. "I like to help people. I think I can help you, if you'll let me."

"Do I need help?" I asked him carefully. But the question felt rhetorical.

Already, my chest felt like it was squeezing, my heart and lungs fluttering like caged birds trying to get out.

He met my eyes; his were golden warm and invitingly open. "I think love is an experience many fail to master."

"That's very poetic."

Truth smiled. "Do you feel experienced in the art of love?"

I huffed a laugh. "Not really, no."

"How about in lovemaking?"

I stared at him incredulously. Did he *know* what I'd been thinking?

"Er, not really," I muttered, my cheeks heating again.

He nodded sagely.

"Do *you* consider yourself skilled in these arenas?" I couldn't help asking. "Are you a master at lovemaking?"

I held my breath, feeling way more energised now than I had when I was doing the yoga poses.

"I'm not a master. There's always more to learn. But I have been studying Tantra for a number of years now."

I raised my eyebrows, waiting for him to say more.

He held my gaze, his lips remaining firmly closed.

"Are you going to tell me more about it?" I eventually asked. "It seems unfair that I've told you I'm not very experienced and you have the knowledge to share with me if you so choose."

"Is that what you want? To know more about Tantric sex?"

I bit my lip. "Yes." My face felt *very* hot now. "Though, not just the sex part," I quickly added. "All the things you were just saying. About … love and stuff."

Truth's eyes were glinting with something new now.

Without saying anything, he stood and rolled up his yoga mat, placing it back in the corner of the room. Then he returned and offered me his hand. I hesitated briefly—what was about to happen?—but then took it, gasping at his firm grip as he pulled me to my feet.

"I have to go to work now, Laura," he said softly, keeping my hand captured in his and held against his chest. "But if you're around tonight, I'd be delighted to teach you."

He squeezed my hand slightly before releasing it, his smile broad and his eyes warm. I couldn't find any words to say as I watched him leave the room, his dreadlocks swaying across the inkscape on his back, but my smile must have been all the answer he needed.

15

I padded quietly down the hallway, my hair still wet from the shower. Kalina had gone out to buy coffee and something for breakfast, and aside from the cats I presumed I was the only one still in the house.

The ginger smoosh-face was glaring at me from the end of the corridor.

"Hello, grumpy," I said, stooping to pet him on the head.

"Meow." He butted his head up into my hand and then began purring. His little tongue was poking out of his mouth, and I was pretty sure he was cross-eyed.

"You're not a very good-looking kitty, are you?" I said, squatting down on my haunches and petting him more. "You know, if you were a bit nicer—"

Smoosh-face bit me on the hand.

"Ow! See, that's exactly what I'm talking about."

Rubbing my hand, I stood back up and walked into the kitchen, jolting when I realised Echo was in there. He was sitting at the kitchen bench, his laptop open before him, and had a smirk on his face as he watched me.

"Oh! I didn't realise you were here." I felt my cheeks heating in embarrassment.

But he just grinned. "Don't worry about it. That cat's uglier than a hat-full of arseholes. Acts like it sometimes, too."

I laughed, feeling the tension leave my shoulders. "That's one way of putting it. So, what do you do for work?" I asked him as I got myself a glass of water. "Have you lived in Byron Bay for long?"

"I freelance," he replied with a smile. "Been here about a month so far. How long do you reckon you guys will be here?"

I shrugged. "You know why we've come. If we can find Ben today, then I guess we won't stay much longer. But it seems silly to leave without finding him, especially after we drove all this way. But we don't have endless time to look either. I'm starting a new job in less than two weeks, and Ben's meant to be starting the week after." I frowned, biting my lip. "So, if you have any ideas on how to find him, we're open to suggestions."

Echo opened his mouth to say something, but then he paused, looking thoughtful. He closed his mouth again and gave a rueful shrug. "Nothing beyond what you're doing, I guess. Byron isn't the biggest town, you're sure to knock into them soon. Plus, sometimes you need to give people the benefit of the doubt. If that girl really is a shit-storm in a glass, then your mate will work it out."

My lips twitched at the absurd image. "Possibly. We just need him to work it out a whole lot faster than he is."

"Well, there are worse places to be stranded."

"Can you please tell Kalina that? Because I'm all on board with enjoying Byron Bay a bit more, but she's determined to be all detectivey twenty-four-seven."

As if summoned by her name, I heard the sound of the front door opening, and a moment later Kalina was walking in with two takeaway coffees and a paper bag with some muffin-shaped lumps inside.

"Alright, Laura," she said as she walked in. "I hope you're ready for another day of staking out the town."

I raised my eyebrows at Echo. He just shrugged and chuckled, his eyes sparkling as he observed Kalina in her tiny denim cut-offs.

"Best of luck, Sherlock," Echo teased.

Kalina gave him a dirty look. "I don't need luck. I have the powers of deduction."

"Of course you do."

"Come on, Laur." Kalina turned around and marched back out again, taking my coffee and muffin with her.

"Wait a sec!" I raced down the hall and shoved my thongs on, then joined Kalina outside. As I took my coffee and sipped thoughtfully, Kalina launching into a tale of the hot barista who'd served her, I realised something was niggling in my mind.

And then, as I bit into the white-chocolate-and-raspberry muffin Kalina had passed to me, it hit me.

That laptop Echo had been using in the kitchen. It was pearl-white and had yellow sunflower decals all over it.

It wasn't his laptop—it was Meadow's.

"This restaurant here looks amazing."

"Eyes on the prize, Laura. We're not here for fancy restaurants."

"Is Ben a prize, is he?" I raised an eyebrow at her, teasing.

She rolled her eyes. "You know what I mean. We're here for a very serious reason. Think about Lucas, back at Los Perdidos, trying to handle everything on his own at the moment. He's counting on us. *Ben's* counting on us, even if he doesn't know it yet."

My smile dimmed.

The thing was, I'd been trying hard *not* to think about Lucas. Up here, far away from home, it was easy to file him and my life back in Sydney away in a dark recess of my mind and squash it down like it didn't exist. I was mentally shoving all aspects of my regular life into a box and sitting on it.

But Kalina was right. Lucas was counting on us to locate Ben and get him back to Sydney. Even though Matty was handling the kitchen and Lucas had casual bartenders filling in, Los Perdidos wouldn't be the same place without Ben or Kalina there.

Reluctantly, I tore my eyes away from the tapas restaurant. It was closed right now anyway, but I still filed it away in my mind as a restaurant that Ben would love. If we ever managed to find him, maybe we could all go there together to celebrate.

A girl brushed past me on the pavement a bit too close, knocking into my shoulder.

"Oh, sorry!" she said, sounding not at all apologetic, and I scowled at the retreating back of her and her friend. They were wearing matching pale-blue t-shirts that had abstract lotus motifs on the back.

"Isn't that the Yogatainable logo?" I asked Kalina, frowning at their shirts. "They're far from work."

She too was watching the girls and she nodded. "Yeah, it is. I've been seeing people wearing those tops *everywhere* in town. Who'd have thought there were so many people obsessed by yoga up here? It's almost like a cult."

Her words sent a wash of unease through me. Maybe that's what had happened to Ben—he and Amy had joined a cult? It would explain why he wasn't using his phone anymore. They'd probably made him throw it into a bonfire while dancing around in a straw skirt.

"Oh my God!" Kalina suddenly exclaimed. I glanced at her and saw that she had her phone out, Instagram open. "Amy just posted a picture at a cafe! And I know which one it is! Come on!"

We took off at a run down the street.

"Where ... where are we going?" I gasped, feeling a stitch materialising in my side almost instantly.

"It's that one on the corner ... on the other side of town! I can't remember ... the name, but I ... I recognise it. Shit!"

Kalina stopped running, doubling over and breathing hard, and I gratefully stopped too, holding my hand over my ribs as if they were trying to escape.

"Fuck, we're unfit," I said with a gruff laugh.

"Okay. Come on," Kalina panted, her face already sheened in sweat. "Slower pace."

We power-walked down the streets, pushing through groups of people when they got in our way.

"Do you think they're still there?" I panted as we neared the cafe.

"I bloody hope so," Kalina replied.

"What are we going to say?" I asked, my pace slowing a fraction. "I mean—what—surprise! We're here to save you from your girlfriend!"

Kalina also slowed, and I saw her biting her lip. "We'll just … have to be really straight with him. Tell him he's abandoned his responsibilities and his whole family are worried about him. We'll need to get him away from Amy, I think. Might need to divide and conquer."

"She won't let us talk to him alone. As soon as she realises we're here, she'll grip her claws in even harder."

The cafe was in sight now. It was called The Flower Pot, and there were tables and plants all spilling outside, beachy-looking people lounging about with plates of avocado toast or poached eggs. No Ben or Amy, however.

"They must be inside. Let's just look … carefully. It might be best if they don't see us yet."

"Good idea!" I agreed. "Then we can always follow them back to their accommodation so we know where they're staying, then wait until Amy goes out or something so we can talk to Ben alone."

Kalina glanced at me with her eyebrows raised. "Now who's sounding stalkery?"

Slowly, like a pair of weirdos, we crept down the street towards the cafe. As we closed in, we hugged the wall, and then we were creeping up towards the wide-open front. Kalina pressed herself against the wall and I ran forward, doubled over, and hid behind a pot plant. A girl at the closest table saw me, and gave me an apprehensive look as she shifted her handbag onto her lap.

"Can you see anything?" Kalina whispered to me loudly.

I poked my head around the plant and surveyed the tables of people inside. "No. Can you?"

Kalina leaned forwards slightly, just enough so that she could peek around the wall. Then she stepped right out and huffed. "They're not here," she said flatly.

"Really?" I asked, standing up. "Trying to surprise someone," I added to the girl and her friend, who were looking pretty alarmed. They shuffled their chairs away from me.

I did a proper survey of the whole cafe, and then turned and scanned the surrounding streets. There was definitely no sign of Ben or Amy.

"Shit. Shit. SHIT!" Kalina exclaimed.

"Come on." I grabbed her arm and led her away. The two girls looked about ready to call the police.

"We must have just missed them," Kalina said, sounding utterly defeated.

"Maybe not. They could have been here hours ago."

"Oh, that's helpful."

"What do you want to do now?" I asked, feeling as defeated as Kalina sounded.

Kalina checked her watch. "It's after twelve. Let's go to the pub."

"Meow."

"Don't look at me like that," I told old Smoosh-face.

"These bloody cats," Kalina muttered, doing her best to determinedly ignore the grey tabby cat that was butting its head against her arm. "How many are there, anyway?"

"Five," Echo answered. "But two are basically feral and slum it outside."

We were all sitting on the couches in the share house's lounge room. "All" being Kalina, Echo, Truth and me, as well as three of the house cats. Meadow was reportedly out for the night, and we had the coffee table covered in pizza boxes (now mostly empty) and the recycling bin lined with beer bottles. Though, interestingly, it turned out Truth was a non-drinker. He'd been drinking nothing but kombucha and water all night. And once I realised this, I'd also switched to water, meaning I was now essentially sober.

I wasn't sure how exactly it had happened, the four of us ending up sharing pizzas and hanging out together all night. It had started with just Kalina and I—plus smooshy—drinking and commiserating about our failure in the late afternoon. Then Echo had turned up and joined us. Then Truth a bit later. And now here we all were.

"There's definitely something wrong with this one." I glared at the ginger cat that was now kneading my thigh with its claws, its crossed eyes pinned on mine and its rough little tongue poking out of the side of its mouth.

"All earth's creatures are equal under the sun," Truth said, his voice a deep, sultry rumble.

"You're lucky some people like you," I told the cat.

It paused its kneading, glaring at me. Then resumed with startlingly sharp gusto.

"So, how's the hunt for your lost sailor going?" Echo asked, his mocking eyes fixed on Kalina.

"We almost had them today," Kalina replied. "I expect we'll find them in another day or two."

"Meanwhile, you're dragging your friend around town for hours on end like rats in a maze," Echo said.

"Laura wants to find Ben just as much as I do!" Kalina retorted, glaring at Echo.

He shook his head sadly. "No time for sightseeing. What bad

holidaymakers you are."

"We've seen plenty of sights," I argued. "Plus, we did that class at Yogatainable yesterday."

"Now *that* place is a sight," Kalina added.

"It must be cool working there." I directed my comment at Truth. He was lounging on the couch next to me, linen harem pants hanging off his legs and his shoulders and chest exposed by his low-cut singlet. His dreads were tied up in a bun on top of his head, a couple snaking out to brush his shoulders.

"It's great," Truth replied. "Meadow's done a fantastic job with it."

"Meadow?" I frowned.

"She's one of the owners," Truth replied, looking surprised. "Didn't you know?"

"*Meadow's* one of the owners?" Kalina repeated incredulously. "But she's so young!"

"Twenty-eight, or twenty-nine, I think." Truth rubbed his chin, looking thoughtful.

"It's a pretty ambitious resort," Echo added. "Sprung up here almost overnight, eh, Truth?"

"It was an old bungalow in the forest that they bought and converted. Didn't have to do much work on it to get it operating."

"It looked like they were doing a lot of work on it when we were there," Kalina said. "Those weird treehouse things they were building looked like a disaster! When are they meant to be finished?"

Truth frowned. "I don't know about any treehouse things. They're extending the accommodation to include private villas, but that's all meant to be finished."

"Haven't you *seen* them? They looked nowhere near completed."

"What did you see?" Echo asked, sounding genuinely interested.

"And where did you see this? It's all off limits, even for employees,"

Truth added.

"Um, we got a bit lost," I hurriedly said. "We might have been somewhere else entirely. Maybe even on a different property."

Truth shrugged, looking unconcerned. "I haven't seen any of the villas. It's not my area of expertise, anyway."

"They're plugging the whole phase-two launch," Echo said, now looking at Truth thoughtfully. "You saying the staff haven't even seen the villas?"

Truth shook his head. "Others might have. I wouldn't know. You could ask about it next time you're there."

"Wait a second," Kalina looked at Echo incredulously. "*You* go to Yogatainable?"

"You don't know everything about me, love," Echo replied with a grin.

"You're *such* a delinquent! I bet you can't even touch your toes!"

"Wanna bet?"

"Kalina's a natural at yoga," I interjected, shooting them both a grin.

"So am I," Echo replied.

"I bet you're not." Kalina eyed him with annoyance.

"Try me," he challenged.

"Fine, come on, then, beardy. Challenge on." Kalina stood up, taking her half-full beer with her, and marched off towards the yoga room. "Show me what you can do!"

With an exaggerated grimace, Echo obligingly stood up and followed her into the yoga room.

"Want to join them?" Truth asked me, making no effort to move off the couch.

"No," I replied, feeling a smile tugging at my lips. "I'm happy here."

"Good. Me too."

For a moment we considered each other, his golden-brown eyes holding mine. Then I bit my lip and looked away, the smile tugging at my lips again.

"So!" I said.

"So," he repeated.

"Alright, I'm just going to say it. I want to hear more about Tantra. What do you do in your lessons?"

Truth smiled. "It varies, depending on what the clients need. Sometimes it can feel a lot like relationship counselling."

"Right. But you said you also teach individuals. So, what would you teach to one person?"

"Again, it depends on what they want to learn."

"What if I was your student? And I just want to learn about what Tantra is?"

"Well, that's easy enough. I'd probably just give you a book to read."

I narrowed my eyes at him, wondering if he was being serious or just teasing me. He had his body turned towards me again, giving me his full attention, and he was still smiling in that open, easy way he had.

"What if I don't want to read a book?" I asked quietly, watching him carefully.

He met my eyes, and I watched as he slowly bit his lower lip. Then he extended his hand out, palm up.

"Can I have your hand?" he asked, his eyes still on mine.

Slowly, I placed my hand in his. He gently squeezed my fingers, then carefully turned them over so that my palm was facing up, his left hand holding it gently in place.

"Tantra is, at its heart, lovemaking rather than just sex," he said softly. While he spoke, he used the middle finger of his right hand to trace a sensuously slow line down from the tip of my middle finger to the centre of my palm. "It's about connection with another person. Being present and open together. And building that connection over time through both physical and spiritual sharing."

His finger kept moving across my palm, tracing a slow spiral out from the centre, making my whole arm tingle right up into my shoulder

135

and chest.

"So, Tantra is only for people in relationships?" I asked, trying not to gasp.

"No. It becomes much deeper when you're with someone you love for a long time. But that's not necessary to experience Tantric sex. Anybody who knows the art of Tantric love can share this with others."

His finger stopped moving, resting now on my wrist right above my pulse point. He looked up into my eyes again, and I struggled to breathe.

"Would you like to join me tonight?" he asked softly, his hands still gently holding mine.

Slowly, I nodded.

He smiled. Then he drew my hand up to his mouth and kissed my palm gently, right over the invisible spiral he'd drawn.

"I'm going to go upstairs and take a shower. Why don't you come and find me in half an hour?" he said.

"Okay," I breathed.

He released my hand and stood gracefully, and I watched him over the back of the couch as he walked to the stairs.

"See you soon," he said, with a smile so warm and relaxed and confident that I couldn't do anything other than return it.

I watched him walk up the stairs and disappear, and my body started thrumming with the most delicious sense of anticipation that I'd ever felt.

16

I'm about to have sex with a gorgeous Tantric-sex instructor!

Two seconds later and I was in the downstairs bathroom, tearing off my clothes and turning on the shower taps. Thankfully, I'd shaved everything that morning (yes, *everything*), and my hair was still clean, so I really could power through an express shower. By the time I'd brushed my teeth and emerged all clean and perfumed, I could hear that Kalina and Echo were still in the yoga room, giggling and shouting at each other.

I raced into my room and scrounged around in my bag, hissing triumphantly as I found the black lacy bra and undies I'd packed (for just such an optimistic occasion), then frowned as I tried to work out what else to wear. I wasted most of the next fifteen minutes trying on different things and discarding them before finally just settling on denim cut-offs and a low-cut singlet.

I know, totally irrational use of time.

And then I realised the half-hour was up.

Oh my God. Should I be feeling this nervous? I mean, I wasn't sure it was nerves as much as excitement.

I tiptoed down the hallway and over to the staircase, hoping Kalina wouldn't suddenly appear and ask me where I was going. (She'd work it out later.) And then I was climbing the stairs, feeling somewhat naughty and a bit giddy with the thrill of it.

Upstairs there was only one light on, coming from a doorway down the end of the hall. I walked towards it, taking deep breaths, and feeling only slightly shaky.

I knocked.

A moment later, Truth was pulling the door open for me.

He was wearing his loose harem pants again, but his chest was bare and gleamed golden in the lamplight. Half his dreads were tied up behind his head, while the lower half hung freely over his shoulders. His teeth and eyes both sparkled when he smiled at me.

"Come inside."

I moved past him into the room, the scent of soap and cologne washing over me from his still-damp skin. His room was large, the roof sloping down on one side and his main window being a skylight above the bed. He had beanbags and pillows scattered across the floor, along with a low mosaicked table which had a collection of ceramic bowls on it. The light in the room was coming from a few antique-looking lamps, and along the top of a set of drawers a collection of candles burned.

"So, this is your room," I said, laughing nervously.

"It is," Truth replied warmly. He closed the door and then crossed to stand beside me, his shoulder brushing against mine. I could sense him looking down at me, a smile on his face, and I forced myself to squash down all my nerves and meet his gaze.

God, he was *stunning*. The low lighting made his skin look even darker, the ridges of his cheekbones, collarbone and abs all accentuated. I inhaled sharply and bit my lip. Truth's eyes dropped down to focus on my mouth.

"I'd like to kiss you," he said. "May I?"

I nodded.

He moved so he was standing in front of me. He shifted his hands slightly and then I felt his fingertips on my arms, tracing slow, soft lines from my wrists to the insides of my elbows, making me shiver. His eyes were pinned to mine, and when I closed mine briefly his fingers stopped moving until I looked at him again. Only then did he resume the slow progression up my skin, around the back of my arms and down across my ribs.

As his hands moved further around my back his body moved closer, his eyes dipping lower until our foreheads were almost touching. And then his eyes closed and I closed mine, too, tilting my face up, and a moment later I felt the featherlight caress of his lips on mine. Softly, slowly, our mouths moved across each other, teasingly gentle and delectably warm.

His hands still traced lines down my back and I shivered. His fingers stopped moving, his palms flattened on my sides and he drew me into him. Our bodies pressed together and I felt my top pushing onto his bare skin, the fabric an unwelcome barrier.

My hands found his bare sides, and I traced my own lines slowly up his back, feeling how soft his skin was and the interplay of muscle and bone across his ribs and shoulderblades.

He growled softly as our kiss deepened and I felt like a fire was igniting inside me. His linen pants left nothing to the imagination, and I pressed my hips further into him, hearing him groan softly again.

Oh God. It was like drowning. I felt energised but weak at the same time, as if my legs were going to give out from beneath me. The kiss was so slow and sensual and unhurried, our lips slowly interchanging as bottom lips were sucked, tongues drifted slowly across each other, and heat and breath were exchanged. Our fingers moved across each other's backs so slowly, so tenderly that I felt dizzy. His hands had moved beneath the hem of my top, and his palms were hot on the small of my back, his thumbs tracing slow circles up to tickle my lower ribs.

And then I really did feel like my legs were going to give out, and I had to grab onto him to stay upright. His mouth moved away, making me gasp, and then he was looking at me with that same warm expression, his eyes shining with desire and his lips swollen and wet.

"Come," he said, stepping back and taking my hand. "It's more comfortable over here."

And then he led me to the bed.

I went to kiss him again when he turned to face me, but he held back, smiling.

"Wait," he said. "I want to undress you. May I?"

I laughed at his repeated question, feeling relaxed, and turned on and *happy* being with him. I nodded again.

He kissed me then, softly. His hands were on my hips, then on my top, and then he was lifting it, pulling upwards. I raised my arms and let him remove it, dropping them slowly down as he stood back and looked at me, his expression delighted. "You are divine," he told me, his eyes devouring everything from my waist up to my neck.

"So are you." I similarly let my eyes dance across his chest.

He stepped forwards again and my eyes found his. He raised his hands and then I felt his thumbs softly tracing outwards across my cheekbones, his fingertips dancing above my ears and down the sides of my neck. I shivered again and tipped my face up towards his, letting him capture my mouth once more. His hands continued down my back, and as our bodies pressed together he released the hooks on my bra. Without breaking the kiss, he swept his fingers across my shoulders and the straps came away; I shifted back slightly and felt my bra drop to the ground between us.

I gasped, a moan escaping between us, as my nipples pressed softly against his bare chest. I stretched my arms up around his neck, and his hands came up the sides of my ribs, his palms brushing the rounded curves of my breasts. And then he broke away again, his mouth moving to kiss my jawline, then my neck, my collarbone. He dropped to his haunches and his mouth captured my nipple, his palms on my lower back holding me to him. My breath was ragged as his hands came around to the front waistband of my shorts, and then he looked up at me with an inviting smile, his fingers paused on the button.

"Is this okay?" he asked, his voice husky.

"Yes," I said, my own voice coming out ragged.

My body felt like liquid. Within moments my shorts were undone and I wriggled my hips as he pulled them down, and then I was stepping out, letting them fall to the floor with my other discarded clothes. My lace underwear was still in place, and Truth seemed to be letting me keep it for now. He stood again, his hands coming up to my face and he kissed me softly, slowly once more.

"I want you to lie down on the bed and let me pleasure you. Are you comfortable with that?" he asked, holding my face gently in his hands and looking deeply into my eyes.

I must have looked uncertain because he smiled encouragingly at me. "I won't do anything you're not comfortable with."

I nodded again, and then we both climbed onto the bed, me lying in the centre on my back, him kneeling beside me.

For a second I felt embarrassed, and moved my arms to cover my breasts. Truth leaned over and kissed me, then pulled away only slightly so we were looking directly at each other again.

"I hope you don't feel shy," he said softly. "I'm really enjoying being here with you."

"You've still got pants on and I'm basically naked," I pointed out.

"Would you like me to take my pants off?"

"Yes," I said.

With a cheeky grin, he jumped off the bed and was out of his pants almost immediately. Beneath he was wearing basic Y-front briefs, and my eyes widened as I looked at the large bulge straining within.

"Better?" he asked me, jumping back on the bed and resuming his spot kneeling beside me.

"Definitely." I obligingly removed my hands from my chest, letting my arms fall to lie at my sides.

"If at any point you feel your mind wandering, I want you to return your focus to your breathing. Take deep, slow breaths. Just like in yoga," he added.

"Okay, teacher," I said, and took a deep breath. And then he began.

It started with light fingertips on my arm, moving in a slow, inward spiral from my wrist to my elbow. When he reached the centre he paused, fingertips pressing gently, then flattened his hand and swept his palm from my inner elbow down over my fingertips, the sensations he'd been causing on my skin dissipating.

"Is this pressure okay?" he asked quietly as his fingers moved to my upper arm and began the process all over again. An oval from my shoulder to my inner elbow was drawn, getting increasingly smaller as he spiralled in.

"Yes," I replied. He leaned down and kissed me, softly, his fingers continuing to dance across my skin, until they paused at the centre of the oval. Then he pressed his palm flat and swept the spiral away, from my shoulder out and down to the end of my hand.

He did the same thing with my other arm, and each time I found my breathing starting to catch I'd close my eyes and focus on taking deep, slow breaths. At one point I felt like I was back in some weird yoga class and had to bite my lip to stop from laughing. But then Truth was there, kissing me again, his mood so relaxed and open that what we were doing didn't seem silly at all.

When he was done with my second arm, his fingers moved to my collarbone. The spiral crept across my throat and ran down the centre of my chest and over my ribs, then up the side of my chest. As he drew slowly inwards around my breast, I felt shivers all the way down to my toes.

"Is firmer better?" he asked quietly, pressing slightly harder so that it was less ticklish and I felt the sensations deeper in my flesh.

"Yes," I managed. "That's good."

"Thank you."

His fingers kept trailing up around my breast, coming slowly inwards to the peak at the centre. He lightly grazed my nipple, then leaned down and took it in his mouth. I gasped at the sudden rush of warmth and wetness on my skin, and I found myself arching up into him, unable to lie still. He released me with a gentle lick, then cupped my breast in his whole hand, gently kneading it as the pleasure dissipated out through my body.

The circular massaging began again with my other breast, and I found myself biting my lip in anticipation. When his fingers were close to my nipple once more, I arched up towards him, and his mouth came down and found mine, kissing and distracting me.

"Keep breathing slowly," he whispered to me, then his mouth was capturing my nipple, his wet tongue and teeth grazing across it. I forced a slow, deep breath, and felt the pleasure emanating outwards up into the back of my neck and down into my groin.

Holy shit.

He released my nipple and moved down my body. Picking up a small pillow, he gently invited me to bend one leg outwards, placing the pillow beneath my knee.

"Is this comfortable?" he asked me.

"Yes," I whispered, feeling like my body was turning into butter.

He began the spiral on my inner thigh. I didn't know if it was deliberate or not, but the heel of his hand grazed across the lace of my underwear, right between my thighs, and I gasped in response. Truth didn't react, other than to keep moving his fingers down across my skin, making his oval smaller.

When he finished with one leg he moved on to the other. I was trying to maintain the deep yogic breathing, but was finding it harder to focus. Every nerve in my body was sparking with pleasure, as if there was an electric current running just below my skin. Truth's movements were igniting and focusing that pleasure on one area, then sweeping it back down to a gentle simmer when each spiral was completed.

He grazed across my underwear again as the last spiral was being completed and my hips shifted in response. His eyes glanced up and met mine and he smiled warmly again, making my breath catch. He looked so beautiful in the lamplight, the light catching on the curve of muscle in his arms. His dreads hung across his shoulders and the hint of ink across his back made him look like something out of a dream.

"Can I take these off?" he asked, his fingers on the elastic of my underwear. I nodded and lifted my hips, letting him slide the lace down over my thighs and then off to drop on the floor.

He came up beside me then, propping himself up on his elbow and leaning over to kiss me. I opened my mouth and my legs at the same time, and gasped when I felt his fingers land gently at the crease of my inner thigh. He kissed me tenderly, delicately, and his fingers began a new spiral with my thighs at the edges. And then our tongues met as his fingers slowly finished their spiral right at the centre of me and I felt like my whole body began to splinter.

I was struggling to breathe now. His fingers were so light, and delicate, remaining at the heart of the last spiral and stroking across different areas like a painter outlining a masterpiece. He kissed my mouth and my neck, then drew back slightly to meet my eyes, his shining with warmth and pleasure.

"I want you to tell me what you want," he said. "Do you like it here?"

"Yes. There! Oh God, there." I was starting to squirm and writhe beneath him, feeling the pressure building to a peak. And just when I thought I couldn't bear it anymore, his fingers stopped moving, his palm stilling and cupping me gently.

"Deep breath in," he whispered in my ear. "Now breathe out slowly."

I did as he said, closing my eyes and letting out a shaky exhale of breath. The pleasure moved out from the core of me down into my toes and up through my fingertips to the top of my head, every single nerve in my body thrumming with heat.

I swallowed and opened my eyes, the wave receding. Truth was watching me, and as his lips drew upwards in a sensuous smile, his fingers began their dance again.

Three times he played this game, bringing me right to the peak so I was writhing and panting beneath him. Then he'd halt just before I went over, making me breathe and relax and let the pleasure spread out through my body.

The fourth time, he didn't stop.

"Keep breathing deeply," he said to me, his fingers dancing. "Relax your body and think only of what you're feeling right now."

I tried to do as he said. I made myself relax and felt the pleasure in my core almost immediately amplify. I whimpered, my muscles begging to clench up again, but I made myself lie still, breathing deeply through the pleasure that was intensifying so profoundly beneath his fingers. He traced circles that dipped almost inside me, the heel of his hand pressing higher where my nerves ached. He kissed me again as the pleasure crested, and I gasped, opening my eyes and looking at him, panting, as I realised this time he wasn't going to stop.

"Oh my God," I cried out, my hands gripping the sheets as he captured my mouth with his.

His fingers didn't stop as I shattered beneath him. His mouth pressed to my jaw and I breathed in the most magical, intensifying breath deep into my belly, feeling wave after wave of pleasure wash over me.

And it went on. Holy shit, but it went on and on, each breath I took in and out spreading through every bone and every muscle in my body, the waves rippling out from where his fingers kept up their movements.

And then it receded, and I was panting, and his hand was no longer between my legs but holding me against his body. He kissed me softly and

I could feel the smile on his mouth and the stiff heat of his erection pressed against my thigh as he cradled me against him.

"Oh my God," I repeated, turning so I could look at him. His eyes were dark with both arousal and satisfaction, and he kissed me gently on the lips.

"You are so beautiful," he said, dropping a kiss on my shoulder. "I love touching you like that."

"*You* are beautiful," I told him, shifting so I was facing him properly. I lifted my hand to run my fingertips across his cheekbone and down over his shoulder. "Now tell me what I can do for you."

Truth kissed me slowly. "I'm the teacher tonight," he said. "And I haven't finished with *you* yet."

With another kiss, his fingers started to dance again.

17

I couldn't believe how amazing sex could feel.

I mean, I'd had good sex before. Obviously. At least, I'd had sex that I thought was good at the time. I guess I'd always figured that if you had an orgasm then it must have been good, right?

But holy fucking cow. Last night with Truth was on another level. It was on another *plane*.

I had five orgasms, for one thing. *Five*. I'd never managed more than one. I'd never *attempted* more than one. I'd always thought that girls who said they could have multiple orgasms were just, you know, lying. But Truth was the most extraordinary lover. He kept doing this thing where he'd hold back and wait for me, and then start again just as the pleasure was receding, making it build up again. He could hold off on finishing for such a long time, where he'd stop and just breathe with this really deep concentration. And then when he did finally let himself release, his whole body shook in what seemed to be the most powerfully intense way that I was immediately turned on even more just seeing how much pleasure he was experiencing.

Also, Truth came *three* times. I didn't even know that was possible. I always assumed that after a guy had finished it was all over red rover for the night and he'd need to wait hours before any kind of stiffening was likely to recur. But Truth was ready to go again mere *minutes* later. So there you go. I learned something new about the male anatomy.

I woke in Truth's bed, feeling the dawn light filtering softly through my closed eyelids.

For a few long breaths I lay there, basking in the warm, liquid afterglow from last night. I'd probably only had about three hours' sleep, but I wasn't anywhere near exhausted.

Opening my eyes, I turned over and saw Truth asleep beside me, his dreadlocks splayed out on the pillow around him. His breathing was soft and even, and the sheet was drawn only up to his belly button, leaving his torso exposed.

Oh, he was beautiful. I felt such an urge to run my hand over his chest, to trace the lines of the tattoo there and feel the softness of his skin. To wake him up and demand a repeat of last night.

But then, I also thought maybe I should sneak back downstairs and return to my own bed before Kalina woke up. Just because ... well, I wasn't really sure what *this* was, and didn't particularly want to get twenty questions from her about it.

Also, I *really* needed to pee.

Quietly, I removed myself from the bed and slipped my clothes on. Truth was still asleep as I closed the door softly behind me and walked as quietly as I could along the hallway and down the stairs. All was quiet in the kitchen, and after a quick trip to the bathroom I found myself outside my own bedroom. The door was shut, and I carefully eased it open, trying hard not to wake Kalina.

Except, as I stepped into the room, I discovered that Kalina's bed was also empty.

I frowned. She hadn't been in the kitchen or lounge room I'd just passed. Could she be in the yoga room? Somehow I couldn't imagine that, but then ...

I turned to go and check and came face to face with her creeping down the hallway.

She jumped when she saw me, a hugely guilty look on her face, and we both froze for a moment and stared at each other.

She was wearing the same clothes she'd been in last night. And her hair was all dishevelled. And she had black panda-eye smudges beneath her eyes.

"Oh my God!" I squealed, my face splitting into a grin. "You slept with Echo!"

"Shh!" With a laugh, Kalina pushed me into our room and closed the door quickly, then gave me a mock-stern look. "Let's not worry about me, what about *you*! You haven't been in here all night either! So tell me, how was old Truthy in the sack, then?"

I laughed. "Honestly, Kal, you wouldn't even believe it."

"Did he get all Tantra on you? Was there rhythmic stroking and weird trance stuff?"

"No! Actually, sort of." I laughed again. "But seriously, spending the night with him was … I can't even describe it. My eyes have been opened, let's say that."

Kalina looked delighted. "Well, I'm glad. I've been a bit worried about you lately, not sleeping with anyone. You can't go too long between guys, you know."

I rolled my eyes at her. "Come on, your turn. I thought you couldn't stand Echo?"

"I can't! He's such a … he's so … he's just *irritating*. Super irritating. He really gets under my skin."

"And into your pants?"

Kalina threw her pillow at me. "Whatever that was last night, it will *not* be repeated. Lapse in judgement aside, I can now go back to just finding him plain annoying. And not spending any more time with him than necessary."

"Uh-uh."

"Oh, shut up. Let's get back to business. Since we're both up early enough, we can go hunt around for Ben and Amy at the cafes. I've got a good feeling about today."

"Ooh, can we also stop at that treehouse-looking place for breakfast?" I asked excitedly. "I mean, since we need to eat and all. Plus, that place was cheap. And looked cool."

"Okay … But only *after* we've done a lap around the other cafes." Kalina slid off her bed and started grabbing clothes out of her bag. "I'm going to have a quick shower."

"Hurry up, then. I'm starving!"

And I was. All that sexercise and all.

We had the most delicious, massive breakfast at the treehouse cafe next to the backpackers' hostel in town. Kalina had evidently also had a rather active night, since we both devoured bacon-and-egg rolls and two huge coffees each. Then we began our tour of the town, systematically checking every cafe and juice bar for a hint of Ben or Amy.

We were just crossing the road near the beachfront pub when we noticed a large crowd of young, trendy-looking people gathered on the grass above the beach. With a glance at each other, Kalina and I made our way over there to see what was going on, squinting our eyes against the morning sunlight reflecting off the ocean.

Spaced uniformly across the grass was an assembly of yoga mats. On top of each one was a person who looked like they were auditioning for a reality TV show. Every single guy and girl was absolutely gorgeous, and all were decked out in the trendiest activewear imaginable.

"Who seriously does morning yoga on the beachfront?" Kalina muttered, sounding disgusted. "Are they even getting a workout, or is it just a bloody fashion show?"

"Yeah ... weird," I agreed. Though, actually, I thought it looked kinda cool.

Suddenly, a girl wearing trendy silver-grey-printed leggings and a relaxed white tank with a familiar logo on it was in front of us, smiling broadly, and holding out a flyer.

"Free guest passes for Yogatainable?" she offered us.

"Ah, thanks," I said, taking them. I mean, you could never have too many guest passes, right?

"What is this?" Kalina asked, nodding at the group of yogis all doing phenomenal bow poses.

"Oh, it's a class we're running with some of our VIP clients," the girl replied. "It's part of the promotion we're running to draw attention to Yogatainable's Luxe Link grand opening."

"What is that?"

"You haven't heard? Luxe Link offers the most phenomenal health retreats in the whole of the southern hemisphere. It's stage two of Yogatainable. The official opening is this weekend, but it's already the most sought-after wellness retreat. We've got a huge wait list of celebrities."

"Can anyone join in with this class?" I asked, my eyes still drawn to all the beautiful people holding warrior two.

The girl laughed. "Oh no, this is just for our influencers this morning. If you look closely over there, you might recognise Phoenix Fox? Or Healing Ashleigh? What Jane Ate and Silver Belle are here, too."

I raised my eyebrows, glancing at Kalina. I was pretty sure by her unimpressed expression that she'd also never heard of any of these "influencers".

Turning back, I looked more closely at the group of yoga people again, and realised that there was a crew of people with video cameras or phones out all recording the session. In fact, each person on a yoga mat seemed to have their own personal assistant standing nearby snapping pictures of them. I suppose it was going to be a social media storm, at least for anyone who followed people like Phoenix Fox.

The promo girl moved away from us to hand out free passes to some other people who'd also paused to watch, and I looked at Kalina sceptically. "You reckon this Luxe Link thing has anything to do with that shambles of a construction site we saw?"

Kalina was frowning at the guest pass, a look of concentration on her face.

"Kal?" I prompted.

"This Yogatainable place really is a bit of a force up here in Byron Bay, isn't it?"

"I guess so."

"Amy would be completely drawn to it."

"Probably," I agreed.

"So she *must* have been there. And will probably go back. She's never able to stay away from excitement for long."

"What are you saying? That we should just go and hang out at Yogatainable all day and watch out for her?"

"Maybe we don't have to. Truth said that Meadow is one of the owners, didn't he? So, she'd have access to all the records on file. If we can get her onside, then maybe she can log into their system and take a look."

"But even if Amy's been there, how's that going to help?"

"We had to write down our phone number, and an emergency contact person, remember? So, chances are we could get the number for Amy's mum or dad."

"Okay ... but what are we meant to do with that?"

"We can call them up. Just play dumb and act like one of Amy's friends. I'll bet they know where she's staying—there's no way she would have cut herself off from everyone like Ben has."

I opened my mouth to object, on the grounds of how insane that sounded, but then I closed it again. In the very slim chance that we could get that information, it was better than anything else we had.

"Alright. But if we *do* get her mum's number, you're the one calling her."

"Deal."

⁓∾

By lunchtime, we'd had no luck running into Ben or Amy anywhere in Byron Bay town. We decided to meet up back at the house and regroup; Kalina went off to the supermarket to get some groceries, while I headed out to buy us some takeaway burritos for lunch.

Pushing my way into the house while juggling the food, I found Meadow in the lounge room, sitting on the floor and using the coffee table as a makeshift desk. She was dressed impeccably in another Lululemon ensemble, looking more like she was about to do a backbend than computer work, and my mate Smoosh-face was purring in her lap.

"Hi, Meadow!" I said brightly. I suddenly realised this might be a good opportunity to see if she'd help us by searching Yogatainable's records, so I made my way over and sat down on one of the lounges near her, putting on my friendliest smile. "How's your day going?"

She looked up at me, and her brows were creased in a frown. But then she reached forward, snapped her laptop shut, and smiled at me, her expression instantly clearing.

"Getting there!" she said. "Lots to do at the moment, but it's all good fun. How's your holiday going?"

"It's good! It's, well … to be honest, we're not really up here on a holiday."

Meadow looked surprised.

"We're trying to find our friend," I elaborated. "Our flatmate, actually. We think he's in trouble."

Meadow looked even more surprised. "What sort of trouble?"

"Well, he disappeared up here with his new girlfriend, and we're all really worried about him. He's in a bit of a vulnerable state, and we think this girl is taking advantage of him."

Meadow stared at me wide-eyed, looking shocked, and I found myself babbling on.

"See, his great-aunt recently died and we don't think he's really processed it, and he's really trusting and generous, and well, he's just not very good at standing up for himself." I took a breath and looked at Meadow. "So, anyway, we're starting to get a bit desperate about finding him before it's too late."

"That's why you guys came here?" Meadow asked, her eyebrows raised. "To Byron Bay?"

"Yeah. We thought we'd come and rescue him." I couldn't help an ironic laugh. "But it turns out just *finding* him is the impossible step."

"Gosh. What are you going to do, then? Are you going to give up?"

I sighed. "We don't want to give up. But we feel like we're stuck. We're starting to run low on ideas about how to find them."

"That sounds like a nightmare. Is there anything I can do to help?"

Yes! Success!

"Oh ... well, now that you mention it, we did have one idea."

"What is it?"

"Well, we're pretty sure that this Amy girl will be drawn to Yogatainable. It's likely she's been there already. So, we were wondering if there's any way you could look up client contact details on your system? Because if she has visited, then she might have listed the hotel they're staying at or at least put a phone number down for herself. Or maybe even listed her next of kin and their contact details?"

Meadow looked at me warily for a second, but then she leaned forwards and snapped her laptop open.

"What's her name? I'll see what I can do."

"Amy Richards," I said quickly. "Or Ben Hartcoat, though I'm not sure he would have been there." I held my breath while she started typing on her laptop.

"This stuff is meant to be pretty confidential, so you'll have to promise me you won't let anyone know where the info came from."

"Absolutely! We really just want to find our friend. We won't do anything dodgy with the info, I promise."

I wanted to move around to sit behind her so I could also see the screen, but while I'd been talking the grey tabby cat had sprung up onto my lap, turned in a few circles, then settled down in a ball. If Meadow's laptop wasn't angled away from me I might have been able to see it, anyway, but from my current vantage point I just had to wait.

"Hmm," she said, frowning at the screen. "I can't see anything here. How do you spell Amy's name?"

I spelled it out—at least, what I thought it was—but after Meadow typed it in, she shook her head and looked up at me apologetically. "Definitely not in here. Looks like she hasn't visited."

"Oh. Bugger." I felt myself deflating instantly. I was so *sure* that Amy wouldn't have been able to resist somewhere like Yogatainable. That was, if she was actually in Byron Bay. Once again, tendrils of doubt started snaking through my stomach.

Meadow was still watching me. "What other ideas have you guys got to find them?"

I frowned while I cautiously patted the cat on my lap. "Honestly? Nothing really. We just keep staking out the town and the beach in the hopes of spotting them."

"Any particular areas?"

I shook my head. "We've pretty much been canvassing the whole town."

Meadow raised her eyebrows. "And no sign of them? What makes you so sure they're here?"

"We saw a couple of photos they posted from Byron cafes. So, we know that they *were* here very recently."

Meadow's look turned pitying. "Well, I suppose you can only keep trying. Although, how long do you think you'll keep looking if you can't find them? Don't you have jobs you need to get back to?"

"Soon, yes. Ben does too, which is partly why we're worried."

Meadow shrugged. "Maybe you're not giving him enough credit. I mean, if he wants to return for his job then he probably will. It's up to everyone to make their own path, really."

"I guess so."

Just then, the front door opened and Kalina came in carrying a few armloads of groceries and groaning with overdone fatigue.

"Hey," she panted, coming into the kitchen. "Oh, hi, Meadow!"

Her eyes darted to me, questioning, and I gave a small shake of my head.

"Well, I'll let you get on with your work," I said to Meadow, carefully pushing the tabby off me. He didn't go without a fight, and left me with some new thigh scratches.

Meadow stood up as well, closing her laptop and picking it up. "I've got to head out, actually. I might see you guys later," she said.

Kalina looked at me again, more urgently, but I shook my head decisively.

"See you then," I called as she gathered her things and left the house.

"Well?" Kalina asked.

"She looked them up in the Yogatainable system. Nothing."

"Fuck!"

18

Kalina and I were finishing off our burritos, sitting at the kitchen counter, when we heard footsteps on the stairs. I glanced at her, frowning, but she just pulled a face, which I think meant she also had no idea someone else was in the house.

"Good afternoon," came Truth's deep, mellow voice as he appeared at the bottom of the stairs. He had his linen pants back on and a loose, faded t-shirt, and I couldn't help the shy smile breaking across my face at the sight of him.

"Hey," I managed, after swallowing my food.

"You're looking chirpy," Kalina said. "Had a good night last night, did you?"

I kicked her foot under the bench, but she still snickered.

"I did," Truth said, his warm eyes turning on me.

"So, um, you don't have work today?" I asked him, trying to prevent this line of conversation going any further.

"No. Day off," he said, his eyes catching mine. "What have you girls been up to?"

"Oh, just checking through town again," I said. "Still no luck finding Ben, though."

"He's *got* to be here somewhere," Kalina said. "There aren't that many places they could be going in Byron Bay, surely! I really don't understand why we can't find them."

"Maybe they're just holed up somewhere in bed all day?" I suggested.

"For this long? No way. No one can spend that long having sex."

My eyes flicked to Truth and his answering smile made me blush. Before last night, I wouldn't have thought that was possible either. But now ... I could definitely imagine spending all day in bed.

Kalina made a kind of scoffing sound, her eyes glancing between us, then excused herself to go to the bathroom.

"I missed you this morning," Truth said, turning his attention back to me with another smile. God, I was *really* loving that smile. "I had a wonderful time last night."

"So did I," I said, smiling shyly back at him. "But I'm sure you realise that."

"I had an inkling." His eyes sparkled. "But it's nice to hear you say it."

I watched as he moved about the kitchen, turning on the kettle and putting together a tea infuser with a herbal loose-leaf blend.

"So, what are you up to today?" I asked him.

"Nothing." He yawned and stretched up his arms, his muscles rippling over his ribcage. I caught a glimpse of the tattoo on his back again, underneath his t-shirt, and realised I hadn't had a chance to examine it more closely last night.

"I was surprised to find you gone so early this morning," Truth continued. "I was going to invite you somewhere with me."

"You were? I mean, sorry, I didn't want to wake you up. What were you going to invite me to?"

"Have you been to the Crystal Castle before?" Truth asked.

I frowned. "I don't think so. Is that a shop in town? I don't remember ..."

Truth smiled. "It's not a shop. The Crystal Castle is a place, about half an hour from here. It's quite an experience."

"Right. It sounds ... interesting."

The Crystal *Castle*? All I could imagine was a bunch of hippies sitting around in some weird decked-out living room smoking weed.

"We could go there this afternoon," Truth suggested, jolting me out of my imaginings. "That is, if you don't have anything else on."

"Really? You want to go there with me?"

Truth smiled. "I do."

For a second, I didn't know what to say. He wanted to spend the afternoon with me? My chest felt all warm, and my mouth was drawing up in a smile again.

"What is it exactly?"

Before he could respond, we heard the sound of the front door opening again and then Echo came fumbling inside, a surfboard under his arm, and his clothes and hair damp.

"Hey, mates," he drawled, standing his board up near the door then coming into the kitchen with a happy grin. "Great surf this morning."

Kalina chose that moment to reappear as well, though she kind of froze a bit when she saw Echo, and then made it quite obvious that she was looking anywhere but at him.

"I was just saying to Laura," Truth continued speaking easily, as if the kitchen hadn't suddenly become an extremely awkward place. "That I think she'd enjoy visiting the Crystal Castle with me. Is anyone else interested in joining us?"

Echo barked a laugh. "That place! Once was enough for me, mate."

"Unless Ben is likely to be there, I don't see the point," Kalina said, looking at me and Truth but definitely not Echo.

"I'd like to go," I heard myself saying, my eyes finding Truth's. But then I quickly looked back towards Kalina. "That is, if you don't mind? I mean, Ben *could* be there. Plus, we were just going to do the beach again this afternoon, right?"

"Right," Kalina said, shooting looks between us. "Well, I guess we can cover more ground if we split up, anyway. I'll stay here and keep looking ... around here again, I guess."

"I can show you around the beach, darlin'," Echo drawled, grinning at her over the top of his mug.

Kalina rolled her eyes, then shot Echo an exasperated look. "Well, I suppose I can't stop you following me, if that's what you want to do."

☙

Truth and I drove to the Crystal Castle in my car, since Truth didn't have one. "It's bad for the environment," he'd said, pointing out the slightly rusted pushbike he used for getting around town.

I didn't mind driving, though. My car was rather old, but it had got me and Kalina up to Byron Bay perfectly well, and had never let me down before. It was the kind of car that just kept on going year after year. Besides, Echo was spending the day with Kalina, and he had a massive dual-cab ute if they desperately needed to drive somewhere, even if Kalina was a bit horrified by it.

I was following the GPS on my phone, driving out through similar burnt-brown farms as when Kalina and I had gone to Yogatainable. We were taking a different route, but it seemed the Crystal Castle was in a similar location in the Byron hinterland.

Truth had put on some music that was ... well, not *quite* my taste, let's just say that. It was that kind of echoey, raw vocals and acoustic guitar stuff that, if anything, tended to make me feel a bit depressed when I heard it. But Truth seemed happy and serene, so I thought maybe I should give the music a go.

I mean, it's not like it was a particularly long drive.

We turned off the road and I drove us up a steep driveway and into a carpark that was surrounded by trees and fences. I couldn't see anything resembling a castle; it looked, from there, more like we'd arrived at a wildlife park or botanic gardens.

"I love this place," Truth said as we got out of the car. "I think you will too. Just remember to keep an open mind."

With that slightly alarming caveat, we made our way to the ticketing booth and paid our entry fees. (Actually, I paid an entry fee; Truth had an annual pass). I was handed a guidebook and then we stepped in through the gate and I found myself staring at a small, yellow sculpture in the middle of the pathway that looked like a children's sandcastle with little staircases and about five cone-shaped spires sticking up.

"Is that it?" I couldn't help asking.

Truth laughed. "That's not the castle. The castle and the gardens are the whole place. Keep walking, you'll see."

As we made our way further in, I realised it *was* like walking into a botanic garden. Huge trees soared overhead, shading the pathway and a multitude of flowers down below. There was a wide pond all covered in lily pads, with flashes of orange koi swimming within.

I started flipping through the guidebook I'd been given, and was a bit blown away by all the things here.

"There's a dragon egg! And an enchanted crystal cave!" I said, my eyes widening at the pictures. "Can we go see them?"

"Of course," Truth laughed. "There are lots of things here."

The dragon egg was just around the next bend, and I was kind of blown away by the thing. Not a real dragon egg, obviously, but a huge egg-shaped volcanic rock formation that was filled with what looked like millions of deep purple amethyst crystals. One side was open, and there was a little mat placed within so you could actually *sit* inside the thing.

Well, of course I sat in it. And it was pretty fantastic.

After the dragon egg we kept walking around, and there were crystal formations everywhere, each blowing away the last one. It felt like every step took us past crystals or rare stones, each placed carefully around the place to blend in with the plants. At one point, we were standing in a courtyard, and the entire floor was paved with a mosaic of rose quartz.

One thing I felt I could say with certainty: there really was no other place around like it.

19

Alright, so I might have fallen a little in love with the Crystal Castle. The gardens were the most beautifully sculpted botanic gardens I'd ever been to—all winding pathways, and beautiful trees and plants and flowers, and then all these fountains and statues of Hindu gods everywhere. Not to mention the ginormous amethyst crystal formations that were everywhere. Named "geodes", they were great towering canoe-shaped things that were lined entirely with the gorgeous purple amethysts, set around the place like gateways. One of the sets was so enormous that I imagined if one was lying flat rather than standing upright, then Truth and I could lie down in it, head to head. Except that the amethyst bits looked pretty spiky.

Down in the gardens, walking along those serene pathways, I felt like my soul was expanding. And beside me, Truth walked along. His dreadlocks swayed across his back as he moved, and each of his steps was careful and light, as if he was walking on water. As we moved through the gardens, he pointed out certain things and gave explanations that were deeper and more moving than what was written in the guidebook. I found myself wanting to emulate the joy he seemed to discover in all things natural. And more and more, I was finding my gaze drawn to him, feeling that experiencing the beauty here through his eyes was somehow more rewarding than simply looking at it myself.

I desired to be like him.

Or maybe it was that I still really desired *him.*

"This is such a strange but amazing place," I said to Truth as we passed a beautiful sculpture of the Hindu goddess Lakshmi. "Thank you for bringing me here."

"Well, you brought me, really." Truth laughed softly. "But I'm glad you wanted to come. I got the feeling from you—and I hope this doesn't sound presumptuous—but when you asked to learn about Tantra, I think you really wanted to learn more about love. About how to experience love fully in both the physical and emotional sense."

"Hey!" I laughed. "I do know about love. I mean, I've *been* in love before."

"Will you tell me about it?"

I looked at him cautiously, feeling thrown. I barely knew him, but then, maybe that was a good thing? For some reason, I felt completely safe and comfortable around him, and that I really could tell him anything. As though he really was a master of love, and I his unintentional student.

We'd stopped right in front of a bench among the flowers that cast a sweeping view out over the countryside beyond the gardens. "Alright," I said, sitting on the bench. "But I don't want you to look at me while I'm talking."

Truth nodded his head solemnly then sat beside me, drawing his feet up to sit cross-legged. He did as I asked of him, keeping his eyes serenely on the horizon, all calm and zen-like, his hands resting quietly in his lap. I cleared my throat, thought for a moment, and then started speaking quietly.

"I still remember falling in love with Jack. We went to the same school, though we were never in the same classes. But I'd see him around all the time and it was almost like I could just *sense* when he was in the same room as me. I was too shy to talk to him, so I just spent years being sort of *aware* of him. It was only when we were in Year Ten that some of our friends started hanging out together. I remember we all went to the movies in a big group and somehow it worked out that Jack and I sat next to each other.

We spent the whole movie whispering and talking to each other—we pissed off everyone in the movie theatre, I'm sure. But I didn't care. He asked me out after that, and we became one of the most stable couples at school. He became one of my best friends, and we just seemed to click and connect so well that I thought we were soul mates. I never for a second imagined that we weren't right for each other. Which is so silly, because when I look back now I can see how different we were. But at the time, I couldn't see any of that. I just started planning my life around his. I remember, at one point when we were talking about our futures after school, he started looking into universities in Melbourne, and talking about possibly moving there. I just thought, great, I'll go study in Melbourne, too, and we can live together. And I probably would have done. I'd have made my life fit around his." I laughed softly, shaking my head at the memory before I continued.

"Neither of us went though. We stayed in Sydney, and stayed together all through uni. There were fights, of course, and lots of up and down times, but I just assumed that was normal. Every couple fights. I thought we were bonded for life. That he felt the same way about me as I did about him. It never occurred to me that he might have doubts. That he was looking at me and wondering if it was right. Because I'd chosen him. And I believed that he'd chosen me."

I realised I had tears pooling in the corners of my eyes, but I didn't bother wiping them away. We were silent for a while, the musical calls of birds and the breeze on my skin interplaying around me. Truth remained silent, his presence calm and patient. I wiped away my tears and kept speaking.

"I still wonder if I pressured him into getting married. I kept dropping all these massive hints about how we'd been together for such a long time. And both our parents were the same, also dropping hints about it. Maybe he still wasn't sure about himself, even then. If he knew what he was and he married me, anyway ... I think that would be the worst. As it was, he waited until I said I wanted to try for a baby before he announced he was gay. So, that was it." I turned to Truth, taking a deep breath and putting on a shaky smile. "Eleven years together. I thought he was my soul mate, but instead he crushed my heart."

Truth looked at me and there was such kindness in his eyes. He held out his hand, palm up, and I put mine in his. He gave it a gentle squeeze.

"Broken hearts can leave some of the worst scars," he said, still holding my hand. "Thank you for sharing your story with me."

I laughed softly. "Thank you for listening."

And I meant it. Even though my chest hurt from the memories, having said them out loud, in this place, was like releasing the pain out into the atmosphere.

"Have you noticed how much rose quartz there is here?" Truth asked. "Like these stones beside us?"

I looked down and realised sitting on either side of our bench were boulder-sized pink crystals, standing sentry among the plants.

"All crystals and stones have mystic lore associated with them," continued Truth. "Pink quartz is the crystal associated with love and relationships. For centuries, it's been used to heal wounded hearts and help expand our love and compassion."

I gave his hand a squeeze. "Is that why you really wanted to bring me here? You could sense a damaged heart within."

Truth smiled at my joke. "I think everybody deserves to love and be loved to the fullness of their being. And I enjoy helping others to understand that and embrace all that they can."

"And you enjoy the physical aspects of love as well, I'm sure," I teased him, giving his hand a final squeeze before letting it go. I didn't know why, but I felt the need to lighten the mood now.

Truth laughed. "You know, I can't understand when people are so closed off to learning about sex and how to do it better. You'd think more men would want to learn how to be better lovers. But so many think that if they acknowledge they want to learn then they're admitting that they're bad in bed. Yet everyone has this ridiculous assumption that men will just somehow be able to naturally intuit how to be amazing lovers."

"You're right," I said, thinking about it. "I guess that's why we have this notion that the more *experienced* someone is in bed, the better they'll be. As if you have to sleep with lots of different people in order to learn."

"Which is pretty funny, because if everyone you sleep with is bad, then you're not learning much, are you?"

I laughed again, thinking about my fairly dismal track record to date. Before Truth, I could definitely say that none of my lovers had been particularly good, nor that I'd learned a whole lot from any of them. Although, I'd definitely got some pointers on what *not* to do.

"One of the purposes of Tantra is to teach us how to open up emotionally, to share a connection with someone on a deeper level," Truth went on. "The more you know someone, and the deeper the connection, then the better your physical lovemaking will be as well. Love becomes about joining two people together both physically and emotionally, rather than only focusing on one element."

I looked at Truth carefully. He was glancing up towards the sky, his expression relaxed but happy. I frowned.

"Do you want that with someone? The emotional connection as well? I mean, I love that you're teaching me this stuff and that you're free to do so … but have you never met the right person for yourself?"

He looked back at me slowly, his expression dimming somewhat. "I'm very happy being a teacher and a guide for others right now. I do have my own emotional journey that I'm … still working through. And I find I can do that better by being alone."

I was going to ask him more, but he jumped to his feet and held his hand out to me again. "Come," he said, his expression clearing with a grin.

"There's still more to see. And I have a challenge for you."

I took his hand and let him hoist me to my feet.

Later, I thought. I'd ask him more about it later.

"Here. The labyrinth."

I frowned as I looked at the small clearing Truth was indicating, having almost missed it. It was tucked away in the bushes near the main "castle" (which was a huge, sprawling, single-level building), and to be honest didn't look like much at all.

"Labyrinths have been used as a focus for walking meditation for centuries," Truth continued, looking in at the clearing with adoration. "Have you ever tried meditating before?"

"Er, no." Well, if we didn't count the fake meditating I did in order to spy on a certain hot volleyball player in Manly that one time.

"Pose a question in your mind before you start. And then walk the pathway slowly, letting the universe send you guidance."

"Are you doing it, too?" I frowned at him, but he shook his head.

"I've done this before. Come and find me inside when you're done."

"Really? What am I meant to ask the universe?"

Truth smiled at me. "You'll think of something."

He walked away, and I turned to face the labyrinth, feeling a bit silly. It was a flat, circular area made up simply of the one narrow winding pathway that switched back and coiled its way through four quadrants towards a small, open centre. The edges of the pathway were created by strips of grass and crystals embedded in the ground, so despite the fact that you could just walk right over the top to get to the centre, that wasn't the point. You had to follow the single track to get there.

I stepped up to the entrance and paused. Hmm. Question for the universe. What could I ask?

To be honest, my mind was whirling with so many thoughts that I found it difficult to focus on any of them. So, after a moment I just stepped onto the pathway and began my journey through.

If I'd been expecting some kind of spiritual connection with the universe while I walked the labyrinth, I would have been disappointed. At first I didn't feel anything. It was just me, walking along a narrow, winding pathway, trying to go slowly, but mentally checking out the rest of the pathway and trying to calculate how long this would take.

I mean, I liked the *idea* of meditating, don't get me wrong. But I always found that as soon as I tried to not think about anything, I would start to think about lots of things, and it just didn't really work. Like right then, when I was supposed to be thinking about some question for the universe, meant to be seeking guidance, I was thinking about how much I wasn't doing that, instead. I mean, what could the universe guide me on, anyway? Love? Presumably, that's what Truth thought I needed guidance on.

My eyes focused on the crystals embedded in the ground, and I realised most of it was rose quartz again. And there were large rose-quartz boulders placed around the labyrinth, among the bushes. I smiled, seeing all the stones of love everywhere.

I knew how to love. I did. There were many people I loved right now— my family, obviously, but my friends, too. I loved Kalina and Ben and Rose. And I loved myself, didn't I? Or … did I?

I turned another corner, the path switching back again and leading me away from the centre of the labyrinth.

I *did* love myself, I thought. I did. Really. Even though sometimes I felt a bit panicky.

But I supposed, well, *why* did I feel panicky? Why, as recently as a week ago, had I been waking up in the night in a cold sweat? And why had that not happened up here in Byron Bay? Was there something I was frightened of in Sydney?

With each step I took, moving forwards on that path, pieces of an idea kept slipping in and out of my mind, something I'd been trying for a while now not to confront. But then it was right there, in front of me, and I couldn't ignore it anymore.

I was scared of moving forwards, of embracing something that might be permanent. I was afraid I'd make a life-altering choice and I'd get it wrong, like I did with Jack.

I was so afraid of making a mistake that I was holding myself back from life.

I arrived at the centre of the labyrinth feeling like I could now see the weight I was wearing around my shoulders. And I couldn't help a rueful smile and a small chuckle at myself. Without consciously doing so, I'd managed to complete a walking meditation. I'd guided myself and my thoughts into something resembling insight.

The walk out of the labyrinth again, along the same path, seemed so much faster than the way in. And when I emerged again, among the bushes, I exchanged a smile and a knowing nod with a middle-aged woman who was just about to start. I hoped she found answers in there, too.

There was no sign of Truth, but then he'd said he'd be inside the building when I was done. I picked my way over, passing by a gorgeous fountain with a huge sphere of rose quartz rotating slowly on a slab of wet granite.

Inside, I found myself standing in a gift shop.

There were crystals everywhere, all sorts of things, from jewellery, to ornaments and loose stones. I found a rack of necklaces that had gorgeous single stones suspended in a silver pendant, in every kind of crystal imaginable.

My fingers strayed to the rose-quartz ones and I carefully lifted down a pendant. Beneath the label on the wall were listed the various properties for each stone, along with a simple mantra. The one for my pink quartz said, "*I feel loved and loving."*

I smiled as I took my new necklace to the counter, deciding that I was taking a piece of this beautiful place home in my heart.

20

"He made me walk up to the bloody lighthouse, Laura! *It's easy*, he said. *It's not far*, he said. Well, it was really bloody far!"

"It's not my fault you're so unfit, love. Though the amount of whingeing you did all the way—*my legs hurt, my feet hurt, my back hurts*. I might as well have taken a bloody toddler."

"I'm not unfit! That took *hours*, it was a fucking marathon!"

"Children were overtaking you."

"They have small legs! And they're closer to the ground, so they have less gravity to deal with."

"How 'bout that group of old men that overtook you?"

"They had walking poles!"

My eyes were flicking back and forth between Kalina and Echo like I was at a tennis match. They were sitting on opposite couches to each other, each with a cat on their lap, and despite the fact that they were theoretically talking to me, I was pretty sure neither would notice if I suddenly stood up and moonwalked right out the door.

"Anyway," Kalina said, finally shifting her gaze back to me. "That was my day. Zero sightings of Ben and Amy. They were *not* doing the lighthouse walk, as Echo so heavily suggested they might be when he convinced me to do it."

"They weren't at the Crystal Castle either," I replied, yawning and running my fingers through my damp hair.

"How'd you like that place?" Echo asked.

"I loved it! It was just … amazing. I've never been anywhere like it before."

"Oh yeah." Echo scratched his beard, looking sceptical. "I went there a while back. Was a bit out there for me."

I smiled. "You've got to be open to the experience. Let the healing energies of the place get inside you."

Kalina frowned at me. "Is that what you did?"

"It was." I sighed happily and let my hand stray to my new necklace. "I really think I've found some new clarity. I understand things so much more now."

Kalina looked at me as if I'd just said I'd developed a fungus under my toenail, but I ignored her.

I heard footsteps on the stairs, and knew straightaway whom they belonged to, since Meadow was away for work tonight. I watched as Truth walked into the lounge room, wearing nothing but his linen pants again, his dreads damp and his clean skin burnished golden in the dim light.

His eyes met mine instantly, and after returning my smile, he kept walking into the kitchen and fetched a glass of water.

I was so intent on watching Truth, that I barely even registered Echo's voice behind me.

"Maybe you can put your newfound clarity to use locating your flatmate, since your friend here doesn't have a hope."

"You're the one that provided zero input today!" Kalina countered fiercely. "Honestly, you would make the most rubbish detective. Don't ever quit your day job to become a spy or anything. Oh wait, you don't even *have* a day job. You just spend all day surfing and reading and shampooing your beard."

"This takes a lot of care to maintain. And I don't shampoo it, I use beard oil."

I stood up from the couch and walked over to join Truth in the kitchen.

"Hey," I said to him, moving past to get myself some water.

"Hey," he replied. He was leaning against the kitchen bench, water glass in hand, and he smiled at me warmly again.

"So, um, have you got any plans for tonight?" I asked, filling up my glass and then leaning on the opposite bench, facing him.

"I was just thinking of hanging around the house here. How about you?"

My stomach leapt up into my throat, but I tried to ignore it. "Oh, same. Just hanging around here." I hid my smile behind my water glass as I took a sip.

"Laura!" Kalina suddenly shouted at me. "Let's go get some dinner!"

My smile disappeared. "Oh, I've already eaten!" I called back, which was half true. I did have a piece of toast when I got back from the Crystal Castle. "And actually, I'm a bit tired. I might just stay in tonight, if you don't mind?"

"Really?" Her voice was tinged with disappointment. "But what about Ben?"

"I'm goin' to the brewery," Echo said. "Can't stop you following me if you've got nothing better to do."

"Really, Laur?" Kalina called again, sounding slightly desperate.

My eyes met Truth's. He was watching me calmly, offering no input, but I'm sure his eyes were shining slightly.

And, alright, part of me knew that I *should* go out and resume my search for Ben. But a much more insistent part of me was really wanting another night alone with Truth.

"Sorry!" I called back to Kalina. "I'll put in double effort tomorrow, I promise!"

I'm such a bad friend, I thought. But with Truth right there, after our day together, and the way he was looking at me …

I didn't feel bad for long.

"Have you ever tried breathing with a partner before?"

Truth's question puzzled me slightly. We were sitting on his bed, both cross-legged and facing each other, barely ten minutes after Kalina and Echo had left the house. Truth was still only wearing his linen pants, I was still fully dressed, and I was trying to keep my eyes up on his face and ignore the fact that, bare-chested, he looked absolutely gorgeous.

"We're all always breathing," I answered. "Aren't we?"

Truth smiled. "True. But when you breathe together, with someone, you start to exchange energies."

I must have looked sceptical.

"Have you heard of aura photography?"

"Didn't they have that at the Crystal Castle?"

"Yes. But studies have been done elsewhere with two people together. There's special photography that makes it possible to see the energy surrounding people, and to show it in colour. When a couple sends negative thoughts to each other, their auras separate. Yet when they send positive, loving thoughts, their auras intermingle and become one flowing energy."

I really tried to keep my eyebrows down, but they just weren't cooperating.

Truth laughed softly. "I know it sounds strange. And it involves believing in something you cannot see, at least without the assistance of special cameras. But exchanging energies is an ancient practice. In ancient Chinese traditions, the female energy is described as being like water and the male energy as fire. During lovemaking, the two energies must merge together slowly so that the fire can heat the water, turning it to steam, otherwise the water will just quickly put out the fire. Other ancient cultures similarly believed in these kinds of energies, or life forces. Either way, the focus is on balancing one with the other and developing a harmonised connection."

"And you're saying you can do that just by breathing together?"

"Breathing is the start of it. When you breathe in, imagine drawing your energy in, from your first chakra at the base of your spine, up to your heart centre, the fourth chakra. Then as you breathe out, imagine sending that energy down and out, through your yoni and up into your partner's body."

"Did you just say through my *yoni*?"

"Yes." Truth smiled. "During lovemaking, that's where you're the most physically connected. It's one way to exchange energies—through the first chakra."

"Uh-uh." I looked at him sideways, one eyebrow still twitching upwards. "And what is this supposed to achieve, exactly, this matching of energies?"

"It'll achieve a deeper connection with your partner. Many people know how to have good sex. But not many people know how to connect with each other while doing so. Have you ever found that you've had good sex with someone, but for most of the time your or your partner's eyes remained closed, or that you didn't feel any more connected to them emotionally afterwards? Or that you can have good sex with someone at night, but the next morning you don't feel any closer than you did before?"

I frowned. "I guess so. I mean, I hadn't really thought about it."

"There are so many layers to lovemaking. Unfortunately, so many people think that lovemaking is all about the physical aspect of the experience. They equate good or bad sex to whether their partner had an orgasm or not. They don't realise that the emotional and energy connection is just as important."

"Yes, well, it's not like anyone's going to have, or necessarily *want*, an energy connection with someone you don't know very well. What if you're only interested in a one-night stand?"

Truth laughed. "People don't need to have energy connections every time they have sex. But knowing *how* to is a good skill to have."

"I see." I bit my lip and then found my lips pulling upwards in a cheeky grin. "So, is this something that you're offering to teach me?"

Truth's eyes sparkled. "I'd be delighted to."

I think my heart skipped a beat.

"So, um, how do we start?" I asked.

"We can start by taking off our clothes."

"What?" I squealed. "Just like that?"

He tipped his head, looking at me curiously. "I saw you naked last night. You're not feeling shy now, are you?"

"Ah ... yes! Of course I am!"

Truth chuckled. "How about I get some mood lighting happening, then?"

"That's a start."

Truth climbed off the bed and walked around the room, switching off half the lamps. My eyes followed him, drifting over the lines of the tree tattooed on his back, up over shoulderblades and down across his hips. I was determined to get a good look at it tonight. But ... afterwards.

He lit the candles that were still sitting on his chest of drawers, then picked up a strip of fabric and tied his dreads up in a loose bun on his head. Walking back towards me, he had a cheeky smile on his face. I was about to ask him what he was grinning about, but then he stopped right next to the bed, pulled the knot tying his pants together loose, and with one quick motion had pants and underwear dropping to the floor.

"Oh my God!" I laughed, glancing at his nakedness then up towards the ceiling in embarrassment.

Truth didn't reply, he just climbed back onto the bed and sat opposite me again, cross-legged, as if he wasn't now completely nude. He closed his eyes, turned his palms up on his knees, and said, "Your turn," with a soft smile on his lips.

I laughed again. "Really?"

He opened his eyes. "How about you can keep your underwear on. To start with."

I bit my lip. "Deal."

Carefully, I removed myself from the bed. Truth remained seated, his back straight and his wrists resting on his knees, as if he was just calmly meditating. He'd shut his eyes again, and I let my own gaze travel all the way down his body. He wasn't hard yet, and somehow that made it easier. I felt like he was going to teach me things again, things that were beyond physical sex.

I quickly stripped off my top and shorts, leaving my bra and undies in place. Then I cautiously climbed back on the bed.

Truth's eyes opened as I knelt on the mattress near him.

"We're going to start back to back," he said, and carefully, he spun himself around so he was facing away from me. "Sit like I am, with your back up against mine."

My eyes caught on the beautiful lines of the leaves and branches across his shoulders. I wanted to run my fingers over them, but instead I did as he suggested, sitting down carefully and pressing my back up against his. Immediately, my skin felt warm all over where we were touching, and there was something beautiful about knowing there was that artwork pressed between us.

"Now what?" I asked.

"Now I want you to concentrate on your breathing and your thoughts. Imagine every time you breathe out, slowly, you're sending all the negative thoughts from your mind. And each time you slowly breathe in, you're drawing positive thoughts and positive feelings up into your heart."

I closed my eyes and tried to do as directed. Okay. Negative thoughts out and away. Did I have any negative thoughts? I supposed I was thinking about how silly and weird this was, so that thought should probably go.

And maybe I was thinking that I'd been a totally bad friend, both in ditching Kalina tonight and in making no effort to find Ben today. So let's breathe that one out.

And I supposed there was that thought of, did I really deserve to be doing this? Who was I to be taking up Truth's time with some private Tantra lessons that weren't really lessons at all and I actually had no idea what this was or what we were doing together ...

"Think about breathing in warmth and love and acceptance," Truth said quietly. "Each time you inhale slowly, imagine drawing in positive energy and letting it disperse right through your body."

Alright, let's forget the negative thoughts. Positive thinking. I could do that ...

My neck is itchy.

"Try to slow your breathing," Truth said softly. "See if you can match your breath to mine."

Alright, that's a bit easier.

I concentrated on the feeling of Truth's ribs expanding and contracting behind me, and matched my own breath with his so we were breathing in together and then out together. Actually, concentrating on that was a lot better, and I did feel my body start to relax.

"Let's now turn and face each other," Truth said, starting to shift around.

There were a few moments of awkward (on my part) scrambling around, before we managed to get into the position Truth wanted. Basically, we were sitting almost nose to nose. My legs were draped over his thighs, his legs on either side of me, and we were both sitting upright, our bodies close together, almost like we were in a bear hug but with a small stretch of space between us.

I couldn't help giggling, and Truth smiled, waiting for me to stop. With a huge effort, I forced myself to revert to a straight face.

"Place your hand here, over my heart," he said, and then he gently lifted my right hand and placed it in the centre of his chest. His skin felt so warm and soft, and I was starting to feel a lot of heat between us, from where my legs were draped over his as well as where my hand rested on his chest. I was also trying to prevent my eyes from drifting down between his legs …

"May I?" he asked, indicating that he wanted to place his hand over my heart.

I nodded, and shivered slightly as he pressed his hand in between my breasts.

"Draw your attention to your heart centre, the fourth chakra. As I breathe out, I'm going to send my heart energy down through my lingam, into your yoni and up into your heart. At the same time, you will breathe in and focus on opening your heart and receiving my energy up into you. Then as you breathe out, you can imagine sending your energy from your heart, down through your yoni, across to my lingam and up to my heart. This way we are exchanging energies in a U-shape."

I really *tried* not to laugh.

Truth smiled. "Just a few times. See if you can do it. And let's see if we can maintain eye contact at the same time."

Alright, this was all a little bit confronting. Plus, I still had underwear on, so was that going to interrupt the psychic flow?

Anyway. Concentrate.

I tried to keep my eyes on Truth's. And I tried to match his breathing, but then, shit, no, we were meant to be breathing at opposite times now, weren't we?

He smiled, and I tried to relax, but honestly, I was sitting with my legs spread around him, and our thighs were touching, and his felt so solid and warm and strong beneath mine, and my hand on his chest *really* wanted to start roaming a bit, and I was having difficulties breathing slowly enough with his warm hand pressing on the tops of my breasts.

Come on, Laura. You're meant to be learning something here.

Alright. I could focus on the energies. I could.

I looked up and let my gaze melt into his.

His eyes were all brown flecks and amber warmth framed by dark lashes and brows. But his gaze was soft, open. Calm. Welcoming.

I thought about my heart beneath his hand, and I did feel like my whole chest was expanding and opening as I breathed in. And as I breathed out I tried to think about the energy moving down through my yoni (?) and across into Truth's …

Hang on a second.

My eyes dropped downwards to confirm what I thought I'd seen from my peripheral vision.

And yes. He was no longer unexcited.

As I drew my eyes back up again, the corners of my lips came with them. Truth's eyes were gleaming in response, a tiny smile on his mouth as well that I thought he was trying to control.

"Alright," he said, his voice close to laughter. "I'm going to call this particular exercise a fail."

"Oh, you're failing me?" I tried to pout, but was still struggling not to laugh.

Truth chuckled. "That's not necessarily a bad thing."

He lifted his hand from my chest and moved it to my shoulder, stroking my arm softly down towards my fingertips. Realising that I no longer had to do as he was telling me, I let my own hand begin to move, trailing it slowly down over his chest and across the ridges of muscle over his stomach. I kept my eyes on his, keeping his own gaze captive so I could see the flicker of surprise, of pleasure, that hit him when my hand finished its descent and stroked softly upwards over velvet skin.

Then he leaned forwards, or I leaned forwards, and my eyes were falling to his parted lips. And then we were kissing, softly, gently. I kept my fingers light, dancing over his length with the same gentleness he'd used to stroke my whole body last night. He growled, a deep rumbling in his throat, and then his mouth was opening and our lips and tongues were sliding across each other. His hand brushed lightly over my shoulderblades and then my bra was falling away. I released him for as long as it took to throw my bra over the side of the bed, and then we were pressing together, my breasts on his naked chest, our mouths locked hungrily, my hand down between our hips feeling how hard he was as I wrapped my hand firmly around him.

Truth's hands came brushing along my back and down over my buttocks until he gripped me firmly and pulled me up onto his lap. I pulled my hand out from between us, letting it join my other hand behind his neck (avoiding the dreadlocks—they're not that nice to touch, as it turned out), and gasped as I felt his hardness pressed against my groin, the fabric of my undies the only thing separating us.

Truth pulled back slightly, making me pause, panting, to look at him.

"Slow down," he gasped, and I wasn't sure if that was for his benefit or mine. Looking deep into my eyes, his hands stilled on my hips and he held me to him firmly while we both tried to slow our breathing. Then gently, he began stroking his hands up my back again. I shivered and arched against him, and he responded by ducking down and capturing my nipple in his mouth. I moaned at the sudden wetness, and tightened my legs around him, feeling the deep pull up through my centre.

He kissed my neck, then his mouth found mine again, and our tongues and lips were sliding across each other.

In one fluid movement, he held me to him and rolled us down so I was pressed into the bed on my back, Truth on top of me with my legs still wrapped around him. I released my tight grip on his shoulders, running my hands down across his back.

He propped himself up on one elbow, separating our bodies slightly, and I was about to moan a protest when I felt his hand drifting lightly over the skin of my inner thigh. Instead, I found myself shifting my hips upwards, our kiss becoming urgent, deeper, as his fingers first gently lifted the very edge of the lace on my underwear, slowly teasing the delicate skin beneath, and then as I moaned and shifted my hips again, his fingers moved right in through the side.

My breathing became ragged while Truth kissed my jawline and my cheekbone, pausing to whisper, "Breathe. Just breathe," in my ear as his fingers played an artful crescendo within my underwear.

He let me shatter beneath him, his mouth slowly dancing over mine at the same time, his fingers moving slowly until they were almost stilled.

Almost.

Gently, he kept playing me, not in the centre where my nerves felt raw, but on the sides and around, like a painter swirling colours together.

I felt my breathing increase again, my nerves twinging, reigniting. Carefully, Truth sat up and then his hands were gripping the lace sides of my underwear and sliding them downwards. I lifted my hips up, letting him remove the last piece of my clothing, and found my eyes drawn to his erection, my hand moving to capture it as he came back up to kneel beside me.

He gasped, and I could feel him throbbing in my hand. Impulsively, I propped myself up on my elbows, and with my eyes looking up into his, I slowly let my tongue run from the bottom of his shaft up to the tip.

He gasped again, his fingers gently twining through my hair.

"Feel free to tell me what you like," I said, and he grinned in response.

And then I turned my attention back to the delightful contradiction of softness and hardness before me.

Alright, now let me just say that I'd never been very good at blow jobs. At least, that would be my self-assessment. In reality, I'd only ever performed the said "job" on one person—Jack—and to be honest, I really did feel like that was a job. He never gave me any verbal feedback, and so I was always just trying to remember the tips I'd read about in *Cosmo* or *Cleo* magazines. Plus, I'd always preferred just having sex. It was easier.

183

But I enjoyed playing with Truth. Maybe because *he* seemed to be enjoying it. Maybe because he'd spent so long teasing and stroking me the day before, and perhaps I was somewhat imitating that slow, teasing nature myself. But also, he had no trouble directing me and giving instructions, which was fantastic. I mean, I'd never dreamed of telling a guy what to do if he was going down on me. It would feel rude. But having Truth tell me what to do was just so informative. Especially when I did what he asked and then he groaned with pleasure and I realised how wonderful this whole thing was.

Maybe Truth was right. Men should stop thinking they needed to be experts and just ask for some feedback.

Anyway, I was really enjoying my new role as the one doing the teasing and the playing when his hand tightened in my hair and he suddenly gasped, "Stop!"

I pulled away and looked up at him.

He had his eyes closed, his whole body thrumming and tensed. And then he slowly released his breath, opening his eyes and looking down at me with a smile.

"That was nearly *too* good," he said, gently pushing me back on the bed and lying down next to me.

"I didn't need to stop," I protested, reaching for him again, but he captured my hand and held it still while he kissed me.

He pushed me deeper into the bed, rolling half onto me and bringing his thigh up between my legs. I gasped at the renewed contact between my thighs, feeling my wetness transfer to his skin, and he groaned appreciatively.

"We're not stopping yet," he said, before kissing my neck again. His hand released mine and drifted down over my shoulder, up and across my breast and nipple, and down the centre of my stomach.

I moaned as I spread my legs, my hands coming around his neck and pulling him up to kiss me again while his hand slid down into the wetness below.

He touched me gently, lightly, testing to see how ready I was. And when I gasped and trembled in response, he pulled himself away from me. I watched him get a condom out and slide it in place, then pulled him back on top of me, growling in frustration when he held himself away, over me, but not touching.

He dipped down to kiss me gently and he let one hand trail along the side of my body very slowly.

"Only slow movements allowed," he said, his eyes glinting with pleasure. "Think about breathing deeply."

I trailed my hands up his sides, over his ribs and across his shoulders. Then I moved them back down to his hips and tried to pull him towards me.

He kissed me and moved his hips down, so slightly, so that the very tip of him pressed on me.

I moaned and tried to raise my hips up, to draw him in, but he drew away. Gently, he captured my hands and moved them so they were together above my head, holding them there in one of his. He moved his other hand down to press on my hip, holding me still on the bed.

His lips danced across mine. Leisurely, the tip of his tongue grazed my lip just as I felt the tip of his erection push against me.

I whimpered again.

His tongue moved sensuously over my lips and I felt him moving, so delicately, pushing just the tiniest bit inside me.

I arched up, wanting to pull him into me more, but his hand tightened on my hip, reminding me to stay still. I took a deep breath, making my whole body relax. And he rewarded me by pushing the whole head inside me, then slowly drawing it out.

And then a bit more. And more again.

I started to lose my grip on reality.

My limbs felt like electrified putty, my breath drawing in and out down to my toes and through the back of my neck.

I focused on our mouths together, feeling his lips and tongue move wetly across mine, as below he was dipping slowly in and out, each time giving me just a little bit more.

I felt my chest opening, my breasts pushing up into him, as he let himself move further inside me. And I could feel the wave building again, my muscles wanting to tighten even as I breathed through them and made them relax.

Truth's mouth left mine and I opened my eyes to find him looking down at me, his eyes filled with warmth. He released my hands and my hip, pausing all movement and stroking my face softly. Then, with our gazes still locked together, he finally pushed his hips right up into mine, letting himself slide into me fully. I arched up, gasping, and he captured my mouth again with his, both of us growling. And barely moments later, as he moved steadily within me, I felt myself peaking and breaking again, wave after wave washing over me, intensified when he tensed and shattered as well.

"Holy fuck," I whispered.

I felt him smiling against my neck before he kissed me again.

21

The tattoo began on the curves of his buttocks as faint tree roots that spider-webbed upwards, growing thicker. They met at the base of his spine and melded into a tapering trunk which stretched up the centre of his back. Branches appeared just below his ribs, arching gracefully outwards, their boughs thick with a wash of green foliage in swirling, asymmetrical lines.

Within the tree, hidden among the branches and the roots, were tiny details that I kept discovering. A lotus flower on his right shoulderblade. A tiny kiwi bird, hidden in the roots. Two cats, lost in the leaves. Up the centre of the tree itself were faint symbols, drawn to be merged with bark or leaf, which Truth said corresponded to the position of the chakras. But my fingers kept drifting near his left shoulderblade, to the place on his back that would shield his heart, where a name would forever live on his skin, almost hidden amongst the leaves.

"Who is Ryan?" I asked him, letting my thumb brush lightly over the word.

We were lying together in his bed, he on his side and I behind him so I could examine the tattoo. We were both exhausted (at least I was exhausted), but at the same time I felt wide awake.

Truth's breathing stilled for a moment, then began again, the silence in the wake of my question stretching a bit too long.

"He was my best friend growing up," Truth eventually said. He shifted around, moving so that he was lying on his back, his arm pressed into me. I turned over too, so we were lying shoulder to shoulder, both staring up at the star-speckled night sky through the skylight above us.

"What happened to him?" I asked softly.

"He ... died. When we were seventeen."

My hand drifted down to his and I squeezed it, linking my fingers through his. "I'm so sorry," I said. And then, "Will you tell me about it?"

Truth stroked his thumb over the back of my hand gently. Then, he took a breath and began speaking.

"He was always the loud one, the outgoing one. The fun one, I suppose. We lived in the same street and had known each other since we were kids. We were like brothers, almost, since neither of us had any siblings. We'd always be round at each other's houses. Just always together, always hanging out.

"We stayed close all the way through school. But in Year Twelve, things started to change. It happened slowly, I guess. We were both trying to study a lot, both feeling the pressure of that last year. I still wanted to muck around and blow off steam, but he never wanted to go out. When I'd try to push him to take a night off, he'd get angry at me. He'd just stay home, not want to do anything. I found out he'd started buying drugs off the kids who had connections. When I asked him about it, he got so angry that I barely even recognised him. He started accusing me of weird shit every time we spoke, which made *me* angry. I didn't know ... I didn't understand what was really going on with him, or how to deal with it. So I guess I distanced myself and ... and I wasn't there for him."

Truth fell silent for a moment. His voice was calm, accepting, as if he'd thought about this a lot already. I remained quiet, waiting for him to continue, even though I had an awful feeling of dread in my gut about where this was going.

"He hanged himself from a tree in his back garden." Truth's voice was hushed. "Two months before the QCE. His mum was the one who found him—he'd left a note in the kitchen, asking her not to go outside. But of course she did. I heard her screaming from down the street in my bedroom."

I gripped his hand, feeling my throat constrict as tears escaped to run across my temples.

"After he died," Truth continued calmly, "I barely made it through the exams. Came close to failing almost everything. I became so angry myself, so ashamed of who I'd become. My cousin, Jess, was heading to Asia to go backpacking and my mums convinced me to go with her. It was there that we discovered the yoga commune, the place that really struck a connection with me. Jess stayed a couple of weeks then kept travelling, but I stayed there for months. It was there that I learned about living in the present, about not trying to change the past or put too much focus on the future. One of the masters taught me a lot about human behaviour and what impact our actions can have on others. I know now that when someone is angry, what they really need is love. That if someone is trying to push away and pull away it's because they don't trust the people or person nearest them to love them."

Truth stopped speaking, and we lay together holding hands. I felt so touched that he was sharing this story with me, this story of his friend. Ryan's death had affected Truth so deeply that he now spent his life trying to teach others, trying to heal others.

Is that what he was doing with me? Trying to help heal me? His words rang true for most of the relationships in my life. What was I doing with Lucas, if not continually pulling away from him? Was it because I didn't trust him to love me?

More tears slipped from my eyes. I didn't want to be afraid to let someone in again.

"It can be hard," Truth eventually went on, "to recognise the signs of someone in pain. No one ever asks for help when they need it. But one thing I've learned is that I want to live a life where both my eyes and my heart are open to others."

I squeezed his hand again. "You're a good friend. I'm so sorry about Ryan, about … everything that happened."

He squeezed my hand back. "*You're* a good friend. You've come all the way up here to find your flatmate, even though he's resisting, because you sense he's in trouble."

His words startled me, but I realised he was right. Ben *was* in trouble. He was pulling away from his friends and his family, trying to push us out. But that just meant that he needed us all the more.

"Thank you for sharing with me," I whispered to Truth. "And for what it's worth, I think you're one of the most amazing people I've ever met."

Truth kissed the tip of my nose. "Thank you. I think you're pretty amazing, too."

⊃⊙

I slipped out of Truth's room early, before he woke.

It was strange seeing the dawn light breaking across the sky, another beautiful day beginning. I felt … different, somehow. Calmer. Or more centred. Like I'd somehow formed a deeply spiritual connection with Truth, with the universe, with just … everything around me.

Unfortunately, that feeling was shattered when I collided head-on with Kalina just inside our bedroom door, both of us reeling back with muttered curses and hands to our foreheads.

"Blimey!" Kalina huffed, flopping down on her bed. "How *hard* is your head?"

"Your head's like a bloody rock!" I protested, sitting on my bed and practically seeing stars in front of my eyes.

"What are you doing, anyway, leaving Truth's room so early?" Kalina asked, still rubbing her forehead. "Not such a good night together, eh?"

"No! I just … wanted to get an early start on looking for Ben today." I pressed my head gently, wincing at the pain there. "Besides, *your* bed looks very much un-slept-in. If I had to guess, I'd say I'm not the only one sneaking out of a boy's room early in the morning. Thought you were done with Echo?"

"I *am*. Definitely. Not going to spend another night with him."

"Uh-uh. You haven't been quietly enjoying your hunting dates with him?"

"As if! I'm trying to take this whole thing seriously. Ben is missing! Why am I the only one who thinks this is worrying?"

"Sorry. I mean … I haven't been …"

"No, no." Kalina waved her hand towards me dismissively. "I'm not trying to have a go. It's just … well, it's meant to be you and I out looking for Ben, not Echo and I. He doesn't even listen to me! He keeps making all these suggestions which are just so … well, they're actually quite good, but my ideas are just as good. And it's like he's just watching me, and waiting for me to fail, so that he can come in with a much better idea."

"Right. So, just to be clear, you *don't* want to get the input of Mr Good-ideas man in the search for Ben?"

"Not unless we're desperate."

"Aren't we desperate yet?" I sighed, turning serious. I drew my legs up onto the bed and pulled a pillow into my lap. "It's been almost a week, and we've gotten nowhere. Plus, you're wrong about being the only one taking this seriously. I *am* worried about Ben. I know yesterday I was a bit … well, not paying enough attention to the Ben situation. But we do need to find him, and let him know how much we love him. And soon."

"Right." Kalina gave me a bit of a weird look, but then she shook her head, stood up, and began pacing around our small room. "We really need to come up with a better plan."

"Are we one-hundred-percent sure they're still in Byron Bay?"

Kalina stopped, shooting me a surprised look. "Oh, yes! I forgot to tell you! According to Lucas, Ben spoke to his mum yesterday morning and told her he was up here with Amy. Didn't say where they were staying though, or how long they'd be here for."

"Hang on, what? You spoke to Lucas yesterday?" I felt an almighty thud in my belly. Why had Lucas called Kalina and not me? And why hadn't Kal mentioned it last night?

"Sorry, I totally forgot. He called in the afternoon to ask how the hunt was going, when I was out doing that stupid lighthouse walk. He sounded like he was pretty stressed."

"Shit. But Ben actually called his mum? Didn't she press him for details? She could have got all the info out of him!"

"She doesn't know the half of it, remember? Lucas didn't want to worry his parents. But he's super worried about Ben now. His mum told him that all the beneficiaries of the aunt's estate have now been advised on what they can expect to receive, and apparently, Ben is going to receive a huge chunk of inheritance in his bank account. Lucas is worried that Ben's not in a good state of mind at the moment to deal with it, that he might go off and spend it all at once on something stupid."

"Oh shit. And we know how much Amy likes to have him spend his money."

"Exactly." Kalina flopped down on her bed with a sigh. "I think our deadline to find him has just escalated."

We were silent for a moment, both processing this and probably both having equally nightmarish thoughts about Amy sucking Ben dry like a vampire. I knew I was.

But my thoughts didn't stay on Ben for long.

"So ... did Lucas ask about me?"

Kalina shot me a look. "He did," she said levelly.

"Oh? And what did you say?" I suddenly felt gripped by fear. "You didn't say I was spending the day with Truth, did you?"

"No, I just said we'd split up to try to cover more ground. But why would you care if Lucas knew you were hanging out with another guy? I thought the two of you were just friends?"

"We are," I said quickly.

Kalina chuckled. "You don't fool me, Laura. You've totally still got a thing for him."

"I don't! I mean ... well, maybe I did. Or I do. I don't know."

"You should just sleep with him. Get it out of your system."

"I can't do that!" I protested.

Even though that *was* what I wanted to do. It's what I'd wanted to do since that first morning out in Manly when I'd seen him playing volleyball on the beach. Was I seriously thinking about sleeping with Lucas when I'd just come straight from Truth's bed?

"Well, just remember, there are plenty of men to go around," Kalina said. "Just look at the state of the guys up here. They're great for a bit of fun, but the sooner we leave here the better."

"Yeah," I echoed, but I didn't quite agree. Truth was more than just a bit of fun for me. He was ... I don't know what he was. But Lucas was something else entirely.

"Come on," I said eventually, infusing my voice with as much positivity as possible. "Let's get out into town and go look for Ben again. He might be out for breakfast somewhere."

"Alright," Kalina agreed. "But I'm going to start praying to all of the gods for a miracle."

22

MIRACLE!!!
Oh. My. God.

Oh my *God.*

OMG.

Alright, I wasn't actually religious. Let's be clear that when I said "God" I was sort of just referring to the forces of the universe. (No, not *that* Force. Although, let's hope it may be with us all the same.)

But seriously, whatever universe vibes we were sending out that morning paid off. Because as Kalina and I were walking down one of the streets in Byron Bay, looking around us and talking about how annoying Echo was again (well, Kalina was talking about how annoying he was; I was having flashbacks to Truth's naked body from last night), when suddenly, SUDDENLY ...

Amy. Was. Right. There.

We both froze. Part of me wondered if it was a mirage. One of the elusive two, just standing right there on the pathway ahead of us, looking into the window of a shop.

Kalina's hand launched out and gripped my elbow, super hard. "It's *her*!" she hissed.

"I know! What do we do?" I asked, feeling slightly hysterical.

Oh God. We'd been hunting Ben and Amy for so long. And here was Amy right here, and we didn't know what to do about it.

"I can't see Ben anywhere." Kalina was frowning, her head turning to look up and down the street. I scanned the pathways also, but there was no sign of him.

"Maybe he's in the store?" I suggested.

As we watched, Amy took out her phone and pointed the camera at something in the window. I glanced up to the shop's sign hanging out over the footpath and felt a stab of misgiving.

"Kalina, that's a jewellery shop she's looking at," I said uneasily.

Kalina scowled. "She's going to spend Ben's money, my arse."

Before I could stop her, Kalina stormed up the footpath, straight towards Amy. I followed her quickly, my unease rapidly increasing.

"Kal, I think we should—"

"Hello, Amy," Kalina said loudly, her voice sweetly sinister.

If the devil had a mistress, I'd bet her name was Kalina.

Amy jumped back, startled, and looked around guiltily. My eyes fell to the display in the window she'd been photographing, and I felt my heart sinking with the realisation that my own suspicions were correct.

It was a display of engagement rings.

"*You* two," Amy said, her startled surprise quickly turning to dislike. She tossed her blonde hair over her shoulder and drew herself up haughtily. "So, it is true. Have you seriously taken to stalking me now? I could take out an AVO on you for this."

"Oh, don't flatter yourself, we're not stalking *you*," Kalina snapped. "We should be the ones reporting *you* to the police—you've kidnapped Ben and brainwashed him."

Something akin to fear flickered briefly over Amy's face, but it was gone in a flash and then she smiled coldly at us.

"You're so deluded. I told Ben you were obsessed with him, but he didn't believe me. But how can he not now? You've literally stalked him all the way to Byron Bay."

"Where is he?"

Amy's smile grew and she shrugged casually. "He's not here."

"Tell us where he is, you cow." Kalina stepped forward menacingly, and Amy took a step back, her eyes going wide.

"I don't have to tell you anything!" Amy's voice turned angry. "If Ben wanted to talk to you, he would. What, you think he's lost your phone number or something? He doesn't want to see you. He doesn't want to know any of you anymore. He's got *me* now." She smiled again, and I could have sworn she'd grown fangs.

"You little—"

"Kal!" I grabbed her arm and held her back. "Amy," I addressed the monstress directly, trying not to grit my teeth. "We're just worried about Ben. He's our friend, our *good* friend. And we only want to know that he's okay. Surely you, being so close to him and of course wanting the *best* for him, wouldn't mind some of his *friends* having a little talk with him?"

I felt Kalina still beside me. I watched Amy carefully, my breath held, hoping she would—

"Oh, fuck off," Amy said, rolling her eyes. "I'm not going to fall for that bullshit."

My mouth fell open. "Well. I tried," I muttered when I managed to collect myself, releasing Kalina.

"Look, you little shit—" Kalina said, stepping forward again.

"No, *you* look!" Amy interrupted, stepping forwards herself. The two girls were standing practically nose to nose, their eyes locked in a staring contest. I felt my chest clench in fear, wondering if this was about to turn into an all-out street brawl.

Amy bared her teeth as she spoke right into Kalina's face. "Ben is *mine*. You're the one that's driven him away with your interfering. But I know how to make him happy. And we're going to have a perfect life together, far away from you."

Amy stepped back, but Kalina just laughed. "You're fucking deluded, you know that? He'll see through you soon enough, whether we're here or not. Ben has *real* friends, something I doubt you even know the meaning of. And you think you know him—but you barely know anything about him."

"Don't I?" Amy smiled, and I didn't like the triumphant look in her eyes. "I know who Ben is. I know the kind of man he is, or at least the kind he wants to be. And he'll always want to do right by his *family*."

She emphasised the last word, and as she spoke it, she placed one of her hands protectively over her stomach, just below her belly button.

Oh ... Jesus ... Fucking ... Buddha ...

"You're not ... no!" Kalina spluttered, looking as shell-shocked as I felt.

Amy smiled again, the triumph written plainly on her face. "I'm going to tell him soon. And then I'm sure we'll be celebrating our engagement in no time."

"You fucking bitch!" Kalina launched herself at Amy and I practically had to tackle her to the side.

Amy stepped back again, avoiding us, looking equal parts fearful and exultant. "You're a fucking nutcase, Kalina. *I* know what's best for Ben. He doesn't need you in his life."

"I'll fucking murder you, you evil little shit!"

"Kal! Stop it!" I was panting with the effort of holding her back.

"Stay away from us, or I'll call the police!" Amy half shouted, from where she was hastily backing down the street.

Through the exertion of restraining Kalina, I noticed people had stopped and were staring at us from across the road.

"We'll just follow you home!" Kalina shouted. "You can't hide him forever!"

"Kal! Ow!" I panted again. She was grabbing at my hands, trying to wrench me off her, and I was struggling to hold her in place.

"You come near me and I'll call the police!" Amy shouted again.

Kalina wrenched my hands off her, and I let go with a yowl of pain. In a second, she was flying down the street, and I realised with absolute horror that she was actually going to attack Amy. She was going to *attack a pregnant woman.*

But then a guy was suddenly tackling Kalina side on, a strong arm going around her waist and swinging her away. All I noticed was the thick beard before I recognised Echo. He literally slung her up and over his shoulder, gripping her legs so she couldn't kick him, and she pounded on his back with her fists, shouting and swearing at him. And that's how he approached me on the street, a scowl on his face, looking absolutely comical with a struggling Kalina squirming over his shoulder.

Behind him, Amy was shaking her head, looking appalled, but then she swiftly waved down a taxi that was passing and jumped inside. Before I could process what to do, she was driving away.

"Stop it!" Kalina was shouting. "We need to follow her! Put me down, you fuck-face!"

Echo dropped her back onto her feet beside me. "You can't follow her now," he said, his voice harsh. "You've just threatened to murder her in public as well as telling her that you're going to follow her home. She really will call the police, and have good cause to."

"I don't care if she does!"

"Don't be stupid, Kalina. If you get arrested you could end up with a criminal record."

"But we need to find Ben!" Kalina said desperately, her eyes fixed on the retreating taxi.

Echo still had her arm held in a firm grip, and she was trying to wrench it out again.

"Unhand me!" She turned and punched him on the shoulder.

"She's already gone, Kal," I said, looking up and down the street. "There's no other taxi here, we've already lost her."

Kalina slumped and rubbed her ribs. Echo finally let go of her arm and stepped away from her.

"You shouldn't have interfered!" Kalina rounded on him, looking furious. "That was the best opportunity we've had since we've been here! Now you've just—"

"I've just prevented you from doing something stupid," Echo replied, looking equally furious. "You can't assault someone on the street! Especially someone who's just told you they're pregnant."

"Oh, you heard that, did you? What the fuck are you even doing here? Are you *following* me?"

"I'm here by coincidence, Kalina. Don't flatter yourself."

"Well fuck off, then, won't you? We don't need your *help*."

I blanched for Echo's sake.

Echo glanced to me, looking equal parts apologetic and frustrated. I shrugged helplessly at him.

"Fine." Echo turned and stormed off down the street.

Kalina growled and turned her back on him. "Fucking bastard. I wasn't *actually* going to attack her."

I raised my eyebrows. "You could have fooled me."

Kalina huffed once, almost a laugh. "Yeah. Well. Maybe I was."

I shook my head at her. "That was a bit intense, Kal."

She sniffed and rubbed her nose, not looking at me. And then I noticed that she was visibly shaking.

I took her gently by the arm and steered her towards the cafe on the corner. "Come on. I think we need to have a talk."

23

"**A**lright, spill. *What* is going on with you?"

We'd sat down in the back corner of the cafe, for once not even pretending to keep an eye out for Ben. Kalina looked the most rattled I'd ever seen her, and she wouldn't meet my eyes as she replied, crossing her arms over her chest.

"Nothing. I don't know what you're talking about."

"Come on, Kal. I'd like to think I know you well enough to recognise that something is up with you. Something has been up with you ever since we came here. No, since before that. You've been acting weird for weeks. I don't want to sound harsh, but seriously, you're starting to lose your shit."

Kalina laughed softly, her whole body kind of sagging. For a moment, she looked down at her lap, her hands twisting together. And then she clenched them into fists, sighed, and looked up at me.

"Okay. You're right. I've been a bit rattled."

"A bit?"

"Alright, a lot," she admitted.

I nodded in satisfaction, feeling relieved that she was finally going to talk to me. The waitress arrived at our table and deposited our coffees in front of us, and I waited until she'd left before I pressed on, being as kind as I could.

"I'm going to hazard a guess here and say it's got something to do with that British guy who turned up looking for you on our doorstep?"

Kalina's mouth flattened into a thin line. Then she nodded. "Adam. My ex."

"Your ex as in … *the* ex? The one that cheated on you with your best friend? When you'd been living with him for four years? The one from London?"

Kalina nodded again, her eyes dropping to her cappuccino as she started stirring. "Mmm-hmm."

"But, what does he want? And what on earth is he doing in Sydney? And how did he find you? I mean, sorry, God, you probably have no idea about any of this. It's just incredible that he'd dare even to show his face and come looking for you!"

"I met up with him."

I almost spilled my latte on my lap. "What? When?"

"The night before we came up here."

I let that sink in for a moment. Kalina had insisted we leave to find Ben the second we figured out he was in Byron Bay. Was part of her eagerness to come here a strategy to get far away from Adam?

"What happened?" I asked, making sure I sounded encouraging rather than accusatory. "I thought you never wanted to see him again?"

"I didn't. I still don't. But the guy flew across the world just to talk to me. And I guess I was curious to hear what he had to say."

"And?" I prompted.

"And he misses me." She laughed humourlessly. "He knows what a huge mistake he made. He thinks I'm his 'one' and he wants to be with me. He wants me back."

My mouth had fallen open. I supposed it was the sort of thing you flew around the world for, but all I could think was, *How dare he!* Kalina was way too good to get back together with him. I wanted to tell her so, but for an awful moment I wondered if maybe she wanted him back. Should I judge her? Or should I just be open and supportive and shower her with love, the way Truth would do?

"What do you want?" I asked softly, my heart freezing in place as I waited for her answer.

She scoffed and shook her head, but I could see tears in her eyes. She sniffed them away.

"Honestly? I want to punch him in the face and knee him in the balls. I want to *hurt* him, as much as he hurt me. I never want to see him again ... and yet, we were together for so long, you know? When I saw his face ... I keep remembering how it was before, as in before I knew about the cheating and stuff. But then that just makes me even angrier. Because how could I have any nice thoughts about him after what he did? We could have had a nice life together, but he *ruined* it. That can't be undone."

"I don't think it's unreasonable to remember the nice times and miss them," I offered, recalling my own old life with Jack. "Even though you know it wasn't right, there are still all those memories of how it *felt* right at the time."

How it felt to come home to someone who loved you (or, at least, was supposed to). How it felt to have that one person who knew everything about your life. To have that person to wake up to every morning, and fall asleep with every night, whom you'd share those silly jokes with that no one else would get.

Someone you could roll on top of on Sunday mornings, just for fun, pretending to be a dugong and squashing them.

God, I missed that.

"That's exactly why I can never trust him again," Kalina said, and I snapped my thoughts back to the present. "Him, or any other guy. He made me feel like I was safe. It's like your heart is made of glass and they're holding it in their hands. You think they'll take care of it, but instead they smash it on the ground, into a million tiny pieces. That shit can't be fixed. It'll never be fixed."

I gave her a look. "Kal, is that why you haven't dated anyone seriously since then? Are you worried it will happen again?"

"Of course I'm bloody worried! And it *won't* happen again, because I won't let it."

"But … don't you want all the nice things again? I mean, not with Adam—I'm definitely not suggesting you get back together with him. But with someone else maybe?"

Kalina shifted in her seat, looking like I'd just shoved a sea anemone under her butt. "You don't get it, Laur. I *can't* go through that again. I was in … a really dark place after it happened. I honestly thought I might die. It felt like someone, at least, had died. And I remember thinking, there's no way I can go back there. You get it, don't you? Weren't you the same after Jack left?"

"I was. And I do get it. But, Kal, there's no guarantee that you'll end up back there. Maybe the next guy you like, who you date, will end up being the one for you, your soul mate. Someone you can just do *life* with, someone who will never hurt you."

Kalina snorted. "You really believe that?"

I thought about it for a moment. "You know what? I believe it's something worth trying for. I believe that no one should be afraid of loving again. And if something terrible happens, I'll be there for you. Your *friends* will be there for you. Your real friends, the ones who will never do something like sleep with your boyfriend behind your back."

Kalina laughed again, but I think she did it to kind of cover a sob. "Well, one of my friends is still MIA and hates me." She wiped at her eyes and sniffed. "Think I'm getting hay fever. Bloody allergies."

"Yeah, that time of year," I offered, laughing. "But Ben doesn't hate you. He loves you. Really. He just doesn't realise that he needs us right now."

"Well, then." Kalina stirred her coffee pensively for a moment, then she looked up at me and locked her eyes onto mine. "How about we make a deal? I'll consider letting the next nice guy in a bit more ... if you do as well."

"Me?" My heart did a weird kind of sideways flutter. "Why do I need to?"

"Come on, Laur. All that stuff you just said to me, it applies to you, too. You want to find that special someone again. You probably have already, you just won't admit it."

I dropped my eyes and was suddenly *very* busy rearranging the sugar packets.

"No rush. No pressure," Kalina said. "But we could probably both do with a bit of ... risk taking."

I met her eyes and laughed. "Fine, then," I said. "It's a deal."

Kalina knocked back the rest of her coffee in one gulp. "Alright. Now, let's go find our loose cannon of a friend."

Later that afternoon, my phone rang and my heart lurched when I saw the caller ID.

Celeste. My new employer. Well, the producer on the film I was starting work on in just over a week. Also, the woman who'd hired Ben. I wasn't sure if she was my direct boss—I was pretty sure there would be a location manager that I'd be reporting to. But she was the one coordinating everything for the production.

"Hi, Celeste!" I answered cheerfully, even though I shot Kalina a worried look. We stopped walking on the pavement, pulling back against the wall of a shop, and Kalina pulled a kind of "eek" face at me.

"Laura, darling, so lovely to hear your voice," Celeste said, sounding as brusque and confident as I remembered her being. "I trust you're all ready to start next week?"

"Absolutely!" I hoped my voice didn't sound quite as strained as I imagined it.

"Of course you are. Listen, darling, I'm trying to get in touch with Ben, but I'm not having much luck."

"Oh, really?" Shit. Shit!

"Yes, his phone appears to be disconnected and he's not responding to my emails. Do you know where he is?"

Oh God. This was bad. This was very, very bad.

"Um, I think he's on holidays at the moment," I replied, giving Kalina a desperate look. She nodded eagerly at me, and made a hand movement like a plane taking off. "On an island!" I quickly added. "One of those islands with really bad reception … and no internet."

"Holidays! That'd be right. Do you know when he's expected back?"

"I'd have to check the exact date … but he'll definitely be back in time for production to start. I'm sure of it."

"Right. Well, we've had a bit of a change to the production schedule. A few of the key scenes have been moved forward quite a bit. Do you think you can get him to give me a call as soon as possible? I need his availability confirmed, otherwise I'll need another sound recordist."

I reached out and gripped Kalina's arm, feeling panicked.

Shit! Ben was looking forward to this job so much, he'd be devastated if someone else was brought in. It was one thing for him to ignore his friends and family, but for him to risk his job like this! It was so unlike him. Kalina was making faces at me and rolling her hands around in circles, though I honestly had no idea what that was supposed to mean.

"I'm sure that won't be necessary!" I quickly said to Celeste. "I mean, I'm sure Ben will get back to you really soon. In fact I'm positive. I'll make sure that he does. I know there's no way he'll want to miss this job."

"Excellent. Tell him I need to speak to him no later than Wednesday, otherwise he's bumped from half the shoot. Thanks, Laura, I knew you were going to be a reliable hire!"

I laughed nervously. "Yes, absolutely!"

"Alright, darling. Talk soon."

I started to say goodbye, but I realised Celeste had already gone. "Shit!"

"Laur? What did you just promise? And ow, you're hurting my arm."

"Sorry!" I released Kalina, leaving bright white bloodless lines across her bicep from my claw hand. "Kal, what day is it today?"

"It's Monday."

"Oh God. We've got two days left to find Ben, otherwise he's going to lose his job. And I think I've just put my new career on the line for it."

You have [2] new notifications

Sᴇɴᴛ Mᴇssᴀɢᴇ
To: Ben Hartcoat at 10.49 am
Ben!! This is not a drill!! For the love of everything you are, if you aren't already wearing condoms then start wearing them RIGHT NOW!! Pregnancy IMMINENT otherwise! Repeat: This is not a drill!

Sᴇɴᴛ Mᴇssᴀɢᴇ
To Ben Hartcoat at 3.17 pm
Celeste can't get hold of you! What are you doing?? Urgent job info—call her ASAP!! And call me too!

YᴏᴜTᴜʙᴇ Aʟᴇʀᴛ
Recommended for you:
"How to Toilet Train your new puppy!"
by Clicker Training Revolution.

Fᴀᴄᴇʙᴏᴏᴋ Aʟᴇʀᴛ
Elle Baker updated her status.
Back in Sydney bitchesss!!!

24

Things were bad. Things were very, very bad.

We'd run out of ideas on how to find Ben. I hadn't seen Kalina looking so despondent in ages, and I'm sure I wasn't looking much better. I had chewed all of my fingernails right down to the quick, and I wasn't even a nail biter.

The morning's encounter with Amy had been like a little beacon of false hope. It was a cruel tease that had just made everything worse. I felt like Ben had turned into a ghost, and my worries were constantly intensifying.

Could Amy actually be pregnant? Or did she just say that to try to throw Kalina and me off? And if she was ... would Ben really marry someone like her? Would he let her control the rest of his life for the sake of a child?

It made me feel sick just thinking about it. Unless he'd *chosen* to try for a baby with her ... but somehow, I couldn't imagine him doing that. Not yet, not when he'd only been dating her for barely two months. I knew from past conversations that he was super careful about birth control, and STD prevention. But Amy was the first serious girlfriend he'd really had. If they'd stopped using condoms, presumably because she was on the pill, then he'd be completely blindsided by a pregnancy.

For now, I'd just have to cross my fingers and pray to every single god out there (Yoda, can you hear me?) that Amy was not pregnant. But even if I told myself that she wasn't, that wasn't the end of Ben's problems.

What if we couldn't find him and he didn't get back to Celeste in time?

What if he got sacked from the film production, a mere week before it started? Or worse, what if he chose not to return to Sydney for it? Amy might be able to convince him to throw in his job and run away with her, further away than this.

Aside from the fact that I knew Ben loved his job, especially when it meant working on film sets, a part of me was terrified for my own selfish sake. Ben was my connection to the film. Would I still have a job there if Ben pulled the plug?

For a few seconds, I let myself imagine a world where that happened. If I didn't have a job to get to in Sydney ... what then? What if I didn't return to Sydney at all but stayed here, in Byron Bay?

I felt like this place had infiltrated my heart. When I found myself in the beautiful garden out the back of this share house, or walking through the relaxed town and eating vegan goddess food, part of me wondered what it would be like to live here.

I could get a job at one of the whole-food cafes and start doing yoga every day. Maybe I could even do my yoga teacher's course and then get a job at Yogatainable! That place was turning out to be a bit of a city in its own right, and I did have the connections to get a job there.

And Truth was here. Every time I pictured him, I felt a rush of warmth course through me. I felt safe and relaxed with him. I could imagine us sleeping together every night, lying lazily together in his bed and staring up at the stars. Eating breakfast together in the mornings and doing yoga together at dawn. We'd shop at the local ethically sourced vegan cotton store and buy groceries from the farmers' market. I'd get beads and cornrows done in my hair, and maybe a beautiful winged bird tattoo across my shoulderblade. We'd both just live in the present, not worrying about the future. Not worrying about the past.

But that was silly. I shook my head, displacing the fantasy. Of course I wanted to go back to Sydney. Sydney was where my family lived, and my friends. I loved my flat with Kalina and Ben (who hopefully would be coming back). I loved Manly and the beach and the Corso and being able to get the ferry across the harbour to the city.

And Lucas. I loved …

Did I?

My ribs squeezed together.

Was Lucas a reason to go back to Sydney? Or a good reason to stay away?

"Hey."

I started, looking up to see Truth standing in the doorway behind me. I was lying in the yoga room in my favourite position (*savasana*, aka "corpse pose"), the cloudy afternoon casting me in shadowy light, and I'd obviously been lost completely in my own thoughts.

"Hey," I managed, giving him a weak smile as I sat up.

"Everything alright?" he asked, coming in and sitting gracefully beside me.

"Oh, just no luck finding Ben still. But now, we're even more worried about him than before."

"What's happened?"

I told him about the run-in with Amy earlier, and her insinuation that she was pregnant.

"Do you think she really is?" Truth asked.

I shrugged helplessly. "I hope not, but I have no idea. Part of me wonders what kind of person would fake a pregnancy, but then I realise that Amy is exactly that kind of person. I'd hope Ben was sensible … but he's a twenty-three-year-old guy. He probably would never even consider that a girl might lie about birth control. And if she's willing to fake a pregnancy, she's probably also willing to get deliberately pregnant to trap him."

Truth shook his head. "It never ceases to amaze me, the lengths people will go to, to hurt others."

"I reckon."

"Do you want some help in looking for him? I don't know what he looks like, but I can accompany you through town if you like."

I looked over at him and smiled. God, he was sexy. And nice. And just such a wonderful human being. "That would be amazing. Kalina and I were going to head out again tonight, and I'd love it if you came with us."

"I'd be delighted to."

Just then my phone rang, and I picked it up from the floor beside me, answering while barely registering who was calling.

"Laura?" came Rose's tearful voice.

"Rose? What's happened?" I asked, once I'd closed the door and I was alone in my room.

"It's Philippe," she said, her voice cracking.

"Oh God. What's happened to him?"

"He's being such a dick!"

I released the breath I'd been holding and sank down onto my bed with relief. For a second there, I thought … Well, it doesn't matter.

"I thought he was Mr Perfect?" I couldn't help teasing.

She made a disgusted sound. "He usually is! Everything has been completely fine up until this point. More than fine, it's been great! I even let him … well, never mind. But this morning we had this huge blow-up! Do you know what he said to me?"

"Er …"

"He said that I was *high maintenance*. And that I was a drama queen! Can you believe that! The fucking arsehole!"

"What a jerk!" I agreed. "So, what, just out of the blue he starts accusing you of this?"

"Ugh, we were having a disagreement before that. It's my nephew's christening next weekend and he's saying that he can't go. Which is ridiculous! Because I asked him about it weeks ago and he said fine, so all my family are expecting to meet him and he's now announced that he's got some football thing on that day and why should he have to go, anyway. Fucking boys."

"Oh, Rosie, I'm so sorry. That sucks."

"You know what's the worst part?" she went on. "Before the fight, we had such an amazing morning together. We'd both taken the day off work and we really took our relationship to the next level. We … well, we did things that I wouldn't do with just anyone. And then he has the nerve to call me high maintenance mere hours later!"

"Er … right."

"He should have been taking me out to a fucking five-star restaurant!"

"Absolutely," I agreed, even though I wasn't entirely sure what she was talking about. Part of my thoughts were suddenly drawing comparisons between Rose and Amy, which was totally not cool. They were nothing alike.

Nothing.

"So listen, I need to get out of the house," Rose continued. "Where are you? Can we please, please, go for drinks tonight?"

"I'm in Byron Bay, remember?"

"Still? Haven't you found your flatmate yet?"

"No, we haven't. Things are getting desperate."

"Shit."

There was silence for a moment and I thought the line had gone dead.

"Rose? Are you there?"

"I'm coming to you, then."

"What?"

"I'm coming up to Byron Bay. Fuck it, I need a break. I'm going to take the rest of the week off work. Let's go out drinking tomorrow."

"Are you sure? What, you're just going to hop on a plane?"

"Yep. Let me have a look."

I waited, hearing the faint *click-clicking* of computer keys in the background.

"Aha!" Rose said. "There's a flight at ten am tomorrow morning. I'm booking it."

"Really?" I squealed in excitement. "Fantastic! I'll come pick you up from the airport!"

"Done!" Rose sounded much happier. "God, Philippe is going to be so fucking jealous! He's gonna freak!"

25

"Any reason we're staking out the Railway Hotel tonight?" I asked Kalina as I slid onto the bench, managing not to spill any of the three drinks I'd just bought. Truth, Kalina and I had arrived at the most delightful little pub in Byron Bay, which was an old railway station converted into a bar. It had a gorgeous outdoor courtyard with benches and bar tables scattered around, and overlooked a wide green park which seemed to be full of hippies lying around in the late afternoon.

"No, not really," Kalina replied, taking her beer and sipping it casually.

I passed Truth over his non-alcoholic ginger beer, trying hard not to let my eyes linger on him or to think too much about how weird our little group of three was, and then turned back to fix Kalina with a look.

She was sitting a bit stiffly, or perhaps she was looking overly casual, and her head was resolutely turned in one direction.

"Oh, look," Truth said, oblivious to Kalina's awkwardness, and looking the other way. "There's Echo over there."

Kalina's head snapped around, colour rising in her cheeks.

Of course. I should have realised. Things between them must be a bit sketchy after this morning. I'd almost forgotten that Echo had street-tackled Kalina and she'd not only hit him but had sworn blindly at him, too.

Though, if she was acting like this now … that meant she must really like him.

She cared.

Oh my God, Kalina *cared about a guy*.

"Don't, Laura." Kalina shook her head at me. I was smiling so broadly at her that my cheeks were about to split open.

"What?" I asked innocently, taking a sip of beer. "Don't what?"

Kalina ignored me and turned to look at where Echo was, as if it didn't bother her in the least. "Do you know who those guys are that he's with, Truth?"

"Haven't seen them before," he replied.

Just then Echo glanced over and spotted our little group, surprise flickering in his eyes. Truth raised a hand to wave, and I followed suit. Kalina stiffened, looking away as if she hadn't noticed him.

"Aww, look at that, he's coming over here," I said, grinning at Kalina, whose cheeks were turning rather pink.

"He can do whatever he wants," Kalina replied haughtily, wrapping her hands around her pint glass as if it was a mug of hot chocolate.

"Hey, mate," Echo greeted Truth first, clapping him on the shoulder. "Laura, nice to see you again." He kissed me on the cheek. "And Kalina." He gave her a nod.

"Hi, Echo," I replied warmly. "Fancy running into you here." Oh, I could just feel the tension between them and it was marvellous. Echo slid onto the bench next to Kalina, leaving a gap that was not quite sizeable, and faced me.

"Pure coincidence, hey?" he said.

"Must be." I shrugged. "We just figured, well, why not check out the Railway pub tonight. Isn't that right, Kalina?"

"Yep." Kalina kept her eyes forwards, addressing Truth and me, as if Echo wasn't even there. "There's just as much chance of finding Ben here as any."

"Or his girlfriend," Echo added, turning finally to regard Kalina with a steely look in his eyes. "Maybe you can tackle her over a table and start a pub brawl."

"As if I'd attack her in here," Kalina snapped. "I'd be much more likely to drag her out to the park over there and beat her up."

I could have been mistaken, but I think Echo's beard twitched with a suppressed smile.

Truth cleared his throat. "Violence is never a good solution."

"Well, you haven't met Amy," Kalina muttered. "But I'm just joking. I wouldn't attack her."

Echo and I exchanged a look.

"Right, well, you all good for drinks here?" Echo eyed our nearly full glasses. "I'm going to grab something."

As he stood up, Kalina jumped to her feet, too. "I'll come with you," she said. "I want to see what else is on tap."

She did a very good job of not meeting my eyes as they left.

"What's all that about?" Truth asked me once they'd disappeared inside the pub.

"I think they've developed a bit of a love-hate relationship," I said with a laugh. "But actually, I think they really like each other. At least, I hope Echo likes Kalina as much as he seems to. I'd hate for her to get hurt by someone again."

"To love someone is to take a risk," Truth said, smiling out into the middle distance.

"Have you ever been in love?" I asked Truth, taking a breath and turning to look at him.

"Yes," he replied, smiling. "I've loved many people."

"No, I mean, have you ever *been in love*. With just one person. A girl ... or guy."

"Yes." Truth's smile broadened, and he looked at me with a glint in his eye. "Again, I've loved many people."

"Oh." Well. I wasn't quite expecting that.

"Most were brief, some a bit longer. But people move in and out of my life and I enjoy meeting, loving and then letting them go. You, for example, will be leaving Byron Bay soon, I think."

I raised my eyebrows at him. "Are you saying that you love me?"

"We are lovers, aren't we?"

"That's not the same thing. Although, don't get me wrong, I'm *not* saying … I mean, I don't …"

Oh shit. I hoped he didn't think I was expecting him to have fallen in love with me. That would be ridiculous.

Luckily, he laughed gently. "We all love in different ways. I've never anticipated that you were going to stick around, and so I've loved you in a certain way, knowing that you'll be leaving. Is it not the same for you? I hope you've enjoyed your time with me. And will continue to enjoy yourself while you remain here."

I bit my lip. Oh, he was so delightfully smooth. And accurate, I realised. There was a certain beauty in being with him, in knowing that it was temporary. It meant that every day, every encounter was enjoyed with such a heightened sense of being in the present.

"I have. And I will," I said, smiling. "You're right, though. I should … I *will* have to leave here in a couple of days, whether we've found Ben or not."

Otherwise, I could kiss my new career goodbye. Blow up my life once again.

"Hey." Truth's hand brushed lightly over my back, and I realised I'd been frowning down at my beer. I looked up at him. "Try not to let the future trouble you too much. You never know what's waiting for you right here, in the present."

Instantly, my mood lifted. He was right, of course, again. Problems rarely solved themselves simply by sheer force of brain power (or did they?). If I *was* going back to Sydney in a few days (was the jury still out? Or back in?), then I had a small window of time to make the most of Byron

Bay. Impulsively, I leaned in and kissed Truth.

His hand pressed more firmly on my back, drawing me to him, as our lips lingered on each other. Eventually, he drew back again.

"We'll have to continue this later, when there's a bit more privacy," he said, kissing me once more, quickly, before dropping his hand.

"Deal," I replied with a grin.

Before I could say more or try to strip his clothes off right there in the courtyard, a lanky guy who looked as if he'd just peeled himself away from a twelve-hour Xbox marathon suddenly appeared in front of us, clutching a wad of papers to his chest.

"Support the long-nosed potoroo," he said to us seriously, thrusting one of the papers down on the table in front of us. It was an amateur-looking flyer showing photographs of a small, forest-dwelling animal that looked like a fat ground possum with a long pointy nose like a bandicoot. Written in comic-sans font around the page were the words, "Protect the Long-Nosed Potoroo! Say NO to deforestation! Native animals are LOSING THEIR HABITAT! Down with Commercial Developments! Protect Byron Shire!" along with a link to a website and an Instagram account.

"Er, what?" I asked, looking up at the guy.

"The long-nosed potoroo, sometimes known as the truffle-eating potoroo, is being driven out of its habitat by greedy developers," the guy droned on, in what seemed to be a practised speech. "Byron Shire needs to be protected from commercial developments. The greedy owners of Yogatainable aren't just deforesting the forests, they're acting as a gateway development to destroy the peace and sanctuary of the region."

"I'm not sure that's true," Truth began, but the guy cut him off, his red-rimmed eyes sparking with excitement.

"Yogatainable is destroying our forests! Down with developers! Support the potoroo!"

The guy walked off, and I saw that there was a girl carrying a similar clutch of flyers talking to people at another table. She was gesticulating wildly, and her hair looked in dire need of a hairbrush.

"That's … interesting," I remarked. "Is it true? Is Yogatainable destroying the habitat of the potoroos?"

"Not that I know of." Truth frowned, looking genuinely troubled for the first time I'd seen. "The main building was already there when the developers bought the land, though some trees were cleared in order to extend it. Also, the phase-two accommodations would have cleared more land, I imagine, but that should have been kept to a minimum."

"Haven't you seen it yet? When Kal and I stumbled across those half-done buildings a few days ago, there was a lot of forest that had been cleared there."

"The area is off limits to staff and guests. I'm surprised you saw it. Every time I walk past that pathway now, there's a security guard directing people away."

"Really? That seems weird."

Truth shrugged. "There's been a reporter harassing the staff, trying to get a sneak peek of the stage-two development before the big opening weekend. I guess the owners don't want the surprise ruined."

"Isn't this weekend the big opening gala?"

"Yeah, it is."

"So, shouldn't everything be finished and open by now?"

Truth shrugged, seeming totally unconcerned. Then his eyes locked onto something in the distance, recognition flickering on his face.

"Meadow!" he called, lifting his hand to wave.

I looked over and saw that Meadow was crossing the park, heading towards the Railway Hotel. She spotted us and paused. Her eyes skated over the rest of the courtyard, and a scowl appeared on her face. She waved at us briefly, then pulled out her phone, tapped at it intently, then held it up to her ear as she turned and walked away in the other direction.

"Uh ... has she got a problem with me?" I asked.

Truth shook his head. "I'd say she doesn't want to run into the potoroo people. If they're handing out flyers here, then she's probably already aware of them."

"Right. So then—"

Suddenly I broke off, my attention snagging on the street corner far in the distance. A guy had just flashed past, a distinctive yellow t-shirt catching my eye.

Ben?

I launched off the bench, almost tripping as I vaulted to my feet.

"Wait here!" I shouted at Truth, darting past people and running out the front entry into the park beyond.

I ran like I'd never run before, blood surging all through my veins. My eyes were fixed on the street corner where I could still practically see the guy emblazoned on my retinas. He'd been with someone, I'm sure it was a girl, but they'd been walking quickly, heading up the street and out of sight.

Ben? Is it you? Please, please, let it be you!

It seemed as if there were people everywhere, blocking my path. In frustration, I had to slow, had to take my eyes off the street corner. I growled at a little girl riding a bike to get out of my way (not my finest moment) and ran across the road through a not-really-a-gap between cars (luckily they braked for me). And then I was there, in the spot where they'd been, and I started pelting down the street in the direction they'd been moving.

People muttered in annoyance and disgust as I flew past them, but I paid no attention. My eyes were scanning all around; ahead, over the road, into the shops, down branching streets. But I couldn't see a guy in a yellow t-shirt.

I ran two more blocks before I began to slow, realisation dawning that I'd lost him. And then my body seemed to realise what I'd just made it do. My legs turned to lead, my chest ached, and I needed to stop altogether and bend forwards, panting and heaving and trying to get my breath back.

No! No, no, no!

It had been him! I was sure of it! At least I was about ninety percent sure of it.

Oh God, *was* it even him? Had I just run a bloody marathon for nothing?

I felt dispirited (though strangely exhilarated?) as I made my much slower way back to the pub. Truth was still sitting calmly at the table, minding the drinks and my bag, and he looked concerned as I slid back onto the seat beside him. Echo and Kalina had also returned and they looked at me questioningly.

"I thought I saw Ben," I said, pulling my beer back towards me.

"What?!" Kalina jumped to her feet. "Where? When? Where'd they go?"

I shook my head. "I lost them. Might not have even been him."

Kalina slowly sat down again, looking shattered.

Truth put his arm around me. "That was a solid effort. I'd barely blinked and you were already out the gate."

"Yeah. Fat lot of good it did."

"This is getting …" Kalina trailed off shaking her head. "You know what? Fuck it. Let's just have fun tonight."

I laughed, simply because I didn't know what else to do. And then with a rueful smile I raised my glass. "Cheers to that!"

26

"I think I'm in love with Byron Bay," I said, scrunching up my kebab wrapper and reclining on the grass between Truth and Echo.

It was late, almost midnight. Way down the sand, the Beach Hotel was going off, the occasional swell of music reaching us on the breeze. But we were further down where it was quiet, and mostly we could just hear the waves lapping the shoreline and the occasional car cruising past in the distance.

"Yeah, I'm glad Ben chose this place to run away to," Kalina said. "Rather than ... I don't know, *Tasmania.*"

"What's wrong with Tasmania?" Echo asked, sounding surprised. "Have you been there?"

"Yeah right! Like I'm going to move to Australia from England and go live in *Tasmania.*"

"Oh, you're in for a shock, darling. Tasmania's the shit."

"Ha! Says a guy from Perth."

"I've been all over."

"Oh right. Because you just endlessly backpack around, don't you? What is it that you do again? Do you even have a job?"

"Sorry, I think I missed the conversation where you told me what *your* profession was? Or is terminal tourist a thing?"

Smiling, I turned away from Echo and Kalina and surveyed Truth. He was resting back on his elbows, his dreadlocks hanging down his back and his gaze soft on the horizon. We were the only people out on the beach this late, and it was really beautiful having the whole place to ourselves.

Truth glanced at me and returned my smile. "This is the best place in the world," he said quietly. "At least I think so."

I snuggled down next to him, ignoring Kal and Echo, who were still going strong at each other. Part of me could hardly believe how easily the four of us had fit together tonight. I felt like the time had passed in the blink of an eye, and still I was drawn to Truth. I liked watching him while he spoke, and the way he kept finding little ways to touch my hand or my arm. Now, I was the one pressing my shoulder up against his, unable to decide if I wanted to be back in his bed or simply just lying with him here, beneath the stars.

"You're so lucky you live here," I said quietly to him, our shoulders pressed together. "It really is such a calm, relaxed place. It makes me not want to leave."

"That's how most people end up here at Byron. They come for a visit and they simply stay. The atmosphere just seeps into their spirit."

His words hung in the air, trapped on the beach in front of us, just as the moon's reflection seemed caught in the ocean. What would it be like, I wondered, to never leave? To stay here in Byron Bay and create a new life for myself, far away from my old one?

I was surprised to find that it was tempting. Very tempting. I could become a new Laura, free from the fears and the shame of my old life. No one would know me up here. I could be whoever I wanted to be.

The wind blew warm but refreshing across my skin, catching a tendril of hair and sending it skating across my cheek. I dug my toes down further into the sand, feeling the cool layers beneath wrap around my feet.

It was easy to imagine a life where I focused only on the present. Everything would be decided based on how much enjoyment it gave me now. I could forget about the future. Forget about things like planning and worrying about money. Life should be lived in the moment. That, surely, was the very meaning of life? What gave me pleasure *right now*.

I felt giddy suddenly. I felt *alive*.

Impulsively, I jumped up to my feet. "Let's go for a swim!" I said, turning to the others. "Come on, guys! I've never swum in the sea at night before!"

"I'm not wearing swimmers." Kalina frowned up at me.

Truth rose gracefully to his feet, and in one swift movement had his shirt off over his head. "I'm game," he said. "And it's night-time. You don't need swimmers at all."

Truth started walking towards the water and I followed him, laughing. Behind me, I heard Kalina say, "Is he talking about skinny dipping?" and Echo reply with, "Bet I can beat you into the water."

Then we were all running and giggling and chucking our clothes off onto little piles on the sand. I got down to my bra and undies and hesitated for a second, wondering if I should just leave them on, but then I saw Truth's bare bum striding into the water and I thought, *fuck it*, and off they came, too.

Honestly, I had no idea where this new Laura had come from.

I felt so daring, so reckless being naked on the beach. Though, thank God it was night-time. Although the moon was quite bright, and Echo was not that far away, also stripping off. I ran to the water's edge and started wading in quickly, not thinking about much else other than, *Must get naked body under water as fast as possible.*

And within moments I was in, and Truth was not far ahead of me, and Kalina and Echo were crashing in nearby. I wasn't sure if I wanted to turn around and look at them or not. I mean, I could just sneak a glance at Echo, you know, to check things out and give Kalina a second opinion ...

But no, once seen these things could not be unseen. And since Echo was sleeping with Kalina, he was kind of like in brother territory for me.

So instead, I looked down. And—wow, the ocean was *dark* at night.

Like, really dark. Darker than dark. It was black.

The water wasn't cold, but still I shivered. Was this night swimming thing really a good idea? I couldn't see *anything* in the water. My body just disappeared beneath the surface like it wasn't even there.

Did something just brush past my leg?

Shit. I was being silly, wasn't I? There was no difference between swimming at night and swimming in the daytime. Just think about someone who was blind. They couldn't *ever* see what was in the water.

"Hey. You okay?" Truth was paddling over to me, his chest all gleaming wet and burnished shadows in the dark.

"Yes!" I squeaked, grabbing onto him as soon as he was close enough.

And oh … *hello.* I quickly became very aware that we were both naked.

Truth gasped as my hand landed somewhere rather inappropriate.

"Laura!" Kalina was swimming over to us. With a grin at Truth, I released him. "I'm not sure if this is a genius idea or I hate you right now!" she said.

"It's great!" I laughed, sounding far more confident than I felt. Although, pressed against Truth's warm body in the water, I wasn't feeling nearly so scared anymore.

"You guys better not be getting it on right in front of me." Kalina eyed us with a scowl.

"We're not that bad!" I said, feigning innocence even as my hand crept back across Truth's abdomen, hidden below the water. Behind Kalina, I registered Echo taking a big breath and then disappearing beneath the surface.

Truth's hand moved around my waist, pulling me closer to him, nothing but our shoulders out of the water. I giggled, looking at his face and the cheeky smile he was giving me.

"Yuck!" Kalina made a fake gagging sound. "I'll just— AARRGGGHHH!!!"

I sprung away from Truth, suddenly alert as Kalina screamed. But a second later, Echo surfaced behind her, laughing, and she began furiously whacking him.

"You dick! Oh my God, I'm going to get you for that! I'm going to—"

I didn't get to hear, or see, what Kalina was going to do, because there was an unexpected, and unfamiliar, shout from the shoreline.

"Oi! You lot!"

Shit! There was a middle-aged man, standing there among our discarded clothes, wearing cut-off jeans and a frayed-looking surfer t-shirt over his paunch.

Squealing, we all splashed around frantically, ducking down to make sure our bodies were *well* out of sight.

"What's he saying?" I asked, because as we were now making so much noise and were also quite far away from the shore, I couldn't make out what the guy was hollering at us.

"He's telling us to get out," Echo said, sounding surprised. Then he raised his voice to shout back at the man, "It's a free country, mate! Bugger off!"

But the guy kept yelling something, gesturing with his hands in an exaggerated "get back to shore" movement.

"No!" Kalina bellowed at him with a laugh. "We're not coming in!"

"Oh my God, what if he tries to join us?" I whispered loudly.

But the guy didn't seem in any way inclined to do that. His volume kept on rising, making it really clear that he wanted us to leave the water.

Kalina tutted in annoyance. "What's up his—"

"Hang on, shh." Truth seemed alert now, cocking his head to listen.

The man called out again, and even though I strained to listen the only words I caught were "closed" and "ark".

"What?" I asked, looking from Truth to Echo, who were both listening intensely. Kalina was still splashing around in a most unhelpful way.

"Fuck!" Echo suddenly swore. "We have to go in!"

"Why?" Kalina was languishing in the waves, looking like she was having a lovely time "We only just—"

"He said there's a shark in the water! The beach has been closed all afternoon!"

I felt like time slowed down then. Here we were, the only people in the completely pitch-black water. We were a sitting meal for a shark. It wouldn't even have to chew through our clothes. It was probably circling us right now, wondering which one to eat first.

Oh God. I *always* had a rule at beaches when I swam: never be the furthest person out in the sea. (Because then if a shark came, it would eat *them*, not you.) But I'd completely ignored my own rule. There were no other meal tickets around except us.

I was about to be eaten by a shark.

And then something really did brush past my ankle.

"AAARRGGHH!!!!" I screamed.

Panic ensued.

I couldn't remember ever swimming so fast in my life. If I thought we were splashing around before, it was nothing compared to the explosion of water around us as we all hightailed it for the shore line. I heard Echo yell, "What the fuck are you *doing*?" and I had the presence of mind enough to look back to see what he was talking about.

Honestly, if I hadn't been so scared, I might have started laughing.

Kalina wasn't even attempting to get back to shore. Despite the fact that even in the moonlight I could make out her face and she looked panicked.

But instead of swimming for land as any normal, rational, shark-fearing person should, she was *spinning around in a circle*.

"Kalina!" I tried to get her attention.

"I'm confusing it!" she called back, her voice high and desperate.

"Swim *in*, you muppet!" Echo called. And then he turned and swam back for her, grabbing her arm and pulling her in with him.

Truth was already out of the water, and I saw the man who'd warned us shaking his head disapprovingly (at the night swimming? At the nudity?) before turning and continuing his walk along the beach.

I dragged myself out of the water, feeling the relief flow through me like an injection. As fast as possible, I grabbed up my clothes and started pulling them on, ignoring how they clung and dragged unhelpfully on my wet skin. I was so focused on getting my clothes back on that I didn't even notice as Echo and Kalina made it out of the sea and started dressing.

Finally I felt the panic leaving me, to be replaced by a giddy, exhilarated feeling. The kind of shaky adrenaline surge you got when you had a near-accident in your car, or you stepped off a roller-coaster. I looked around, panting and wide-eyed at my friends, and found them all with priceless looks on their faces.

I started laughing.

Then Echo joined in. And Truth and Kalina. And then we were all laughing so hard that I had tears running down my cheeks.

27

Alright, so I learned a couple of things last night.

Firstly, we probably didn't need to panic *quite* so much about the shark. After checking out the Byron Bay news website, it turned out that, yes, a shark was spotted off the coast yesterday afternoon and the lifeguards had closed the beach. But the chances of the shark still hanging around when we were in the water were very slim. Plus, the beach was open again the next morning, so the shark must have been long gone.

Also, I did some googling and couldn't find anything to support the claim that spinning around in the water would deter a shark attack. I mean, sure, sharks apparently had electrical receptors in their snouts which could be disrupted. But there was nothing to indicate that the slow spinning of a human trying to swim in a circle would manage to do that.

So, lucky for Kalina that she didn't actually meet the shark.

Truth left the house early to go to work, so I took the opportunity to have a sleep-in in his bed. Kalina seemed to also be lying in with Echo, because there was no sign of either of them when I finally dragged myself out of bed and went down to the kitchen.

Despite the late hour, Meadow was bustling around putting out saucers of food for the cats, who seemed to eat on top of the kitchen bench. Smoosh-face looked up and glared at me when I walked in, as if daring me to make an attempt on his food bowl.

"Hi, Laura," Meadow greeted me cheerily. "How was your night last night?"

Oh God, was she referring to the bedroom I'd just emerged from? Suddenly, I wondered to what extent she was aware of the updated sleeping arrangements at the house, since neither Kalina nor I had slept in the room we'd actually rented for the past few nights. But then, I also remembered waving to her outside the Railway Hotel yesterday afternoon and decided that she must be referring to that.

"It was great!" I replied, coming over and patting the grey-striped tabby cat. "You should have come in and joined us. Though I suppose those potoroo people can be a bit of a nightmare."

Meadow looked confused for a beat, but then her expression cleared. "Right. Yes, they've been turning up at Yogatainable and trying to campaign out the front about the potoroos. Absolute waste of time—*of course* we have all the right permits and approvals for the expansion."

"So, it's going ahead this weekend, then?" Grey-stripes took the opportunity with my lapsed attention to whip his (her?) head around and bite my hand sharply. *Ow.* I quickly withdrew it.

"Absolutely!" Meadow didn't seem to notice the bench-top assault. "It's going to be huge. We've got our core influencers all lined up and DJ Beatrix will be playing. We've got curated health packages and luxury workshops. Guests from Lonely Planet, Trip Advisor and all the travel mags are coming. Yogatainable will be put on the world map for luxury health retreats, literally."

"Wow! That sounds really exciting."

"Definitely! And it's such a good opportunity. You know, we still have investment options open for anyone with vision." Meadow was getting on a real roll now with her speech. If that potoroo guy last night had even half of Meadow's passion about his cause, he might have got a bit more traction. "You know, people can own a little slice of Yogatainable for themselves. It comes with annual retreat options, VIP packages, first options on luxe stays. The works."

"Right. It sounds like a great opportunity for people into … that stuff."

Meadow nodded her head, then seemed to notice that one of the cats had tipped over its food bowl and was now playing chase with one of the biscuits across the bench. With a tut of annoyance, she picked up the cat and put it on the floor, then swept up the biscuits.

My eyes followed what she was doing, but then they snagged on the pile of stuff she'd left on the bench. Sitting beneath her keys and phone was a glossy Bali brochure.

"Oh, are you planning a holiday?" I asked.

"What?" she looked up at me with a frown.

I nodded at the brochure. "Bali? I've heard it's amazing there."

Meadow glanced at the brochure distractedly then shrugged. "I'm thinking about it. You know, after the opening, I might get away for a bit."

"I can imagine it must be tough at the moment, with the rush of trying to get it opened on time. How are the treehouse things going?"

Meadow frowned. "How do you know about those?"

"Oh … I stumbled across them when I visited. They were still under construction, back then … I mean, well a few days ago."

Meadow's gaze turned uneasy. "Yes. Well, that area's currently off limits for everyone. But it's all under control."

Her phone beeped with a notification and she jolted as she saw it. "Bugger, I'm running late! Sorry, Laura, hope you have a good day." She picked up her pile of things and left the house, already dialling a number as the front door swung closed behind her.

I turned back to Smoosh-face, who was still on the bench.

"Looks like it's just you and me now," I told him.

He glared at me for a moment. And then he *winked*. Although, that might just be because his second eye didn't close properly.

After giving him a final wary glance, I turned on the kettle and pulled out a mug and tea bag. And then I found myself gazing out the window, a frown on my face.

I couldn't shake the feeling that there was something off about Yogatainable. Like there was a secret lurking beneath the shiny surface. I wondered, with Meadow being a part owner, how much she knew about it? She certainly seemed passionate about the place, but then, also wary when I mentioned the treehouses. Could those things really be finished in time? And if not, well, what was the point in lying about it? Surely, the opening could just be pushed back until they were done? Unless, it *had* to be finished by a certain date for some reason. Like, if it wasn't done on time the local council would requisition the land for native wildlife again.

Hmm. Maybe those potoroo people really were a threat.

And if they were, well, then, what was really happening to the potoroos? Honestly, I'd never been much of an activist. Should I be doing something to help the potoroos? Was I just sitting back and ignoring the plight of an adorably fluffy ground possum?

I'd just finished making my tea when my phone bleeped with an incoming text message. Sighing, I pulled my thoughts away from Yogatainable and the potoroos. After all, Meadow *had* said that they had all the right permits, and I couldn't imagine that a luxury eco-retreat would be into native animal habitat destruction.

The text message was from Rose, letting me know she was now waiting at Sydney airport. With a grin, I double-checked her flight details, and was mentally working out what time I'd need to leave to go pick her up when an incoming call from my mum suddenly lit up the screen.

"Hi, darling!" Mum's cheery voice greeted me when I answered. "What are you up to today?" In the background, I could hear some high-pitched *ark, arks* going on.

"Hi, Mum. I'm still in Byron Bay."

"Oh, shoot. I was hoping to bring the dogs to visit you! They're desperate to go out, and Elle's trying to unpack her things and the dogs are getting a tad too interested in this strange furry thing she brought back from Columbia."

"Elle's back?!" I squealed in delight. "That's great! How is she? Is she there?"

"Oh yes, she's here somewhere. ELLE!" I flinched and held the phone away from my ear as Mum shouted through the house. "Your sister's on the phone! Oh, I don't know where she is. In the shower maybe. Muffin, stop that!"

"How are the dogs going?" I smiled as I picked up my tea and headed out into the backyard. "Any word on when Margaret's coming back for them?"

"Didn't I tell you? She's now staying in Denmark for at least another month. Her mother is *very* ill, but is clinging on desperately to life, poor Margaret. So, the pups are staying with me for a while yet. I'm getting quite fond of them."

"So I've seen. You're being very ... enthusiastic with the Instagram pictures."

"Isn't it great? It's so easy now, this photo thing. Every time I snap a picture of the dogs, I just whack it up online!"

"Yes. Although, you know, you don't need to post *every* picture."

"But I'm getting so many people liking my photos and commenting on them. People love seeing pictures of Baxter and Muffin! I've even got the hang of this hashtag thing. And you know, I've got so much time to take photos of them, I can really put a lot of effort into it. I can make it quite a thing. So," Mum took a deep, momentous breath. "I've made a decision."

"Yes? And what's that?"

"I've decided that I want to go viral. I'm going to be a social influenza."

A social *influenza*?! Oh dear. Should I correct her? No, best not to crush her dreams.

"Er, that's great, Mum. Do you know what's involved with that?"

"It seems simple enough. You just keep putting up photos and then bang, you're 'trendy' and people want to send you things!"

I heard a bit of a scuffle happening with the phone, and then it was my sister's voice blaring down the line at me.

"Laura! I'm back in Sydney! And you're living in Manly! And we've got a TON of stuff to catch up on, but first, can I move into your old bedroom?"

"Elle!" I gasped, starting to laugh. "Nice to hear your voice again!"

"I know, it's been so long and I've got so much stuff to do and Mum's insisting I unpack all of my shit—like, all of it—but I've run out of room and these dogs have apparently made my bedroom their home, so now it smells like dog and I've got nowhere to sleep!"

In the background, I heard Mum saying loudly, "It doesn't smell like dog!"

"Right!" I managed to say. "Well, yeah, I guess so. I'm not planning on moving back home."

"Great! See, Mum, told you she wouldn't care! Anyway, so how've you been? Mum said you're on holiday in Byron Bay? I'm so jealous!"

"Jealous? You've been on holidays for the last *year*! How was *your* trip?"

"Oh it was *amazing*. We did so much weird, cool stuff. But I'm so glad to be back somewhere that you can just drink water straight from the tap! Honestly, it's the little things that really get to you."

"I can imagine!"

"So, what are you doing in Byron Bay?"

"I'm here with my flatmate, Kalina, and we're trying to find our other flatmate, Ben. It's a bit of a long story. You'll have to meet them both soon!" I wondered if Ben would be returning to Sydney at all. And could I imagine him and Elle in the same room? Huh. They were pretty close in age, actually. Kalina and Elle, I could tell, would get on like a house on fire. And Elle and Ben … well, that was a weird thought.

"What do you mean, you're trying to find him? Where is he?"

"He's here, in Byron Bay, we just don't know where *exactly*. So, we're just sort of … looking around."

Wow. That really was all we were doing, wasn't it? But what else *could* we do?

"That sounds … kind of weird. And a bit boring."

"Oh, I'm doing other stuff, too. Like, going to the beach, and going out to the pubs." *And having the most amazing sex of my life with a Tantric-sex instructor.* "Plus, I've been doing some yoga. Did you know, there's this place here called Yogatainable and it's going to be the largest health retreat in the whole southern hemisphere? It's only just opening at the moment." Why did I feel the need to impress my sister? I had no idea.

"Wow. There were *heaps* of those wellness and yoga things in Mexico. Like, every hotel and every resort had some health thing. Marika and I were going to go to one, but they were all way too expensive. Though one of them turned out to be a massive scam—it was all over the news. The owners had stolen all this money and done a runner and the government was trying to track them down. And there were all these American tourists from Florida moaning about how they'd booked into these long-term health stays and now they wouldn't be able to get their seaweed back peels or whatever."

"Seaweed *back* peels? God, the things these places come up with!"

"I know! We saw a sign for a chilli-scrub foot soak, which apparently makes you have 'happy feet' for hours!"

We laughed and continued talking for another few minutes, but then Elle had to go because apparently, Baxter had started zooming around the lounge room while Muffin was stealing all of her socks from her suitcase. I hung up, still smiling, my mind transported back to Sydney.

But as her voice faded from my mind, I found myself gazing around at the beautiful tropical (if slightly overgrown) garden. Birdsong echoed from the surrounding trees, and the warm air carried the scent of the sea on it.

I realised I could imagine staying here. Waking up every morning in this beautiful town. I thought of Truth as he would be right then, shirtless in the yoga studio and leading an asana. He was a part of this town ... or was it that Byron Bay was part of him?

And was it becoming part of me, too?

28

At one pm I met Rose at the nearby Ballina airport. Even though she was apparently in crisis with her boyfriend, she still looked stunning in a white summer dress and wedges. Her hair and makeup could have been done by a professional, and if I didn't know better, I would have guessed she was a model just arriving back from a glamorous photo shoot in Fiji.

"Rose!" I hugged her at the gate. "Welcome to fabulous Byron Bay!"

"Look at you!" Rose squealed back, releasing me from her arms. "Laura, you look so tanned! And relaxed! And, I don't know, it's like you're glowing!"

"Really?" I laughed. "Well, there must just be something in the air up here."

"I want to hear all about it." She linked her arm through mine as we made our way out to the carpark. "Tell me everything you've been doing, starting with your hunt for the flatmate. Has there been *any* sign of him?"

I filled her in on our mostly futile search as we climbed into my car and began driving towards Byron Bay's town centre.

"Do you think she's really pregnant?" Rose asked when I'd told her about our Amy encounter.

"I certainly hope not. Ben is way too young to deal with something like that. He's only twenty-three!"

"The poor guy. It happens a lot, though, you know. Girls who get 'accidentally' pregnant on purpose."

"That just makes me feel sick thinking about it. The worst part is, now that she's told me and Kalina she's pregnant, I think that even if she wasn't, maybe she'll try to now."

"Is Ben sensible enough to use condoms every time?"

"He's sensible, but he's also super trusting. If she told him she was on the pill, he wouldn't doubt her."

"Ugh, that's so messed up. How can girls *do* that?"

"We think she's a gold digger."

"Well, that's hardly surprising. But what gold digger goes after a twenty-three-year-old chef? No offence, but she's not a very smart one if that's what it is."

I laughed. "Yeah, well, did I mention he's super generous? He'd do anything to make her happy."

"Poor guy. Sometimes that's the only way for them to learn, though, isn't it?"

"Let's hope not. So anyway, your turn. As much as I'm loving this last-minute trip, I'm guessing there's something not so good going on back in Sydney. What's the deal with Philippe?"

Rose made an elaborate groaning sound. "I'm pretty sure I'm messing everything up even more by being here. You know, it wasn't until I was on the plane that I realised I was doing exactly what he accused me of. I'm being a massive drama queen."

"You're allowed to be!"

"Well, either way, I'm still going to let him do the grovelling. I keep wondering if he's worked out that I've gone yet."

"You didn't tell him you were coming here?" I asked.

"I left a note for him on the bed. But he'd already gone to work when I left, so he won't find it until this afternoon. Now, I just need to relax and enjoy my mini-break and not think about him at all."

"Well, this is certainly a great place for that. I feel like my life in Sydney is so far away right now. It's easy to forget."

"Is that right?" I could sense Rose looking at me, her eyebrows raised. "And is there someone in particular you're trying to forget while you're here, Laura?"

"I don't know what you're talking about," I replied innocently, before quickly changing the topic. "Did you have lunch on the plane? Because I've found the most amazing restaurant here that does these vegan nourish bowls that are to die for."

⁓᧚〇

We walked into Half Cooked and got a table near the front of the restaurant, right by the open glass doors and terrace tables that spilled out onto the pavement. The place was filled with a slightly more upmarket crowd than the sandy-clad hippies that usually rolled in off the beach. I realised we were actually quite lucky to get a table here at all, given how packed it was.

"Alright, give me the lowdown on Byron Bay so far," Rose said, once we'd sat down and the waiter had brought us some water and taken our order. "I'm sensing there's more to tell in the way of this guy you're living with."

"I wouldn't say I'm living with him—it's a share house. There's a number of people all staying there."

"Uh-uh. But only one hottie?"

I couldn't help smiling at that. "He is pretty gorgeous."

"Ha! I knew it! So, have you slept with him?"

"What do you think?"

Rose laughed. "God, I miss being single."

"Rose! You were single for all of about five minutes after you left Christian, remember?"

She waved her hand dismissively. "I know, I don't actually want to be single. Philippe is … well, when he's not being a dick he's actually pretty cool."

While Rose was speaking, a group of people stood up from a table on the other side of the room, and my attention was caught as I realised Meadow was one of them. She was wearing a smart black skirt and floaty blouse, which was a far cry from the activewear she'd been sporting a couple of hours earlier. Her hair was tied up in a textured ponytail that managed to look both relaxed and professional at the same time. The two men she was with, whose hands she was now shaking, were also dressed smartly in chinos and collared shirts.

They all began filing out of the restaurant, and I waved to Meadow as she passed.

"Laura!" She came over with a broad smile. "Fancy seeing you here."

"Small town, I guess," I said, and tried not the think of the irony that this was exactly the sort of run-in encounter I'd been hoping to have with Ben. "This is my friend, Rose. She's come up for a few days. Rose, Meadow is … well, I suppose the landlord at the house I'm staying at."

Meadow laughed. "I'm not sure 'landlord' is very accurate, but yeah, I'm organising the rental rooms there."

The two men were now standing out on the street and they'd turned to look back to see where Meadow was. She gave them a quick smile and held up a hand to halt them. "Well, lovely meeting you. I've got to dash though."

As Meadow turned to leave, the folder she was carrying knocked into Rose's chair, and its contents slipped out. She managed to grab most of them, but a few papers dropped down to the floor.

"Shit!" Meadow swore as she stooped down to grab them.

One had fallen near my foot, so I quickly bent down and picked it up. As I turned it over to hand it back to her, I couldn't help reading the top line of the document, which was in bold text, and said, "Investment Agreement". I gave Meadow a knowing smile as I handed it back. Obviously, those guys were the sorts of visionaries who wanted to invest in a place like Yogatainable, but she looked irritated as she snatched it out of my hands and stuffed it back into the folder along with the other papers.

"Sorry." Meadow shook her head. "That was clumsy of me." She seemed to pause and take a breath once the documents were safely tucked back in their folder, then her tight expression cleared and she was all relaxed ease again, smiling at us broadly. "Well, I must dash. Lovely to meet you, Rose. Bye, Laura."

She walked more carefully out the door, holding the folder tightly into her chest. Once she'd left with the two men, Rose turned to me with her eyebrows raised.

"That was a bit weird," I said. "She's been the queen of chill every time I've spoken to her before." I frowned, wondering if maybe Meadow was just a bit worried about having dropped some confidential documents on the floor. But then the waiter appeared with our meals and I forgot all about it.

"So," I said to Rose once the waiter was gone. "What's going on with Philippe? I thought things were going really well between you two?"

"They were." Rose sighed. "He was so perfect up until now. Every morning he'd get up early and bring me a cup of tea while I was still in bed. And he'd go out for a morning run and come home with croissants."

"Wow. Tea and croissants. How could a man even *get* more perfect?"

Rose rolled her eyes at me. "Oh, stop it. I know he's been spoiling me and that I shouldn't expect the breakfasts in bed to continue. And I also know that nobody is perfect. I guess I just wasn't ready for the bubble to burst."

"What happened?"

Rose shook her head, her eyes going distant. "It was so *stupid*. Especially because we've been getting so close lately. Honestly, Laura, we've started having these really romantic nights in together. Like with scented candles, and baths and massages. And even in the mornings, we'll go out for breakfast and then come home and just spend all morning in bed. It was like that just yesterday. We had this amazing morning, where we walked around Pyrmont and went to our favourite cafe, and then came home and had the most *intense* session together. But then after lunch, that's when this whole incident started when I reminded him about the christening and he acted all surprised and said he couldn't go."

"Is it really such a big deal?" I asked gently. "I mean, maybe he really did forget about it, and maybe his football team is really counting on him."

Rose scoffed. "It's football. This is family. He should know which one to pick."

"Right. So, then what happened?"

"To be honest, I can barely remember. All I could think was how much this reminded me of Christian, and how his work would always come first."

"Oh, Rose. You didn't transpose your old frustrations with Christian onto Philippe, did you?"

Rose grimaced. "I may have accidentally called him Christian. Just once."

"Rose!"

"I know! Oh God, I'm the bad guy here, aren't I?"

"I wouldn't say..."

"Oh, you don't have to say. I can see it in your expression."

"Well, if there's one thing I know about Philippe it's that he seems to be really, *really* into you. So, I don't think you need to worry about him turning into another Christian."

"Ugh. I suppose I'll have to buy him a nice present while I'm here."

I laughed. "That might be a good idea."

"Anyway." Rose shook her head. "Let's not talk about Philippe anymore. This little getaway is about me, and I want to have some fun. So, come on, Laura. Tell me all about the guy you're now sleeping with."

I returned her grin and bit my lip. "Well. Did I mention he's a yoga teacher?"

"No! Didn't I tell you they were the *best?*"

"That's not all, though." I leaned in, dropping my voice to a conspiratorial whisper. "He's also a Tantric-sex instructor."

"Get out! Alright, I want to hear about this from the beginning. How did it start?"

Trying not to smile too broadly, I began telling Rose all about Truth and what had happened between us (without going into *too* much detail). Our lunch arrived while I was talking, but I managed to continue the story between mouthfuls.

"So, let me get this straight," Rose interrupted me after a while. "You and Kalina are both sleeping with guys who just happen to live at the house you're renting?"

"Yeah! Weird, hey? But also, very convenient."

"Have you done a foursome or anything?"

"No!" I laughed. "God, no ... though, actually, we all went skinny dipping at the beach last night."

"Seriously? Did you check out the other guy? Which one of them is more hung?"

"Rose! I'm not that bad. But the funniest thing happened! Kind of scary at the time, but funny now."

I began recounting the shark incident, and by the time I got up to Kalina spinning around in the water, Rose and I were both in fits of giggles and I struggled to even finish the story.

"We were all swimming in, and Kal was just spinning around!" I managed to say between giggles, wiping tears from my eyes. "The man on the beach must have thought she was a nut job!"

Rose was laughing uncontrollably as well by this point, and I was glad to see her back in a good mood.

"Oh my God, that's so funny!" she said, wiping tears from her face. "She

243

found Amy's theory so hilarious, and then she did it herself!"

I was laughing so hard that I found I had to hold my stomach to keep from falling off my chair. But then I realised that Rose had quite abruptly stopped laughing.

I looked up to find her frozen, her eyes wide, a look of horror creeping over her rapidly paling face.

"What is it?" I whispered urgently, glancing over my shoulder to try to work out what she was looking at. Had someone she knew just walked in? Had Philippe suddenly arrived, having followed her up here? But I couldn't see anyone that could possibly have triggered this reaction.

Turning back towards Rose, I looked more closely at her face. Her eyes were sort of out of focus, and I realised she wasn't actually looking at *anything*.

"Rose? Rose, what is it?" I whispered, my heart dropping unpleasantly. Oh God, was she about to have a seizure or something? Was Rose a closet epileptic and I never knew?

Her face was so pale it had started to take on a greenish tinge. But then she unfroze slightly, blinked a few times and finally focused her wide-eyed stare on my face.

"Oh. My. God." she said, her voice low and urgent. And then she gulped.

"What? What is it?" I repeated. What was happening?

"Laura, something horrible has just happened."

"What? Rose, you're freaking me out."

Rose shook her head the tiniest bit, closing her eyes and looking like she was in pain. Her body was completely stiff as if she was terrified of moving at all. "No, I mean something awful has just happened to me," she whispered.

I looked her up and down—did she spill something on herself? Or did she just realise she'd forgotten to take the pill and she must be pregnant?

Then a thought dawned on me. "Is it your period?" I glanced dubiously at her white dress. (This was precisely why I would *never* wear a white dress.)

Rose shook her head slightly. "Worse," she said.

"Worse? What on earth could be worse than that?"

Rose was gripping the table like it was the only thing grounding her at the moment, her knuckles as white as her face.

"I've. Just. *Leaked*," she whispered, mortified.

A leak? Oh. Ooohhh ...

"Well, gosh, I mean bladder leakage isn't that bad, there are all those ads about it nowadays so people understand, and really lots of women get it ..." I trailed off as Rose opened her eyes and looked at me furiously.

"Not bladder leakage!" she hissed. "I'm not that old! I meant," she dropped her voice, her jaw gritting together as if she'd just eaten a bee, "yesterday, Philippe and I had anal sex and I've. Just. Leaked."

"Oh!" I sat back in my seat, a little stunned. "What, and it's only just come out?"

Alright, that was probably the stupidest thing I'd said all afternoon. But, honestly, I was just trying to process the logistics of this. I mean, was that even possible?

Rose screwed up her face and made a little whining sound in her throat. "I thought it was all gone! I mean I've heard that sometimes you can have a bit of spillage a few days later, but I've never had this before! Oh my God, Laura, I'm wearing a *white dress*! What am I going to do?"

I couldn't help myself. I started giggling again.

"Laura!" Rose hissed. "This isn't funny!"

But the giggles just kept coming out. My stomach muscles were out of my control.

"I'm sorry!" I managed to gasp. "But it's ... I don't know what else to do!"

"Laura!" Rose hissed at me again. "Stop it, this is serious! What am I going to do? I can't stand up, I'm wearing a fucking white dress!"

I took a few deep breaths, forcing myself to calm down. Rose was looking at me like she might start crying, so I quickly banished any remaining giggles.

"Okay, okay, don't worry, we can deal with this," I said, flipping into action mode.

"I need to get to the bathroom," Rose said urgently, eyeing the doorway on the other side of the room. Between us and the bathroom, there were about five tables of people all sitting and talking over their lunch.

"Alright." I cast around for something that could help. "We've each got a paper serviette, which probably … won't help. Can you use your bag to cover yourself?"

Rose glanced at her handbag and looked doubtful. "It might help a bit. So long as nobody's looking."

"Okay, how about this. You stay here and act calm and I'll run out to the car and grab my sarong. You can wrap it around yourself to get to the bathroom."

Rose looked uncertain, but then she nodded. "Can you grab me some new clothes out of my suitcase, too?"

"Of course! Good idea. Okay, sit tight. I mean," I started laughing again, "not tight … just … I'll be back."

I took off out of the cafe and ran down the street to where I'd left my car. Ignoring the rush of inferno air that came when I opened the door, I managed to get Rose's suitcase open and pulled out some denim shorts and a top. Grabbing my sarong as well, I ran back to the cafe, slowing as I arrived so I could enter calmly and not draw any attention.

"Mission successful," I whispered to Rose, handing over the items.

"Alright. Tell me when no one is looking."

I surveyed the cafe while Rose got the sarong ready around her hips. Once the waiter had disappeared back into the kitchen and the other diners were all calmly eating or staring at their phones, I whispered, "All clear! Go!"

I shouldn't laugh at my friends. I really shouldn't. But there was something immensely funny about watching Rose try and slide herself off the chair and then do a very stiff walk towards the bathroom with a sarong wrapped around her waist.

Once she was safely inside, I went up to the counter and paid for our lunches, then went to join her in the bathroom.

"Rose?" I called, standing outside the one occupied cubicle.

"Oh my God, Laura, it's terrible!" she moaned from inside. "My dress has a stain on it that looks unmistakably like shit!"

I covered my mouth so Rose couldn't hear me choking back some laughs.

"Don't worry about it. Just get changed and you can figure out what to do with the dress later."

"Laura?" Rose asked, her voice low and meek.

"Yes?"

"I need another favour."

"What?"

"Could you please get me some clean undies?"

PUSH NOTIFICATION
Lunar Period Tracker App
Feeling moody? Based on your predicted period cycle, you have a high chance of PMS today.

NEW MESSAGE
From: Yogatainable Lifestyle Retreat at 2.19 pm
Namaste, Laura. Join us this Saturday for the launch of Yogatainable Luxe Link—a yoga love event. Free goddess workshops, Oracle Card readings and custom Yogatainable organic vegan smoothies by Juice Essence from 11–3. Special appearances by Phoenix Fox and What Jane Ate on the mats. We hope you have a radiant day! 🙏

NEW MESSAGE
From: Kalina at 12.07 pm
🖼️
OMG I think I can see Chris Hemsworth at the beach!!! Is it him???

29

After making it out of the cafe, I dropped Rose off at the luxury five-star hotel she'd booked herself into. I'd offered to take her back to the house for a drink and to get cleaned up properly, but she'd insisted that she just wanted to organise a hotel room where she could take a long, hot shower followed by a soak in a luxurious bathtub.

To be fair, Rose still looked pretty traumatised when I dropped her off at the uber-luxe reception area of the Byron at Byron Hotel. Part of me wondered what it would be like to be able to afford to stay there. But then I wouldn't have met Truth, I reminded myself.

"Where's Rose?" Kalina asked as I arrived back at the house.

She was lying on one of the couches, phone in hand, her hair wet and her skin peachy, as if she'd spent a good chunk of the day in the sun. Echo was sitting on the other couch, doing something on his laptop.

"I dropped her at her hotel. She's had a ... tiring day."

Kalina yawned. "Well, I spent a few hours at the beach walking up and down. You can guess how successful that was."

I flopped down on the couch next to her with a sigh. "I didn't see Ben either. Though I ran into Meadow again. Obviously, getting some new investors for Yogatainable."

"What?" Echo looked up sharply. "What do you mean?"

I shrugged. "She was having a business meeting. And she told me this morning about how Yogatainable is such a great investment opportunity for people with 'vision.'"

Echo frowned at me for a moment, then turned his attention back to his laptop and started typing rapidly.

"You know, I feel like there's something a bit off about Yogatainable," I continued after a pause.

"It's killing the potoroos?" Kalina offered.

"Not just that. I drove past so many promo people in town this morning, all on the street corners. They're really talking up this whole Luxe Link thing and the big opening gala that's happening this weekend. But there's no *way* those treehouses would have been finished. Remember how we overheard that scary woman on the phone, Kal?"

Echo glanced up again, looking interested.

"Vaguely." Kalina scrunched up her nose. "I just remember hiding and trying not to make any noise."

"The skills of a true detective," Echo commented.

"Hey!" Kalina threw a pillow at him. "It had nothing to do with Ben!"

"Did *you* hear anything of interest, Laura?" Echo asked.

"The woman was talking about some deadline having to be met, and no option to push the date back, I think. Also, something about a supplier and the terms. And whoever she was talking to sounded like they were about to lose their job."

"So?" Kalina said. "It was obviously nothing. The things must all be finished if they're going ahead with the launch party. They certainly have no shortage of money based on all the marketing stuff they're doing!"

Kalina laughed, but Echo was still frowning, his expression matching the unease I was feeling.

"That's just it, though," I said. "Why is Meadow still running around getting investors if the place is already finished? I mean, I don't know much about finance—"

"Says the girl who used to work at Tiger Finance," Kalina interjected.

"But surely, the investments come in *before* the thing is even started?" I finished, ignoring Kal. Honestly, I worked in the *marketing incentives* team at Tiger—totally different to financial investments. "I'm just saying," I went on. "There's something … not right going on there."

Echo took a breath and opened his mouth to say something. But then he kind of paused and closed it again, exhaling slowly.

Kalina, who was facing away from Echo, shrugged. "Maybe there's going to be a phase three? An Ultra Luxe Link or something. Maybe *that's* what the treehouses were for."

"Maybe," I said. Could it be that simple? "It's funny how big all these eco-resort things are becoming. My sister, Elle, said they were all over the place in Mexico."

"Maybe that's where Meadow got the idea from," Kalina said. "She used to live in Mexico, didn't she?"

"She did?"

We both looked over at Echo for confirmation.

He scratched his beard thoughtfully. "Yeah, she did. So did Truth. That's where they met, at a yoga centre there."

"Right. So Meadow travels in Mexico, falls in love with eco-yoga-luxe things, and decides to come back and open one in Byron Bay." Kalina shrugged again. "It's hardly a conspiracy."

"Unless she's just really bad with money. Though she has business partners here, doesn't she?"

Echo nodded. "Meadow's one of the smaller partners. There are two others who own eighty percent of the company and do most of the running of the business, a married couple. I'd guess that's the woman you saw talking on the phone."

"Still, hardly a conspiracy," Kalina said, shooting Echo a curious look.

"You know, Elle mentioned something else about Mexico. Something about a scandal with one of the yoga places where the owners had taken off with all the money and the government was trying to track them down. Maybe that's somehow connected with this!"

I glanced at Echo and Kalina hopefully, as if I'd just hit on something really good. Echo was staring at me with a frown on his face, and looked like he wanted to say something again but was reluctant to.

Kalina just looked sceptical. "That sort of shit doesn't happen in Australia, surely?"

"It can do," I said. "At Tiger Finance, there was a whole team dedicated to bad debt recovery, because people would take off overseas without repaying their loans."

"Well, lucky Ben doesn't know Meadow and doesn't give two tosses about yoga," Kalina said. "Because he's just been told that he's getting half a million quid to do whatever he wants with."

"Half a million *dollars*?" I gasped. "Are you serious?"

"Yeah. That's what Lucas said. That's Ben's inheritance from his great-aunt."

I looked up at Echo, who was looking equally shocked. "Oh my God," I said. "Let's definitely *not* tell Meadow about that."

"Er ... hopefully she's not listening."

"What?!"

"I thought she was here?" Kalina sat up and looked around.

I glanced about in surprise as if Meadow was going to jump out from behind the couch and yell, "Surprise!"

Shit! What had we just been saying about her?

"Her bedroom door's been shut all afternoon. I thought she must be taking a nap or something." Kalina stood up off the couch and headed for the stairs. "Hopefully, she's not here ... but I'll go check."

Echo and I sat and listened to Kalina's footsteps disappear up the stairs. There was silence for a few moments, and then ...

"Hey, Echo?" Kalina's voice floated down to us, sounding confused. "Is

Meadow usually super neat and ... minimalist?"

"What?" Echo rose off the couch.

Kalina appeared at the top of the stairs, looking worried. "Because either she likes living in a totally bare room, or else she's cleared out all her stuff."

There was a beat when none of us moved or said anything. Then Echo dropped his computer on the couch and took off up the stairs, and I followed close on his heels.

I gasped when I saw Meadow's room. Kalina was right. It was completely stripped. The bed and mattress were still there, and two chests of drawers and a TV. But a quick investigation showed that the wardrobe was almost completely empty (save a few hideous tops that were rightly abandoned) and the drawers had been emptied.

Echo swore and took off back down the stairs again. Feeling perplexed, I glanced at Kalina and saw her mirroring my expression. We ran down the stairs as well and found Echo disappearing out into the back garden with his phone held to his ear. He closed the door behind him, shutting us inside.

"*What* is going on?" I asked Kalina. "I'm so confused."

"This is now just a bit weird," Kalina said. "I thought this was Meadow's house? Or, at least, she's in charge of it?"

"I saw her just this morning. No, I saw her only a couple of *hours* ago. She acted totally normal."

Just then, my phone bleeped with an incoming text message and I distractedly picked it up to take a look.

"It's from Rose," I said, frowning as I unlocked it. And then I gasped, my attention fully engaged.

"What does it say?" Kalina asked, coming over to me.

I looked up at her, my eyes wide. Then I held out the phone so she could read the text, all three words it contained:

I've found Ben.

30

"Rose? Where are you?" I asked as soon as the phone connected. I pushed the loudspeaker button so Kalina could hear too.

"I'm behind a plant."

"What?"

"I'm behind a big pot plant," Rose repeated in a stage whisper. "I'm looking right at Ben and Amy."

"But where? Where are they?"

"They're here, at my hotel."

Kalina looked at me questioningly.

"The Byron at Byron?" I asked.

"Yes. They're standing in the lobby. I think they're staying here. Ben's in board shorts and Amy's in a dress, and it looks like they've been hanging at the pool."

Kalina punched her fist into her other hand with a loud huff of frustration. "I called that hotel! I bloody called them and asked after Ben and they said he wasn't staying there!"

Behind us, Echo came back in from outside, looking agitated, his phone being tucked away in his pocket.

"Trust Amy to pick the most expensive hotel around here," Kalina fumed.

"What are they doing?" I asked Rose.

"I don't know. They're talking to the concierge. Ben looks a bit lost or something. Amy's doing all the talking."

Kalina made a scoffing sound. "We have to go there, now, before we lose them again."

I nodded.

"Oh, hang on a second," Rose said, and we all froze. "A girl's just come and met them. She looks ... Yeah, I think it is. It's that girl we saw at the restaurant, Laura, your landlord."

"What?" My eyes snapped up to Kalina's, and she also looked shocked. "Meadow? Meadow is there with them? Are you sure?"

"Yeah, it's definitely her. She's giving them both hugs. And now they're talking and laughing."

"Shit!" Echo swore. "It makes sense now!"

Kalina and I both stared at him like he was talking gibberish. "What makes sense?" Kalina asked.

"We've got to get there, now," Echo said, grabbing his keys off the table. "Your friend could be in big trouble."

"How do you know this?" Kalina demanded.

"Just ... Laura, make sure your friend doesn't lose them. We'll be there in ten minutes."

I had no idea why Echo was suddenly so involved, but at least we were all on the same page that we should hightail it to the hotel. "Rose, did you hear that? Don't let them out of your sight!"

"Roger that," Rose whispered in her best covert voice. "They're on the move, but I'll tail them. Text me when you're nearby."

"Got it." I hung up and raced outside along with Kalina and Echo. We all piled into Echo's dual-cab ute, me in the back, and moments later Echo had thrown it into gear and we were screeching out onto the road, leaving a huge cloud of dust in our wake.

"Alright, explain," Kalina demanded. "How do you suddenly know more about this than we do?"

Echo looked a bit uneasy and he shot Kalina a slightly guilty look before responding. "Okay. So, I haven't been entirely honest with you about what I'm doing in Byron Bay."

"You think? I may not be as on the ball as Sherlock Holmes, but even I worked that out. What is it, then? You and Meadow aren't drug traffickers, are you?"

"No!" Echo laughed. "You don't seriously think I'd do that?"

"Well, I don't know what to think! There's something sketchy about you, I know that."

"Sketchy? Me?" Echo feigned being offended.

"You're dodgy. Even Laura thinks so."

"Hey, don't drag me into this!" I protested.

"What did I do to you, Laura?" Echo gave me a mock-hurt look in the rear-view mirror.

"Back to the point," Kalina snapped. "*Explain.*"

"Alright." Echo's knuckles whitened on the steering wheel. "I've been working a fairly discreet freelance contract up here. Investigation work."

"Right ... for whom? And investigating what?"

"I can't say for whom. It's a private contract."

"What, is it ASIO?" I leaned forwards, intrigued. "Are you actually a spy?!"

"No! And I didn't say that. I'm freelance, working for a friend. Anyway, the point is that I've been looking into Yogatainable. It's a pretty dodgy set-up, and we're trying to work out just how deep it goes."

"And *you're* looking into it? You're not even good at yoga!" Kalina seemed most affronted by the fact that Echo was the chosen spy.

"I'm a data engineer, usually. As I said, I'm not a spy, I'm just doing a favour for a friend."

"Well, I'm glad you're not a spy, because you'd be a terrible one! Honestly, have you even heard the term 'subtle'?"

"Look, my spy skills are not what's important here. The thing is, Meadow has been taking investment money from people for something that doesn't exist. This whole 'Luxe Link' thing they're plugging is a massive sham. And now we've just found out that your flatmate's about to inherit a chunk of money, and he's meeting with Meadow right now."

"Oh, shit." Kalina turned to look at me, horror on her face.

"But how did Meadow know that?" I protested. "We never told her much about Ben at all! She certainly had no idea he's got any money."

"His girlfriend," Echo answered. "I've been trying to work out how Meadow was targeting certain people. There are links to a second operative who lures them in, and I think this girl might be it."

"*Amy?* An *operative*? Surely not." I couldn't get my head around it.

"I fucking *knew* there was something wrong with her!" Kalina shouted, punching her hand into her fist again. "Of course! Wasn't it just so convenient that Amy turned up literally *days* after Ben's aunt died! She's a fucking maggot, that's what she is!"

"This all sounds so far-fetched! I mean, I don't like Amy either, but could she really be that ... predatory?"

"Of course she could! How else do you explain what's going on now?"

I certainly couldn't.

"We're here," Echo said, turning the car abruptly off the road and barrelling way too fast down the driveway of the Byron at Byron Hotel.

While Echo found a parking space, I texted Rose that we'd arrived, and just as we were clambering out of the car she called me.

"Laura?" she whispered.

"Yes! We're here! Where do we go?" I pressed "loudspeaker" again so everyone could hear.

"Alright, you're pretty close. They're sitting at a table together near the pool. I'm sitting a few tables away, pretending to read a magazine. It looks like they've got some sort of paperwork with them."

"Not good!" Echo called as we ran through the carpark towards the entryway to the hotel.

"Rose! Don't let Ben sign anything! Oh God, how do we get to the pool?"

"He's ... hang on a second, Ben's now standing up and walking away from them. Shit! He's coming this way."

"Rose? Where do we go?" We slowed down as we came up the steps to the entrance hall, which was all lush wooden floorboards and wicker lounges, pale beechwood tables and arty ceiling fans. A concierge looked up at us and smiled, and there were two girls lounging nearby sipping herbal tea. I held up my head and walked straight ahead as if I knew exactly where I was going.

"Ben's walking off!" Rose said urgently. "I don't know where—he's just storming away. Shit, I don't know if I can follow him! The other two are now getting up as well and heading the other way. Where *are* you guys?"

"We're in reception! Where do we go?"

"Just walk straight ahead, and you'll come to the pool. I'll meet you there."

"Alright, we're on it." I put down the phone and quickened my pace, Kalina and Echo right beside me. We emerged on the other side of the lobby onto the most gorgeous deck that was all inviting lounges overlooking the swimming pool, a wall of rainforest rising up not far away.

I began scanning all the people around us, and a second later Rose appeared, wearing a sarong tied over swimmers, huge sunglasses and an enormous wide-brimmed hat.

"Ben went that way!" Rose pointed at the pathway that led straight ahead into the rainforest. "Amy and the other one took off in that direction, towards the rooms."

"You guys go find your mate," Echo said. "I'll go after Meadow."

We all nodded, and I gave Rose a quick hug. "Thank you so much! Do you mind …?"

"I'll stay here and make sure Ben doesn't escape." Rose nodded enthusiastically. It seemed she was rather enjoying the excitement.

"Okay! Let's go!"

Kalina and I took off towards the rainforest pathway at a run. We were so close now! I could hardly believe that after all this time, all this searching, we were finally about to find Ben!

Within moments of entering the curving rainforest pathway, we lost sight of the resort area and all human sounds became muted. Now, we were on a narrow wooden boardwalk that twisted and turned through a sea of paperbarks and palm trees, the air filled with the buzzing melody of birdsong and cicadas.

It felt wrong to keep running in such a place, so I slowed to a brisk walk, Kalina right beside me. My heart was pumping madly in my chest, and I felt like I was in a James Bond movie or something. But although I kept peering ahead, trying to see through the screen of trees, there was no sign of Ben on the pathway. Surely, he couldn't have got so far ahead?

The path twisted again and then we were at a fork, two very different directions spiralling off before us.

I glanced at Kalina.

"You go that way, I'll take this," she said. "Text me if you find him."

"Got it."

I quickened my pace, passing beautiful wide ponds covered in waterlilies and a raised tranquil pagoda. I realised that I had no idea what I was going to say to him when I found him. But that wasn't important right then. The important thing was just finding him.

Minutes passed and I couldn't believe just how long this rainforest walkway was. I kept passing all these gorgeous little meditation spots and bridges and things which would have been lovely to spend an afternoon at if I was staying at the hotel, but right then all I could think was: *Where does this bloody pathway end?*

And then I hit another fork. Shit! I had to pick a direction, and I had no idea which one Ben would have gone in. The sign pointing left indicated that was towards accommodation, and I had the vague sense that was the direction Echo had taken, so I went right, instead.

Now, I broke into a run again. The path had become straight, running along the bank of a river filled with ducks and birds and waterlilies. I was sweating and panting, and telling myself that I really *had* to get fitter when I saw the end of the pathway in sight.

And oh, no! It ended with a small lookout overlooking the river. A small lookout that was currently empty.

I slowed as I approached, deciding I'd stop briefly to catch my breath before backtracking. But as I entered the wide platform of the lookout, I realised there was a bench seat hidden behind the trees.

And there was someone currently sitting on the bench.

"Laura?" Ben looked up at me.

"Ben!" I flung myself at him, practically knocking him right off the bench as I pulled him into a tight hug. He sat stiffly, evidently rather surprised, then gave me a hesitant pat on the back.

"What are you doing here?" he asked as he gently pushed me off him.

"We've come to rescue you!" I started babbling, still feeling completely breathless and slightly hysterical. "Ben, you have n*o idea* how long we've been looking for you! I mean, okay, this will sound ridiculous, but, Ben, Amy is crazy. Like, legitimately crazy! Didn't she even tell you we were here? We've been trying to get in touch with you for ages! And Lucas is worried about you, and Celeste can't get a hold of you, and Amy—oh God—please tell me that she's not pregnant and that you're not engaged to her, because we saw her and she implied she was pregnant and we've been freaking out and now we know what Meadow's really like and why were you meeting up with her and please tell me you haven't handed over all your inheritance to her!"

"*What?*" Ben looked a little bit freaked out by my outburst, which was probably fair. I paused and took a really long, deep breath.

"Sorry. Hang on, let me just ..." I trailed off as I shot a quick message to Kalina saying, simply, *Found him.*

Then I tucked my phone away and looked at him. And I mean really looked at him.

He seemed exhausted. Dark circles under his eyes. Shoulders slumped. Not at all like someone who was staying in a luxury hotel resort.

"Ben? Are you okay?" I asked carefully.

He sighed and rubbed his face, his eyes casting around at the river before us rather than meeting my gaze.

"What's happened?"

He shook his head, appearing a bit shell-shocked. Then he turned to regard me warily. "Why are you here, again?"

"Um, well. Kalina and I thought we'd better come up here and rescue you," I muttered, feeling a bit sheepish. It seemed a bit ridiculous now, saying it to him.

It wasn't any surprise, then, when he started laughing.

"So, Kalina's here as well, is she? I should have known."

"She's only worried about you. She's not trying to sabotage your relationship or anything. Not really ... it's just. Well, she's just being a good friend."

Ben shook his head, but he was smiling ruefully as well. "You know, if you'd come here yesterday I would have been furious. But now ... all I can think is that she was right all along."

I was silent for a beat. "What do you mean?"

Ben ran his hand through his hair in a movement that was so similar to Lucas, it sent a pang of—what, longing?—lancing through my chest. "About Amy. Kalina was right. Amy wasn't—isn't—who I thought she was. But don't

261

ever tell Kalina I said that. She'll never let me live it down."

"So ... what's happened exactly? I mean, why do you now agree with Kal?"

Ben looked at me sideways, his mouth pressed in a thin line. "Amy is ..." He trailed off, shaking his head again. Then he sighed. "She was trying to get me to invest in some yoga-resort thing. I couldn't care less, but she really started pushing it. And just now, well, it was like she wouldn't take no for an answer. Her sister runs it or something, and they both seemed really desperate to get me to commit to it today."

"Her *sister*? Are you talking about Meadow?"

Ben looked surprised. "How do you know Meadow?"

"Oh my God," I said. And then it hit me. "Oh my *God!* That lying cow! She knew you were here all along!"

Ben looked even more confused. "What's going on?"

"We've been staying at the same house as where Meadow lives. I even asked her if she could see if you or Amy had been to Yogatainable—so she knew exactly who we've been looking for! But, Ben, you haven't invested in it, have you? Isn't Meadow here, now, trying to get you to?"

"Yeah, I don't know what to think. I mean, no, I haven't invested."

"Thank God. Because apparently, it's all a massive scam. And Amy's ... well, she's probably in on it."

Ben looked thunderstruck.

"But it might not be that bad!" I offered, even though I really didn't believe it. "We just thought ... well, we were so worried that you'd sign over all your inheritance to them."

"Hey, I'm not that stupid."

"Well ... I mean, you did run away with Amy and ignore all your friends and family for a while."

Ben smiled. "Alright, I deserve that."

"And, um, well, have you been staying here the whole time?"

"Yeah, why?"

"Well … whose paying the bill? I mean, this place is rather pricey."

"Oh Christ, I haven't even thought of that! They've got my credit card on file, but I've got no idea how much it is. Is it really expensive here?"

I cringed. "Um, it might not be *that* bad. Maybe you'll get a discount for staying so long?"

"Shit."

I patted his shoulder and we sat in companionable silence for a moment. But then, I needed to get some answers out of him.

"Ben, why did you ignore us? I mean, we're your friends and you just totally cut us all off. Why didn't you respond to our messages? Did you get any of them—from Celeste or Lucas or anything?"

Ben looked a bit panicked now. "I lost my phone when we first got here. I didn't think … I mean, it hasn't been *that* long, has it? What's happened? Fuck, I *told* Amy I needed to get in touch with people and she kept convincing me that I needed to just relax and unwind and that we should be doing a digital detox … fucking hell, she was just grooming me all along."

"Right. And so … when you took off from Sydney without a word? What about that?"

"Oh." Ben hung his head sheepishly. "Yeah, that. I guess I just didn't want to be told what to do anymore. I didn't want other people telling me they were right."

"Like Kalina?"

"Yeah, like Kalina. I just thought Amy … well, I thought she was something else."

"I'm so sorry, Ben." I gave his arm a squeeze. The poor guy was looking shattered.

"I have to leave here." He stood up. "I need to get my stuff and check out."

"We've got a car if you need a lift."

263

"Yeah? Thanks."

"Come on. Let's go meet Kalina in the lobby."

Ben groaned. "God, she's gonna have a field day with this."

"No, she won't." I knew I didn't sound convincing. "But if you want to tease her back, she's basically dating a guy called Echo. Though, he's actually pretty cool."

"What, she's stuck around for more than a night, then?"

I smiled. "I have a feeling this one's different."

31

The gang was back together.

I sometimes still had to pinch myself that this was my life now. That after having my world torn down and shattered after Jack left me, I could call these wonderful people not just my flatmates, but my friends.

Opposite me, Ben was grilling a waiter about exactly what was in the *sotto sobrese* croquettes, asking where the *jamon* was sourced from and exactly how long it had been aged. Beside me, Kalina was engaged in a heated argument with Echo, opposite her, about precisely what age hipster beards went out of fashion and whether Echo had reached his threshold yet.

I smiled at them all while I sipped my wine. This was what I'd been missing. Hanging out with my flatmates over Spanish food. My friends. My people.

Kalina, I thought, had been quite magnanimous in her restraint over the teasing of Ben. She'd even kept herself away while Ben packed up his room and checked out of the hotel, dumping Amy along the way. (I didn't ask about the hotel bill, but based on his expression when he saw it, I thought he was doing his best to forget.)

Now, of course, we were all having dinner at St Elmo Dining Room and Bar, the cool Spanish tapas restaurant that Kalina and I had passed repeatedly and knew that Ben would love. Rose had declined to join us, saying she wanted to just get room service and lie around in her hotel room all night. I didn't blame her—if I'd had a horrifying public accident like she had, I'd probably also be keen on days of hibernating. But the rest of us wanted to go out and celebrate. Or commiserate, in Ben's case.

"Alright, Ben, I've waited long enough," Kalina said, eyeing Ben off across the table.

"Here we go," Echo quipped, and I exchanged a grin with him.

"Do I have to hear this?" Ben moaned, but his voice had a sense of fatalism to it.

Kalina gave him a mock-stern look before continuing. "Laura and I have travelled halfway across the country to come and find you, and spent all week holed up here in Byron Bay wasting our time in the hunt."

"I'm not sure *wasting* is the most appropriate term," Echo muttered.

"Yeah, Kalina's always having her own party," added Ben, and I saw Ben and Echo share a humorous glance.

"Can I finish? Right. Well, now you know what we've been doing, so I'd like to hear your side of the story. What have you been *doing* all this time? And don't give me any more 'I lost my phone' excuses."

Ben looked a bit sheepish. "Well, funny you should say that. When I was packing up the room, I found my phone among Amy's things. I don't think I lost it so much as she hid it."

"You're joking!" I exclaimed. "Do we need any more proof that that girl was nuts? Sorry, Ben."

"But where have you *been* the whole time?" Kalina pressed. "We've been scouring town every day with no sign of you. What have you been doing?"

Ben scratched his chin. "We stayed in at the hotel most of the time. Or I'd go to the beach and surf."

"No way. We were at the beach *every* day."

"You were? The beach across the road from my hotel?"

Kalina frowned and looked at me.

"Oh," I said, realising. "Right. We were at completely different beaches, then."

"Brilliant," Kalina muttered. "So, you didn't go into town at all? You didn't go to any of the pubs?"

"Actually, we were meant to meet Amy's sister at one of the pubs last night," Ben said. "We were almost there when she rang and cancelled and then Amy insisted we leave too." He looked slightly confused and he rubbed his chin. "I still don't know why we couldn't have gone in for a drink."

"Oh my God, it *was* you!" I squealed. "The Railway Hotel, right? That's where you were going?"

Ben nodded.

"I chased after you down the street, but I lost you! And—of *course*, that's why Meadow saw us and bolted. It had nothing to do with the potoroos!"

Ben looked mystified.

"Honestly, Ben, Meadow and Amy must have been scheming about this all along. And Meadow deliberately prevented us from finding you. Seriously, those sisters are a real piece of work."

Ben sort of deflated a bit in his chair.

"Don't be too hard on yourself, mate," Echo offered. "I've been tracking Meadow's business dealings for over a month. She's conned people much older and wiser than you."

"Did you catch her at the airport?" I asked, suddenly remembering. Echo had lost Meadow at the Byron at Byron, but later had raced off to the airport after receiving a phone call from the mysterious friend he was working for.

"No, she'd already gone. Booked a flight to Singapore, it seems, but we don't know where she's planning on running to. We'll have to keep an eye on it."

"Bali?" I offered. "She had a brochure for it yesterday. I think that's where she was planning to go."

Echo looked surprised but gave me an appreciative nod.

"I think Amy was left out of the loop a bit," Ben said. "Like, her sister had promised her all this stuff but then screwed her over."

I glanced to Kalina in alarm. "That doesn't excuse what she did to you, though, Ben. Did she … um … do you know if she is pregnant?"

Ben's head jerked up, surprised. "No. I mean … no, she's not. At least, she got her period this morning, so she can't be."

"Thank fuck for that!" Kalina said.

"Why would you ask that?" Ben frowned.

"Didn't she tell you about seeing us in town a few days ago?" I asked. Ben shook his head. "We ran into her. She basically implied that she was pregnant and that she was going to get you to propose to her."

Ben looked appalled. "Shit."

"Yeah. Just more crazy talk, I think. But lucky escape for you there."

"Yeah. Jeez. I know it's only been a few hours since I left, but shit … I don't know what I was thinking with her. There's a couple of months of my life I'll never get back."

"You know," I said. "If there's one thing I've learned from my time up here, it's that sometimes you just have to let the universe guide you. Even when in hindsight something seems like a waste of time, it still helped to shape you into the person that you are right now, in this moment. And that always has to be a good thing, because without our past experiences we can't be who we are, or who we're meant to be."

"Did we mention that Laura has waxed philosophical?" Kalina said. "And she's been shagging the yoga teacher."

Echo looked at me with feigned shock. "Who, Truth?"

I punched Kalina on the arm, and ignored her loud "ow!". "He's been teaching me a few things, that's all," I said.

Echo laughed. "Truth's a good guy. But still, that's one household I'll be glad to see the back of."

"You can hardly talk! Your name is *Echo*."

"Well, it's actually not." Echo rubbed the back of his neck. "My real name is Owen."

"What?!" Kalina's jaw fell open. "Are you shitting me?"

"Like it?" He grinned at her.

After a moment, she shut her mouth and looked thoughtful. "Well, I suppose anything is better than Echo."

"So, what's going to happen with Yogatainable?" I asked, looking at Echo—wait, *Owen*. Hmm. This was going to be weird. I wasn't sure if I was ready to think of him as anything other than Echo yet. "Truth still works there. Do you think he's involved with any of this?"

Echo shook his head. "He's not. I ruled him out already. But as to that place ... I don't know. Some investigators arrived here this afternoon and they're taking over the project. My contract has come to an end, so I'm not going to be involved anymore."

"What are you planning to do now, then?" I asked. "Are you going to stay here in Byron Bay?"

Echo's eyes slid over to Kalina and my heart melted a little as I saw the way they smiled at each other. "I'm going to do a stint in Sydney, I think. I have a couple of mates there that can hook me up with some work."

He spoke with his eyes fixed on Kalina, and I could barely believe the look of fondness I saw in her own gaze back at him. Echo reached across the table and squeezed Kalina's hand, and my heart swelled.

"Well, I can hardly get rid of him now." Kalina rolled her eyes at us, even though her cheeks were turning pink. "I mean, he did help save your bacon, Ben, so we basically owe him."

I laughed, and suddenly realised I had tears in my eyes. It was so beautiful, seeing Kalina happy with a guy. To know that she'd finally broken down her barriers—at least some of them—and that she was letting someone else in. The way Echo looked at her, and the way she looked back at him was one of the sweetest, tenderest things I'd seen.

And it hit me unexpectedly: I wanted that. I wanted someone to look at me like that, and hold my hand, and smile at my jokes. I wanted someone who would move cities to be near me, and make me laugh, and struggle to keep their hands off me.

And I knew, straightaway, exactly whom I wanted. Because it wasn't just anyone, it was *him*. The guy it had always been. The one with the sky-blue eyes and the teasing smile and the eyes that laughed with me.

I wanted Lucas. I didn't want to run away from him anymore, or be scared of what we could become. I wanted to open my heart and watch him open his, and laugh with him and cry with him and just be near him every day. I wanted to see what we could become, and if it all ended in disaster then so be it. It was worth taking a risk because the reward could be everything.

"What about you, Laura?" Ben asked, pulling my thoughts back to the present. "Looking forward to your new job next week?"

"I am." I smiled at Ben, while Echo excused himself to go examine the blackboard wine list. "I think ... I'm definitely ready to go back to Sydney."

And I was. Now that Ben was back with us, I couldn't imagine staying in Byron Bay while my friends left. Even if Truth was here. But he was a part of Byron Bay and I just really wasn't.

I was a part of Manly.

"Hey, Kal," Echo said, sliding back into his seat with a grin. "Chris Hemsworth is over there."

"I'm *so* not falling for that." Kalina rolled her eyes.

But I looked, my head whipping around to check out the tables near the blackboard.

And.

Oh.

My.

God.

It really was him. He was sitting there with his family—his gorgeous wife, Elsa, and their three kids were sitting at a table, talking and smiling and laughing with each other. They had plates of food spread out before them, and a bottle of wine on the table and soft drinks for the kids. They looked so happy and, well, *normal.*

"Kal!" I whipped back towards her, squealing. "It's actually him!"

Kalina spun around and gasped. And then she turned back to face us, looking a bit shell-shocked.

"Well, go on," Echo teased her. "Go and say hi."

"No!" Kalina looked mortified. "I mean ... this is Byron Bay. You don't disturb the celebrities up here."

We all laughed while Kalina turned red. And then we forgot about everything other than our little table of four and had the most amazing dinner and the best night out together.

32

That night, I didn't sleep in Truth's room. Instead, I lay awake trying to sleep in the room I'd actually rented while Ben snored on Kalina's vacant bed beside me.

The night felt long, the hours ticking by in that restless, half-asleep state I got when my mind was preoccupied. But at the same time, the night couldn't ever be long enough.

Tomorrow I'd be leaving Byron Bay. And I hadn't said goodbye yet.

At the first hint of the sky lightening outside, I got up and pulled on my yoga clothes. Ben was still sleeping deeply, and I couldn't help but feel surprised at how haggard and exhausted he looked for someone who had just spent a week and a half at a luxury hotel.

Leaving him, I tiptoed down the hallway and took myself into the yoga room. There, with the faintest trace of dawn light washing across the sky and filtering in through the huge glass wall, I rolled out a yoga mat and started doing some asanas.

I felt peaceful. My body moved through positions unhurriedly, and I felt my heart beating firmly, not from stress, but from that delicious feeling of just *working*. I took a deep breath in and exhaled slowly, letting the movements flow with my breathing.

Outside, a chorus of magpies began greeting the morning. Soon, I found myself no longer stretching but just sitting, looking out at the gradually lightening day washing across the garden outside.

I guess I was waiting for him.

Sure enough, it wasn't long before I heard the soft creak of the staircase and then I felt my neck prickle, sensing him enter the room behind me.

"Good morning, Laura," Truth said softly.

I turned around and there he was, serene and beautiful, walking into the room. He was wearing his linen pants and his chest was bare, his dreadlocks loose and falling over his shoulders.

I smiled at him, and waited while he unrolled a mat beside me. He didn't start any asanas, he just folded himself down, cross-legged, to sit next to me on the floor.

"Good morning, Truth," I said.

"I was disappointed you didn't come up to my room last night," he said lightly, his voice holding nothing more than curiosity.

"Sorry. I was just tired after yesterday."

Truth's brows drew together slightly, as if he could tell I was lying, but he didn't remark on it.

I cleared my throat. "Do you know about Meadow? And Yogatainable?"

"Yes, I do." He nodded once, looking disappointed. "Echo told me yesterday. It seems all of the owners have disappeared, leaving behind a mountain of debt. All the staff have been called in for a meeting this morning, but I'm guessing we won't be getting paid again."

"Right. Gosh, I'm so sorry. Did you have any idea Meadow was like that?"

Truth shook his head, but he smiled. "She's a good person, really. Sometimes even the best of us can be led astray."

Meadow? A good person? I wasn't so sure.

"Really," Truth continued, watching my expression. "She's loyal and generous. It saddens me that this has happened to her."

I tried to hide my look of scepticism at his words. Meadow wasn't loyal to anyone except the God of Money. She'd been planning to steal

Ben's inheritance without a moment's thought! Plus, she'd abandoned and screwed over her own sister, who was just as bad as she was.

But I wasn't sure I needed to say this to Truth. He had known Meadow for a lot longer than I had, after all. And I doubted he could see faults in *anyone*. It was one of the things that made him so special.

"So, you found your flatmate, then?" Truth asked after the silence had stretched on for a moment.

"Yes! We found him finally. And luckily, he wasn't in too much trouble."

"I suppose you're heading back to Sydney soon?"

My eyes found his and were lost in golden-brown depths, shining in the morning light. I remembered the first time I'd seen him, standing in the light from the fridge. How awed I was by those cheekbones, by the chiselled ridges of his collarbone and muscles, by that swirling tattoo across his shoulder, a tribal tribute to his mother's heritage. For a moment, I was lost in how beautiful and sexy he was, and I wondered, quite ridiculously, why I hadn't gone to his room last night, why I hadn't spent one more night in bed with him.

But then I remembered my life in Sydney and all that was waiting for me there. I couldn't let my heart stay here in Byron Bay.

It was time to go home.

"I am," I said, hearing the sadness in my voice. "It's been such a dream being up here, and meeting you. And ... thank you. I'm not sure if that's appropriate, but I want to thank you for everything you've done for me. And with me."

Truth smiled, that slow sexy smile of his. "I'm glad you enjoyed your time here. I won't lie and say that I'm not sad to see you go. But I'm also honoured that you spent your time here with me. I hope I've helped show you the pathway to love."

"You have!" I couldn't help laughing. "Oh, you definitely have. And so much more than that." I bit my lip, feeling my heartbeat suddenly accelerate.

"You've shown me so much more."

And with the magpies outside singing their greetings to a glorious new morning, I leaned over and kissed Truth goodbye.

Later, with the morning hours rapidly disappearing, Kalina, Ben and I loaded up my car with all our stuff. I'd spoken to Rose this morning, and luckily she didn't seem bothered that I was heading back to Sydney straightaway. She'd already booked herself in for a three-hour spa treatment at her hotel, and was quite happy spending a few days having some R and R at the resort before flying back to Sydney on her own.

"How much shit did you bring with you, Kal?" Ben asked as he tried to play Tetris with the bags.

"We didn't know how long we'd be away for!" Kalina responded, practically disappearing into the boot as she tried to squash another bag in. "Besides, you're the one who brought absolutely everything he owns. How long did *you* plan to be away for?"

"I was just making a point," Ben grumbled, slamming the boot shut with a definite crunch. "Alright. No one open that until we're back in Sydney."

"Agreed." Kalina rolled her shoulders and looked around.

"Where's Echo?" I asked.

"He went to get us some coffees. A while ago now."

Just then, as if summoned by our voices, Echo walked into view carrying a cardboard tray loaded with four takeaway coffee cups, and a paper bag with some muffin-shaped lumps in it.

"Amazing!" I squealed, taking my coffee gratefully.

"Thought you could use some sugar for the road," Echo said, handing Kalina the bag of muffins along with her coffee.

"Aww, is this your way of saying that you're going to miss me terribly?"

she teased.

"I think you're going to miss *me*, darling."

"However am I going to cope without seeing this beard every day?"

I caught Ben's eye and nodded towards the car.

"Bye, then, Echo," I said pointedly. "Thanks for the coffee. And see you in Sydney soon!"

"Bye, guys," he replied, shaking Ben's hand and giving me a hug. I got into the driver's seat of my car and switched on the engine, while Ben climbed into the back.

"Do you think it's actually serious?" Ben asked me as we watched Kalina and Echo speaking outside the car.

"Yeah, I do," I answered with a smile. "At least, it has the potential to be."

Kalina and Echo embraced, kissing and cuddling for what seemed like a long while. Then he dropped his hands and squeezed her bum and she swatted him away with a laugh.

I snorted with laughter, but glancing back at Ben I saw he was looking at his phone, a frown on his face.

"Any word from Amy?" I asked him gently.

He huffed a laugh. "Yeah. Only about fifty messages and voicemails."

"Oh. Shit. Do you know where she's gone?"

"Don't know, don't care."

"I'm so sorry this has happened to you, Ben."

He glanced up at me, a scowl on his face. "It's my own fault, I guess. I should have known."

"Why do you think that? I mean—*how* could you have known?"

Ben shook his head, as if trying to get his thoughts straight. "It was so much, so fast. *She* was so much. I thought … but, no. Now I know, she was only interested in money all along."

"That might not be true. I'm not trying to defend her or anything, but surely, I mean, some of it might have been real."

Ben pursed his lips and stared out the window for a moment. Then with a sigh, he threw his phone down on the seat beside him. "I doubt it. It's a pretty big coincidence that my great-aunt dies—one of the richest women in South Australia who also doesn't have any direct descendants—and then just days later I happen to meet a girl at a party who seems to fall in love with me on sight. No, I'd say she knew exactly what she was doing."

"But *how* would she have known? Did she know your great aunt?"

"I don't know, exactly." Ben frowned, rubbing his chin. "There were a couple of times when she mentioned being in South Australia just before meeting me, but she never wanted to elaborate on it. And I never asked because, well, it never seemed important. But there was a big feature in the newspaper about Maurine the day after she died. And the funeral was so big, apparently, it was like half the city was there. I don't think it would have been hard working out that my family were her closest relatives. And I guess I was the easiest target."

"I'm so sorry, Ben," I said again.

He laughed. "Well, joke was on her in the end. I don't think she realised that inheritance takes a long time to actually come through. Plus, she was stupid and tried to use me to reconnect with her sister. But Meadow took *her* for a ride there."

"Good riddance to both of them, then." I offered Ben a hopeful smile and after a moment he returned it with a nod.

Just then, Kalina opened the passenger door and climbed inside. "Right. Let's do this!"

I looked out the window and saw Echo raise a hand in farewell.

"When is he coming to Sydney?" I asked Kalina as I waved back at him.

"In a couple of weeks. He's going to Canberra first to debrief with his friend. Then his contract will be over and he's going to come up."

"Aww, so romantic!"

Kalina rolled her eyes. "Come on, let's go before Echo starts crying or something."

Laughing, I put the car into gear and then we were cruising out down the road, heading back through the centre of town.

"Goodbye, Byron Bay," I said, navigating us through a series of roundabouts. Even though it was still before noon, the streets were buzzing with people walking around carrying fresh juices or sitting at cafe tables spilling onto the pavement.

"I barely saw any of this stuff," Ben said, sounding disappointed as he looked out the window.

"We'll have to come back for a proper holiday," I replied.

Kalina snorted. "I'm not chasing after Ben if he absconds with a crazy girl again. You hear that, back there? Don't pick any more psychos, please."

"I didn't know she was psycho," Ben protested.

"Was she at least good in bed?" I grinned at Ben in the rear-view mirror. "Crazy girls are meant to be good in bed."

"*I'm* good in bed and I'm not crazy," Kalina said.

Ben laughed. "I feel like both parts of that statement are incorrect."

"Hey! You've got no idea how good I am in bed!"

"Nor do I want to!"

"Guys, let's all just agree that we are all awesome in bed and leave it at that."

Kalina shot me an impressed look. "You're awesome, are you, Laur? This sounds interesting."

"Aww, I didn't get to see the yoga guy!" Ben sounded disappointed. "Bugger. I wanted to get a look at him."

"You didn't need to get a look at him! He was ... my Byron Bay fling, that's all. Although, I will say that he definitely taught me a thing or two."

"Ooh, what sorts of things?" Kalina asked.

"Guys, I don't want to hear this!" Ben called from the back.

I laughed. "I'll tell you later, Kal."

She made a disappointed sound. "Well, I for one am very glad to be going back to Sydney."

"Is that because your Byron romance is coming with you?"

"He's not my Byron romance! He's just ... I don't know. He's Echo."

"Should we be calling him Owen now?"

"I've told him once he gets rid of the beard, then I'll call him Owen."

"His beard is awesome," Ben said.

"No, it's not!" Kalina and I said in unison, then we laughed.

"Aren't you looking forward to getting back to Sydney, Laura?" Kalina asked me.

"I'm looking forward to my new job starting."

"And something else, perhaps?"

I shot her a look. I wasn't sure Ben had any idea about the Lucas-and-me situation, but I didn't think he needed to know.

Turns out, he was more switched on than I'd imagined. "Yeah, what's the deal with you and Lucas now?" he asked. "You guys aren't seriously still doing the 'just friends' thing, are you?"

"No! I mean, we *are* just friends! What do you know about it, anyway?"

I saw Kalina and Ben exchange a raised-eyebrow look via the rear-view mirror that definitely left me out of the loop.

"Sometimes you just have to take a chance," Kalina said. "*You* told me that, remember?"

"I know, I know. But look, we don't need to talk about this. I've already ... I mean, let's just concentrate on getting back to Sydney, okay?"

I tried not to notice Ben and Kalina giving each other more cryptic looks, and to just focus on driving, instead.

Kalina plugged her phone into the car and set the music, and I watched the town of Byron Bay disappear around us while the electropop beats of Confidence Man began playing. Soon, we had exchanged urban streets for forested highway, and I found myself thinking of Lucas.

Kalina was right. I *was* looking forward to seeing him again, even though the thought sent butterflies racing through my stomach.

It was time to tell him how I felt about him. And I knew how I felt now. I wanted to be with him. I wanted to kiss him and date him and spend all of my time with him.

I was in love with him. And I was fairly confident that he could be in love with me.

My heart raced when I thought about telling him. I wanted to be close to him, to see his eyes light up. I could just picture it. I'd arrive at the bar. He'd be all alone, cleaning down for the night. His eyes would light up when he saw me, and I'd make myself look at him, really look at him. No more evasion. No more looks that skated away. I'd tell him that it was him, it had been him all along. I knew, deep down I *knew* he'd feel the same. He'd been waiting for me for months, hadn't he? He was ready to take a chance on a relationship again.

And so was I.

33

It was after nine pm when we finally arrived back in Manly. We'd been sitting in the car for so long that I actually enjoyed carrying my bags up the stairs just so I could stretch my legs.

Of course, the first thing that became apparent upon entering the apartment was that Kalina and I had forgotten to take the bin out before we left.

"Ugh!" I gagged. "Oh my God!"

"What is that *smell*?" Ben came in behind me.

"It's rotten something!" I had my shirt up over my nose.

Ten minutes later and the situation was under control. (Ben had removed the bin, while Kalina and I opened every window, threw open the balcony doors and turned on all the house fans.) But then, just as we had finished bringing up all our bags from the car, there was an unexpected knock on the door.

"Great, the neighbours could probably smell our flat from the hallway," Kalina muttered as she went to answer the door.

Ben was in the bathroom, but I was standing in the kitchen, drinking a glass of water, which gave me a good view of the doorway as Kalina threw it open.

But it wasn't a neighbour come to complain.

I nearly choked on my water when I recognised the tall, skinny guy with spiked brown hair.

Kalina's ex-boyfriend was on the doorstep again. And Kalina was staring right at him, her face a mix of shock and horror.

"Adam?" she said stiffly. "What the fuck are you doing here?"

"Kalina." He took a step into the apartment. "I came here for you. You said you'd think about things and I can't wait any longer. I want you back."

"Hey, I didn't invite you inside," Kalina snapped. "But you're right. I have thought about things. And the answer is that there is no fucking way in hell I'd ever give you another chance with me."

He blanched visibly. "But ... when we spoke, you said—"

"I was just in shock then. But you're seriously deluded if you think I can ever forgive you for what you did."

"But, Kalina, I love you. And you love me, I know you do." He reached out for her, and she hastily backed away.

"Fuck off, Adam."

"But, Kal—"

"Hey!" I called, storming around the kitchen bench to come and stand beside Kalina and face down this unwelcome visitor. "She told you to fuck off."

He glanced at me uneasily, his cheeks flushing pink. "Don't do this, Kal. I flew all the way here for you. Come home with me."

"Who's this, then?" came Ben's voice behind us, and I felt enormously relieved. I mean, Kal and I could probably take Adam down, but Ben (who was not a small guy) could *definitely* take Adam down.

But that probably wouldn't be necessary. Adam was already backing away, looking kind of flabbergasted.

"Go home, Adam," Kalina said, her voice not quite as harsh as it had been. "You've wasted your time flying here. Go back to England."

"Is that *him*?" Ben came up behind us, sounding outraged. "The fucking *ex*?"

Adam looked a bit freaked out now. "Ah, I'll just ..." he muttered, backing away.

"Just go home, Adam! Go home!" Kalina snapped.

"Fucking Adam!" Ben was now right behind us, and I was half tempted to let him pass just to see what would happen. "You've got a lot of nerve coming here, mate!"

With a final look of anguish at Kalina, Adam finally turned and left, and she slammed the door after him.

"Want me to go bash him?" Ben offered, only half joking.

"No!" Kalina laughed. "Tempting, but no. I think his punishment is all the money he's wasted on this trip."

"Good for you, Kal." I put my arm around her and pulled her in for a hug.

"Yeah, yeah," she muttered, shrugging me off even as her cheeks flushed. "Anyway, I'm not game to eat anything still in the fridge. Let's order pizzas."

"Definitely," Ben agreed.

"Hang on a second!" Kalina suddenly exclaimed, stopping us all mid-step, and I realised she was looking at our wall. The wall that had been the scene of the crime in the Amy spaghetti-throwing incident. "Is that it?"

Ben glanced at me warily.

"That's it," I replied. "Sorry, Ben, I told her about it."

"Ben, seriously, how could you *not*—"

"I know, I know!" He ran his hands through his hair. "Can we just not talk about it anymore?"

"Oh, let me say it just once."

"Say what?" I asked.

Ben sighed. "Fine. Say it."

"I told you so!" Kalina squealed. And then she started doing a weird little jig on the spot. "I told you, I knew she was nuts, I knew better than you, and I bloody told you!"

"That was about four times!" Ben said. "And stop dancing like that." He was laughing though.

"Alright, fine." Kalina stopped dancing and picked up her phone, instead. "I'm ordering pizza, then."

Ben shook his head and went to flop down on a couch. I checked my watch—it was almost ten. Los Perdidos often closed early, depending on how busy it was. So, Lucas could be closing up anytime now.

"I'm going to take a walk," I heard myself saying. "My back's pretty sore from the car. Save me some pizza?"

Kalina raised an eyebrow at me, a knowing smile on her face. But she just nodded.

"See you later," I called, heading out the door.

Soon, I was back on the beachfront, strolling along the walkway towards the heart of Manly again.

It was just as beautiful down here at night. The water was a darkness stretching to the horizon, a stunning mirror for the clouds and almost-full moon up above. Rounded lampposts lit the way along the beachfront walkway, illuminating the path for the many people out for late-night jogs or making their way home. It was all exactly as if I'd never been away.

I breathed in the sea air, and felt my heart starting to race as I came up to the Manly Corso. This would be the perfect time to catch Lucas as he was closing the bar. It would be exactly as I imagined it—his eyes would light up when he saw me. I wondered if I'd even need to say anything? Maybe I'd look up at him, and he'd just say, "I know," and then we'd end up in the storeroom together again.

But no. I had to *tell* him how I felt. That was the important part. He couldn't read my mind. But, oh God. I hadn't really thought of what to say. I just knew it had to be now—this was it.

I was going over the cliff.

I saw the artfully faded sign for Los Perdidos up ahead, and my pace increased, adrenaline suddenly making me shaky. My heart was *thud, thud, thudding* up in my throat and I felt short of breath. Then I was in front of the glass doors and there he was, inside, turned away from me. Lucas was smiling and leaning one arm on the bar, his t-shirt clinging to his bicep, his shaggy hair slicked back off his face.

My lips broke into a smile and my hand reached out to push the door open. But then I noticed something that surprised me, something that made me freeze.

Despite the "Closed" sign on the door, there was a girl inside with him. A girl who was unfamiliar. She was standing behind the bar, facing Lucas, and smiling at him.

I wondered if it could be a new bartender, even as I felt my lungs squeeze in pain, the air inside them abruptly unable to shift.

Because, I realised, the girl *wasn't* unfamiliar. I'd seen her before. Or, rather, I'd seen her photo before. Looking exactly like this—gazing at Lucas and smiling.

It was his ex. The girl he'd once proposed to. The one who'd broken his heart.

And as I watched, she leaned towards him, her eyes dropping to his lips. Her hand shifted across the bar, to within centimetres of his. I wanted to scream at them both to stop. I wanted to barge inside and commandeer Lucas's attention.

But I couldn't. And as I stood there, frozen and watching, I hoped, for the most excruciating heartbeat, that he would pull away from her.

But he didn't. He closed the distance between them and he kissed her.

My whole chest felt like it caved in as she wrapped her hands around his neck. His own hands moved around her back and he pulled her into him, crushing her body against his in exactly the way I'd imagined him doing with me.

I felt it then, standing on the doorstep of Los Perdidos, the night dark around me.

I felt my heart break.

My vision blurred as tears filled my eyes. I couldn't look away, yet I was mortified to be found standing there. I forced myself to turn, forced myself to stumble away. I crashed into someone coming in the other direction, but I barely noticed. I couldn't feel anything.

I was too late. Lucas had moved on, without me. I'd missed my window with him.

I heard Rose's voice swimming through my mind, words she'd spoken only weeks ago. *"You'd better be careful. A guy like him won't stay single for long."*

Part of me wanted to go back and barge into the bar, to tell him that I loved him and to make him look at me. But what right did I have? Lucas had been just as broken as I had. If he'd decided to get back together with a girl he used to love, he must have thought about it long and hard. She obviously knew how to make him happy. That photo I'd seen of them together was proof enough of that. And Lucas deserved to be happy.

I couldn't destroy that for him. Especially because I was the one who'd insisted we could only be friends.

I found myself breaking into a run back down to the beach, as if there were demons chasing me. And once I was there, with the dark sea stretching before me, I stopped and sat on the low stone wall above the sand, dangling my feet over the edge and staring out at the ocean. The moon was still visible, both in the sky and in the sea, casting white light across the dark beach.

Here I am, I thought. *Just as desolate and alone as the empty beach was.*

But no. Not alone. Never alone. Because I had friends.

My fingers found the crystal around my neck, the one I'd bought myself at the Crystal Castle. I carefully undid my necklace and gazed down at the smooth pink quartz now sitting in my open palm, trying to remember how I'd felt that day.

I feel loved and loving. That had been the crystal I'd chosen. But this love wasn't dependent on other people. Lucas …

I squeezed my eyes shut.

Lucas wasn't the one for me. Not now. Maybe never. But that didn't mean I couldn't find love out in the world. As Truth said: love is an experience many fail to master.

But that wouldn't be me.

I put my crystal necklace back on and tucked it under my top, next to my heart. Byron Bay may be far away now, but I'd brought something wonderful back with me.

I'd brought a heart open to love.

34

When I entered the apartment, Kalina and Ben were sitting on the couch, eating pizza, drinking wine, and watching *Rick and Morty* on the TV.

"How was the *walk*?" Kalina asked me smugly, but her expression quickly changed when she caught sight of my face.

I just shook my head, feeling tears pricking at my eyes.

For a second she stared at me, her mouth agape, and then she shifted over to make room for me on the couch.

"Come!" she said. "Sit, eat, drink. There's so much food here."

With a small smile, I went and sat between them on the couch. Kalina got me a plate of pizza and Ben poured me a glass of wine.

"Did you go to the bar?" Ben asked, oblivious to the current mood.

"I went past," I replied, my voice threatening to crack. "It seems ... well, it seems Lucas has gotten back together with his old girlfriend."

"What?!" Kalina shrieked.

"Who, Holly? No way, he wouldn't do that!" Ben protested. But he stopped protesting once he saw my face.

"Oh, Laur." Kalina put her arm around me.

"It's fine!" I said, holding back the tears. "Really." And I made myself laugh for good measure. "It's ... I mean nothing was ever really going to happen between us, anyway."

Kalina and Ben exchanged a glance.

"I'll bloody kill him," Ben muttered.

"No! And God, please neither of you say anything to him, okay?"

Kalina squeezed my shoulder again and Ben looked a bit uneasy.

"Really," I assured them. "It's fine. I'm just happy that I've got both of you guys here with me."

"Well, you've definitely got that," Kalina said. "Right, Ben?"

"Hell yeah. I can't afford to go anywhere else."

I laughed, which turned into a bit of a sob. Ben seemed alarmed and topped up my wine, right to the top of the glass.

"I can't drink all that!" I protested, laughing again.

"Wine cures all ills," Kalina instructed. "And pizza. And friends."

"Lucky I've got all of those, then."

"We're lucky we've got *you*," Kalina said.

"Aww, guys, this is getting a bit deep!" Ben protested.

"Okay, okay! I'll be fine, really. You don't need to worry about me."

"Are you sure you're okay?" Kalina asked, her eyes full of concern.

I thought about it for a second, taking a bite of my pizza.

The truth was, you couldn't plan everything. And there was no point in worrying about the future when tomorrow was going to be a brand-new day full of possibilities. I was about to start a new job. I had the best friends in the world. And I had a heart made of elastic that was ready to spring again.

"I will be," I told Kalina with a smile. "In fact, I'll be better than okay. I'm going to be fucking fantastic."

LAURA'S JOURNEY WILL CONTINUE

GREAT SEXPECTATIONS

LAURA THE EXPLORER BOOK 3

COMING 2021

Acknowledgements

I had a lot of fun researching this book. Thank you to the city of Byron Bay for showing me a great time during my research trip, especially the Crystal Castle and Shambhala Gardens, the Byron at Byron hotel, Creature Yoga, and the many restaurants and cafes I visited. Also a huge thank you to the Byron Bay library where many of these scenes were written or edited.

A massive thank you to Diane Riley of The Australian School of Tantra for your insights and help with some of the conversations and scenes involving Truth and Laura. Many books were consulted when creating Truth's character, but the most essential title was *Tantric Secrets for Men* by Kerry Riley with Diane Riley, as well as *The Emotional Wound Thesaurus* by Angela Ackerman and Becca Puglist.

This book wouldn't have been written without the support for *Laura the Explorer* that came from so many of my friends, but also from so many complete strangers. Thank you to everyone who has joined Laura on her journey, and especially thank you to the wonderful book bloggers who took a chance on a debut indie author and agreed to read and review my book. You guys are superstars and your time and effort is so hugely appreciated.

Thank you to my amazing cover designer, Hazel Lam, for once again creating such a beautiful, perfect cover. Thank you to my copy editor, Alexandra Nahlous, for making my words shine so much more.

Once again, thank you so much to the friends and family members whose real-life experiences were used as inspiration for some of the scenes in this book. A special shout-out to Lidwina, for your wonderfully witty "social influenza" aspirations, and a huge thank you to Elliot for coming up with the perfect title for this book.

Thank you so much to my early readers for your feedback and comments—Caroline, Jeanette and Elizabeth, you guys are the best! Hannah, thank you so much for supporting me and for being my proof-reader. Thank you to my Mum, for being my biggest fan and my first reader, and to my Dad, whose story-telling abilities still hold me in awe.

Even though she'll never read this, Ruby you are the best doggo in the world. Thank you for making me get out of the house every day, even if you only ever want to go to the cafe. And the biggest thank you to Linden, for supporting my dreams and being the most wonderful husband ever. Without you, this book would never have happened.

Support an Author

Leave a Review

Even a single sentence can make a huge difference!
If you enjoyed this book, please post a review on Goodreads.

SARAH BEGG lives in Sydney with her husband and a dog named Ruby. She loves to travel and has been writing fiction for as long as she can remember. She decided she was going to become an author when she was seven and realised that was a real occupation. When she's not writing, she works in digital marketing.

Eat Pray Shag is the sequel to Sarah's first novel, *Laura the Explorer*.

Follow Sarah on Instagram, Twitter and Facebook
@sarahkbegg

Subscribe to Sarah's email newsletter at
sarahbegg.com

www.ingramcontent.com/pod-product-compliance
Lightning Source LLC
Chambersburg PA
CBHW021411110726
47901CB00008B/2138